THE UNFORGIVEN

THE UNFORGIVEN

Howard Clewes

HUTCHINSON LIBRARY SERVICES

HUTCHINSON LIBRARY SERVICES LTD
3 Fitzroy Square, London W1

London Melbourne Sydney Auckland
Wellington Johannesburg Cape Town
and agencies throughout the world

First published by The Bodley Head 1948
This edition 1973

Printed in Great Britain by litho on antique wove paper
by Anchor Press, and bound by Wm. Brendon,
both of Tiptree, Essex

ISBN 0 09 116280 7

Thus am I slayn sith that Pité is deed:
Allas the day! that ever hit shulde falle!
What maner man dar now holde up his head?
To whom shall any sorwful herte call,
Now Crueltee hath cast to sleen us all
In ydel hope, folk redelees of peyne?
Sith she is deed, to whom shul we compleyne?

GEOFFREY CHAUCER'S *Complaint to Pity.*

1

THE FOREST on the western slopes of the mountain is a little hostile at night. With the dusk it becomes a temple whose columns are the great trees that awaken and whisper sagaciously to one another when the night wind moves and the hissing is prolonged like the pious sibilation of communicants or the salacious wheezing of music-hall comedians. Then the snow that clings to the outflung branches falls and the forest is alive with movement among the trees as though they are brushed against by some ghostly herd in flight. The track is swathed in drifts but under the trees there is no snow and there the earth is dry and black and the traveller should take care not to look too long at the shadows lest they move in his own image, nor too closely at the rigid foliage above lest the tears of melted snow the sunshine left are shed and the sorrow of the forest overwhelms his own.

There are few wild creatures: rabbits, a hare or two perhaps, sometimes a marmot; yet there is malevolence. When the moon rises and the mist stirs among the trees, then you can sense it most strongly of all. Then the traveller is beset by his own soul and by the souls of enemies both dead and unborn and loves found and lost again and loves yet unmet and the pine cones snap before he steps on them and his spoor precedes him in the snow.

None has ever reached the easternmost flank of the forest, below the great escarpment. They turn back early, discouraged and afraid. Crosby certainly went further than the rest, being maybe a little less susceptible, and then the tall fair woman called Erica, she being unusually coura-geous, but none has ever reached the end. They rarely know why they begin the ascent, much less what they seek there, and so the initial momentum is quickly spent; the track is very steep and the distractions are many; it is lonely in the forest. They turn back. And when they turn, that is a moment of great importance. If, having once decided to go no further, the traveller faces about and proceeds with non-chalance and a whistle on his lips downwards to the open spaces that lie below the forest, he has little to fear; if, however, he stands too long or looks behind him, he pays dearly for the weakness, human though it may be. He experiences terror. For then the mountain rouses and stirs and utters a deep sigh and the mighty steeple of rock that soars dizzily some thirteen thousand feet above the earth stirs in its bed and teeters dreadfully and after a moment of sickening hesitation topples slowly unbelievably immensely downwards on the traveller, growing nearer and larger till it is as big as a continent and the sky is filled with it and the snow cascades from the spurs and rifts on its naked face and the air screams in its flight from beneath.

The thing is a hallucination, an optical illusion, I sup-pose one would call it, attributable doubtless to the play of moonlight through the cumulus with which the summit of the peak is always shrouded—always; indeed nobody has ever seen the summit itself; even when the wind is high the cloud clings stubbornly to the lee side like a pennant and will not be shaken off. But for the man in the forest the phenomenon is no joke. His tongue cleaves to the roof of his mouth and his knees turn to water. He utters a brief scream and claps his hands to the back of his neck and breaks into headlong flight down through the forest, stumbling and pitching in the deep drifts till his hands and his face are lacerated by the brambles and the bitter crust of ice upon the snow, down the narrow path with the

8

mountain tumbling about his head. It is a foolish, irrational thing to do, and this is what Crosby did precisely, turning to fire his revolver wildly at the oncoming mass and shout shrill obscenities.

He stopped only for lack of breath and sat down sweating and ashamed as though he had been observed in flight and looked about him a trifle furtively, but there was no living creature at hand except the ancient birds he had awakened with the inane banging of his gun; they hovered over him in the pale moonlight. Now he brushed the snow from his clothes with trembling fingers. The damp moss numbed his buttocks where he sat on the rock. Below and beyond him and behind strata of black rock hove up in a monstrous staircase to the foot of the peak which, now at his back, reared stiffly into the starry sky, as though indeed it had never budged an inch. In the chasm where Otto, he remembered, would be working, the cataract rumbled dully.

Otto often painted at night when the moon was high. He was painting a mural—he was always happy to speak of it—on the southern wall of the chasm which was called, colourfully, the Wall of the Oblique Death. He would let himself down the face of the cliff in the cradle he had built and paint sometimes all night and the fine spray would rise like smoke from the depths of the fall and obscure the light and he would return in the morning wet to the skin and ridiculously angry.

The others would be asleep in the camp now, Erica and the Commander and Hans and Slobadov and little Josef and Luca Pugnini and the rest. Soon, as soon indeed as he regained his breath, Crosby would go down to the camp himself and lie down on his mattress and close his eyes and drive himself along the tunnel of his mind towards the light he never reached. God alone knew why he had ever left his bed at all. Looking back, he could not recall his motives in trying to reach the foot of the peak. For

9

curiosity perhaps : the others were so damned reticent about it. But it seemed a little pointless.

He looked at the gun in his hand, still warm with the firing. He had had it already a long time, having found it in a ditch going towards Graz one afternoon in the thin mountain rain soon after the escape from the camp. It was Hungarian and there had been a full magazine in the worn leather holster; nine, he remembered, nine bullets; now he had fired seven, no, eight. There was one left. Idiot, he told himself. Nearly everybody got one that day, of one kind or another, though what the guns were doing there in the ditch nobody could say. They fired them into the gaunt valley at the wild roses, as foolhardy a bit of braggadocio as ever there was, in view of their plight, and the echoes ran to and fro a long time and the two pale Austrian girls in the tavern came out in their slippers in the rain to see what was happening and wanted the men to stay a bit, they had seen no men for months, they said, and were frightfully lonely.

Crosby said at that time he would sell his revolver to an American, but he never did, he would not be parted from it. He had it in his pocket even when he came to the mountain, after he had been separated from the rest, and the others there, the Divisional Commander and Roberto and Slobadov and the armourer's assistants, when they invited him to join them, wanted badly to try it, to fire it; æsthetically, they said. But he wanted the bullets for something else. Might they not have to fight? he asked. They nodded and said it was a possibility, always, if somewhat remote. Now he had wasted eight of the nine he had found in the magazine. But he preserved the one remaining bullet and when he got home, much later, long after his release from the mountain where he sat now, he prized it greatly.

In Five Elms he carried the gun with him everywhere, showing it to people who were tired of guns and taking out the magazine with the bullet nestling in the top to let them cock the action and press the trigger on the empty chamber. People were reluctant to report the matter to the police, though they felt it ought to be done; let somebody else do it. Crosby had fought for democracy for seven years and O'Leary had published a paragraph in the *Five Elms Observer* about how Crosby had won his medal and escaped from a prison camp and became a partisan trapped on a mountain and was a credit to the community and one thing or another and to complain of his trifling souvenir would seem a little churlish. It was not very serious after all; naughtiness is relative. And look at that wretched business with the boy's wife. Nevertheless it was curious that he should derive so much pleasure from the toy.

All they ever thought about nowadays, people said, was guns and bombs. Haven't you had enough of them? they would ask, and he would answer, if in expansive mood, that he loved the gun not so much for what it was—a scrap of metal that would serve a more useful purpose as a bicycle hub—but for what it could do, and what could you do with a bicycle hub? There was no answer to that. It made him feel better, he explained. He liked the way it felt in his pocket, banging against his thigh. It gave him power. With it he could fix everything, could set the world to rights, and God knows it needed setting right. We won their war with guns, he would say, warming to his subject, why not also ours? And then the listener, catching the drift, would turn away sickened and bored and titter to his neighbour.

But when he saw somebody in a bar or elsewhere who, on account of his attitude or conversation, might be held responsible in however small a measure for the way things seemed to be, then he would go suddenly silent and smile absently and finger the gun in his pocket, sweet and warm with the warmth of his body, and reflect with what ease he might deal with this much of the opposition, how simply and effectively he could silence at least this hostile tongue, and the great pleasure of the power he carried in his pocket tempered the despair in the pit of his taut belly and he would say afterwards, ' I could of fixed that little bastard all right,' quite happily, but if he was without his gun and a trifle lonely, it would be, ' I wish I'd had my little gun, I'd of fixed that fellow good and bloody proper.'

Later, to himself, he would say that he was only saving it, saving the bullet for a bigger fish, a fish of considerable importance, whose annihilation would be severely felt. But sometimes he was unable to restrain himself and would spend a little of the splendid resolution in a hopeless fight with his fists. His wound had left him weak, however, and either he suffered immediate and humiliating eclipse at the hands of a more powerful opponent or, as was indeed more often the case, would be ejected from the bar by two or three together and with immoderate hilarity, and Chubb would find him there and pick him up in his arms and carry him to the little house in York Street where Mrs. Chubb, a bitter blonde woman already so stout that her immense pregnancy was hardly visible, would make tea for them both and maybe bathe Crosby's face while Chubb talked to him earnestly,

' I'm just a copper, Jim,' he would begin.

But Crosby would not listen. He smoked fiercely and watched Mrs. Chubb till the woman left the room, not driven thence by the pitiless stare but because she could no longer tolerate in silence her husband's patience with the man.

' He's bad,' she would say, ' bad, bad, rotten.'

But Chubb persisted. ' You're all twisted up inside,' he would tell Crosby gently.

The restless eyes now would pause for a moment on the great blue bulk under the white light. Then they went back to the wedding group on the mantelpiece and the Chinese print and the bit of cracked Delft that Chubb had glued together after he had broken it and the pathetic handful of books so generously displayed on the sideboard and the damned geometrical neatness of everything. They were all and always right-angles. He did not reply.

Chubb shifted his weight uneasily. ' I've got to do what I'm told, Jim,' he muttered.

' Naturally. 'Course.'

The bellicose rasp of the voice was a perpetual insult. In fact Chubb should have taken him straight to the police station and let him face trial and a few days in jail for this last assault, but he found it hard to be so objective; he had known Crosby too long, they had fought too long together, had shared altogether too much. Prison, he knew instinctively, would serve only to crystallise the bitterness that a measure of tolerance might dissolve. So instead each time he talked, aimlessly because he did not understand the nature of the problem, it was always just out of his reach, and clumsily because he was naturally clumsy. He always returned to the gun.

' Why not just give it to me, Jim? You might go and do something you'd wish you hadn't one day. It's against the law to have a gun.'

' Come and get it.'

' I'm not supposed to know you've got it, or I'd have to.'

Crosby grinned, showing his teeth. ' Now you know. I'm telling you. I still got it.'

' If I did what was right, I'd have to report you.'

' Don't talk about it so damn much.'

' You're cleverer than I am, Jim.' He looked down at his hands and smoothed the black hair on the knuckles. ' I don't know, I don't know.'

And Crosby thought suddenly how pitiful the policeman was and how grotesque, and leaned forward to pat the great

13

arm once or twice. 'Never mind, Chubby,' he said, 'just you keep out of it.'

'Jim, some time this has got to stop. Folk are fed up with wars and elections and conferences and revolutions and being badgered about all the time. They want to be left alone a bit, that's all. All they want is a bit of peace and quiet.'

Crosby said, 'Christ,' and drew breath deeply.

'A bit o' peace 'n' quiet, that's all.'

'The way you talk you'd think it was nothing, peace 'n' quiet,' he said. His voice began to rise. 'For God's sake what's everybody been wanting the last couple of thousand years but a bit of peace 'n' quiet? Yet they still talk about it as though it was a packet of fags. And look where it's got them. Every twenty years a war. Everybody wants it and think they deserve it, just as though it was some sort of right and fighting a war was enough and so nobody does a damn thing to keep it, like a lot of ostriches burying their heads in the sand. Nobody's learned a damn thing. Might just as well not have had a war, for all the good it's done. Better. I tell you, Chubb, it's wanting a bit of peace 'n' quiet that's the matter with everything. Cancer, that's what it is. Dry rot. Ask Brett what he thinks about people wanting a bit of peace 'n' quiet. You ask him. Ask old Henderson. Ask anybody. That's what they live on. Folk being nice and quiet and doing as they're bloody told because it's easier. So nobody interferes till it's too late and we're at it again with another because all they want is a bit of peace 'n' quiet. Ah, people are damned fools. People make me sick. Sick.'

'Me, too, I suppose. I suppose I make you sick.'

'Yes, you too, you're one of them.'

Chubb said, 'Jim, I don't believe you mean a word of this.'

Crosby looked at him sharply. 'Why not?'

'The only one you're fooling is yourself.'

It was not pleasant to be told so bluntly a truth you had set aside and ignored because it would capsize your canoe if you accepted it; and doubly teasing when the truth was only half a truth, for Crosby was not certain that he fooled even himself. He put it behind him again.

'You'll see,' he said.

'Better give it to me, Jim.'

'I'm keeping it.'

'Why?'

The policeman was simple, in all conscience, but coupled with persistence it was painfully irritating. 'Souvenir,' he said briefly. He smiled suddenly. 'My little souvenir of the war.'

'Always in your pocket.'

'It feels nice. I like the way it feels.'

'You don't want any more trouble, Jim.'

'I'm saving it.'

'What for?'

'Who for, you mean.'

'Listen, Jim.' He leaned forward and tapped Crosby on the knee and the knee shifted away from the finger. 'Listen to me a minute, there's a thing I want to tell you—'

'Iris,' said Crosby shortly, 'has nothing to do with it. Nothing.'

Chubb rubbed his nose slowly. 'She's still waiting for you. I heard to-day. Maybe if she sent the kid away for a bit. Relatives or something. Any girl can make a mistake, Jim. I think we ought to remember that. We were away a longish time. She thought you were dead about then, while you were with the partisans and couldn't write.'

'I wasn't dead.'

'Everybody thought so.'

Crosby said again, 'I wasn't dead.'

15

'All right, Jim, I know, I know. 'Course you weren't. What were you, then?'

Crosby looked at him steadily. 'Meaning what?'

'What happened that year, Jim?' Chubb was rubbing the hairs on his knuckles to and fro. The man was either extraordinarily perspicacious, Crosby thought, or more than usually bovine; he had been chewing the same cud now for a very long time.

'I was on a mountain. I told you.'

'Yes, you told me.' He had asked the same fumbling question many times, but the answer was always as evasive.

They knew one another very well, these two, as well, that is to say, as was within their several capacities for human relationship, but Crosby had seldom spoken of the year (it was ten months, in fact) he lived on the mountain. Before that time, as a soldier, he had seemed human enough, bitter and maybe a little harsh, but human certainly; and happy, you would have said, within his self-imposed limits, happy at least in the white heat of his hatred of injustice. Fighting had satisfied his vitality, his profound craving for simplification, his lust for action. The enemy for him had been a personal enemy, a hostile individual standing between Crosby and the achievement of his objective and to be destroyed for that reason. He had been, Chubb remembered, a splendid soldier, cool, methodical, quite fearless; much respected by the company and not a little feared. He had no friends other than Chubb, whose company he accepted rather than encouraged, and seemed to need none. Indeed he avoided attachments, having instead a purpose. He was moved by something more, or less, than friendship or necessity or courage; indeed he was never considered a purely brave man : his fighting was too cold, his ferocity too studied. He had an aim and he seemed never to lose sight of it. It lent him some nameless inner radiance, a spiritual serenity that set him

16

apart from the men with whom he lived and suffered. They did not understand him and did not know what his purpose was; nor did they ask, having none themselves and therefore scant interest in another's; and he in any case was not sufficiently articulate to put his motives into words, even had he succumbed to the desire to do so. He had grown up and come to manhood in the war, into a state of mind that was without expression, that came from some recess deep in his slight body and all you could say of it was that it allowed no shading of opinion; there was for and there was against and those who were for he mistrusted and those who were against he encouraged in their hostility, relieved and even pleased at the pristine clarity of his relationship with them; they were opposed to him and he knew where he stood and there could be no compromise. The rest, the majority, those whose attitude was unidentifiable, he tolerated during the years of battle because their objective was perforce akin to his own; afterwards they must be alienated. And he was good at that. He could do that very well indeed. The little managers, he called them, the small fry of the big fish. Here maybe you would catch a glimpse of his soul and you might see distantly what he was against; but what he was for you never knew. Nobody knew. Chubb did not know. Not even Crosby knew.

Now he thrust the gun into his pocket where it bounced against his hip as he set off down the mountainside with the sweat cooling on his face and bile at the back of his tongue. The moon cast his shadow long and thin and black down the slopes below him into the dark lake of the valley. The wind dropped. The sky bristled with stars . . . holes in the floor of heaven, my child, to let the glory shine through. She had smacked her lips over it, he remembered, the sanctimonious old witch whose whole life was an aphorism, whose collection of saws had passed for wisdom, whose daughter, Crosby's mother, learned them parrotwise at the witch's knee so that she might pass them to her own child, Jim, whose wife, too, Iris, had learned them somewhere, the sum of the knowledge of a hundred generations . . . the mist hung over the cataract in the still air like smoke above a great fire and with it, in it and of it, the steady thunder of the falling water hung, so that the noise appeared to have substance, heavy and vaporous, and might be captured and bottled and kept. Here, whipping about his legs, the weeds grew long and rank and the small sharp rocks were hidden. He went down the long slopes towards the head of the chasm and bore away to the left through the scrub and up the spur to the edge of the southern cliff, the Wall of the Oblique Death—he smiled to himself at the name—and through the drenching spray to the crane Otto had built.

It was a tree trunk, scarcely more, pinned to the earth by its own great weight, jutting out over the chasm. The rope and pulley hung from beneath. On one end of the rope the cradle was suspended, swinging idly against the face of the cliff; on the other Otto had bound a rock whose weight, roughly equivalent to that of Otto and the cradle together, constituted the necessary compensation; the rock hung far below the cradle. Thus the artist was able to hoist himself up and down without great effort. Immediately below the brink of the cliff he had constructed a small platform or landing-stage to facilitate movement to and from the cradle; a short flight of steps led down to it.

Now the rope was taut and trembling, for Otto was beneath at work, far below against the face of the wall in the cradle. He was generally supposed, in the camp, to be epileptic, but nobody had ever seen him in the terrible agony of a fit nor heard him utter the unearthly cries usually associated with epilepsy. However, his claim was accepted readily enough. The wide amber eyes burned dully in the gaunt face from whose chin the red beard burst like a bomb. It was somewhat embarrassing, in the middle of a conversation, to be told by your companion that he was epileptic; it was difficult to know whether to express sympathy, or envy, or only a passing interest. In any case you found yourself flinching thenceforward; it arrived without warning in his case, he said. He had a curious liking for Crosby, and the latter for the artist. They rarely spoke a word to one another—Otto was not talkative—but there existed a mutual sympathy, a respect by each for the other's isolation.

Crosby went down to the platform and dropped on to his hands and knees and finally flat on his belly to crawl to the edge and look over. He was conscious of a great urge to establish human contact again after his experience in the forest; it was irresistible; he would wave to Otto, that was all, to see the answering flourish of the brush. But there was nothing to see, only the spume rising slowly out of the depths and the rope dropping down the smooth, bald face of the cliff. He was tired and confused and disappointed and it would have been restful, but for the stealthy advent of nausea with the vibration of the platform, to lie peacefully there for a few minutes. But already the blood was beginning to drum at his temples. He lay rigid and gripped the edge of platform till the muscles of his fingers ached, gritting his teeth against the faintness. He swore at himself aloud, angrily. The rolling mists oppressed him like the walls of a windowless room. He opened his eyes and tried to focus them and then below him the mists parted slowly and the artist, far beneath against the shining rock, was visible for a moment in the moonlight. He shouted but there was no power in his lungs, and waved, but Otto was working. He reached out for the rope and shook it and watched the tremor flee down the living stuff to the cradle below and set it rocking gently. Otto looked up, brush in hand. The white face glistened for a moment against the dark void beyond and then was drowned in the swirling mist. The face left its imprint on the mind. Crosby vomited suddenly and lay still a long time with the clamour of the cataract and the blood booming indivisibly in his ears. He knew he must move soon now, for the instinct to drop quietly over the edge of the platform was strong. He bit on the edge of the platform till the wood splintered in his teeth. The earth rolled drunkenly and then came slowly to a standstill. He shoved himself away from the edge and got on to his hands and knees and crawled to the steps. In a minute he lay in the wet grass on the brink of the cliff and retched without effort.

But they were not all sleeping, as he had anticipated, when he reached the camp. There was a light beneath the blanket that did for a door to the Command Post and he came up to it on tiptoes to listen for a moment to the warm voices beyond. Soon, he told himself, he would enter so that they might look up and he would see recognition in their eyes and hear them speak his name. That would be enough.

The Chief of Staff swung about and half rose from the box on which he was seated at the Commander's desk, his pince-nez flashing suddenly in the candlelight, but the Corps Commander did not raise his head from the map that lay on the table between the two men. He was getting very thin on the crown, Crosby thought absently.

'It's you,' the Chief of Staff said irritably.

Crosby looked at the man, disliking him now more than ever. A dry grey little man, Crosby thought, a stationmaster, an unchartered accountant, a manager: small fry. 'Yes, it's me,' he said, ' Crosby.' In a moment he said again, ' Crosby.'

'You ought to give more warning,' the Chief of Staff told him. He peered at the stiff white face. ' What's the matter?'

20

' Nothing.'

' You're looking badly.'

' I'm all right. What . . .' he hesitated. '. . . I saw the light beneath the blanket.'

' We're studying the attack,' the Chief of Staff said.

' What attack?'

' The attack on the reservoir.' He spoke irritably again, as though Crosby ought to have known; and indeed he did know : he had forgotten for a moment.

' Eight months now you've been studying that damned attack,' he said with sudden heat. ' It's all humbug.'

' There are many aspects of the matter,' the Chief of Staff told him primly. ' We have hardly begun.'

' Who d'you think you're fooling?' The Corps Commander raised his head at the violence of the soldier's voice. ' Yourselves?' But the anger ebbed from his fingers quickly. ' You're crazy, the whole bloody lot of you. You make me sick.' He turned to go, fumbling with the blanket. ' Funk, that's all it is,' he muttered, ' blue funk.'

Now the Corps Commander spoke, the candles throwing the shadow of his vast shoulders across the addled plaster of the walls. The heavy jowl rose and fell with the movement of the jaw. ' How far did you get, Crosby?' The voice was gentle, absent, innocent.

Crosby turned. ' Where?'

' Through the forest.' He waited, fingering the lobe of his ear and watching the soldier with flat grey eyes. ' You went up into the forest, didn't you?'

' Yes. How d'you know?'

The shoulders moved. ' I saw you set out.'

' Not very far,' he said.

' No?'

' It's a long way,' Crosby said.

' Yes, it's a long way.' The Commander had seen them all try; Erica, Luca Pugnini, even the Chief of Staff; and

21

presently return, subdued, reticent and frightened. ' I shall want you to cut my hair to-morrow,' he said.

' Yes, sir.'

The Commander lowered his head and the Chief of Staff bit on a yawn and adjusted his dentures with his tongue and turned also to the map. Crosby left them and went out into the moonlight. The track lay smooth and white between the little dwellings. The stream sang softly beneath the bridge.

He took off his clothes and lay down on the mattress. The pattern of the broken slates moved slowly across the floor as the moon went over the roof. In a little while he reached out for the haversack that lay on the floor beside the mattress and opened it. When he had found the comb and the scissors and the clippers he laid them on the floor beside the pillow and lay back. In a minute he put out his hand again and felt for the clippers; and then the scissors. Then he turned over and began the long walk along the tunnel towards the light.

2

NOTHING stirred in the camp when the aircraft circled the plateau. Twice the ancient cottages, crumbling under the sun, ignored its passage and the blithe shadow, rising and falling with the configuration of the earth, acknowledged their presence on the mountainside with scarcely a flip of the tail. A few scraps of mortar, loosed by the sudden vibration, trickled from the walls of the half-dozen that still remained as habitable places. The rest were already low mounds of rubble and white dust beside the track. The aircraft flew off towards the south. The cottages drowsed in the sun.

Until the Corps Commander and the Chief of Staff, under pressure of circumstance, selected the place as the site of the headquarters, the little hamlet had not been inhabited for some ninety-seven years; the figure was supplied by Father Domenicus. The Chief of Staff had held that, as partisans, they should live in caves, but the Commander felt that a measure of comfort was not wholly incompatible with partisanship, and in any case there were no caves; they occupied the hamlet. It was not easy, by any means; the accommodation was limited. The women lived together, Erica and Paula, in the house near the bridge; Maria, the Divisional Commander's wife, was accommodated with her husband. The men were scattered among the dwellings as and where they had found roofs that defied all but the heaviest rain. The mill was devoted exclusively to the armoury; it stood on the banks of the stream above the bridge. But the presence of ten or twelve people made really very little difference to the village. The walls continued to rot, the weeds continued to blossom from the floors and ivy roamed freely from window to door and roof and smokestack. It had been dead many years. It had not even a name.

It stood on level ground. The track came up from the south to the village between the cottages and over the bridge below the mill and down into the valley in the north. Near the great reservoir which lay a mile or two beyond the village to the north, the track joined the sandy road that led to Ronc. The reservoir, fed by the stream that came tumbling across the plateau from the chasm, was largely natural, standing in a kind of bowl of which only the fourth, the lowest, side was artificial. The dam there was the key to the irrigation of the whole plain and of the cities that sprawled across it, many miles away. You could barely see them even on a clear day. Mostly the haze was too dense, or the clouds that came to rest on the mountainside below Ronc were too languid to shift easily or often. The reservoir glittered gaily in the sun.

The village of Ronc stood two miles below the plateau. From the Corps Commander's headquarters on the shoulder of the plateau you could see nothing of the village but the square campanile of the church, rising above the intervening wood. Sometimes, when the wind was blowing from the west, you might hear the bells when Father Domenicus tolled them; he was clever with the bells and often passed messages to the partisans by that means. The code he used was childishly simple but the occupying forces, while entertaining considerable doubts as to his piety—there were three or four infants in the village whose repulsive faces bore a distinct resemblance to that of the priest—gravely underestimated his wit, and left him to his bells unsuspecting; or so it appeared. In an emergency he could also signal to the headquarters trapped on the mountain by lamp or flag from the top of the tower.

'It is good to have an agent in the enemy's camp,' he said, explaining his particular position to the Chief of Staff in the early days of their resistance. 'I can keep you fully informed of all their movements so that the timing of your attacks, if any, will be the more deadly. We shall catch them, in God's mercy, with their trousers down.' He flicked from the end of his long bleak nose the drop that trembled there summer and winter, raised his pale eyes to heaven and crossed himself.

'It's a dangerous game, Father,' the Chief of Staff told him. 'They have little respect for the cloth.'

'We are all in God's hands,' Father Domenicus said simply. He needed a shave; the bristles grew on his cadaverous face in little tufts here and there. The drop formed again on the end of the nose.

He did not at that time feel it expedient to mention the fact that he was, as indeed were the majority of the good people of Ronc, on equally intimate terms with the occupying forces, whose commander, Walter von Langenburg, he kept as fully informed of the activities of the partisans as the latter of the movements of the garrison. He was, as the local authority, hardly less important than the mayor himself, consulted by partisans and Germans alike and was therefore able to forestall, with an impartiality that befitted the Church very well, the activities of both. In this way he enlivened what would otherwise have been a somewhat humdrum existence, protected his parish and parishioners from liberation, prevented loss of life and blood irrespective of nationality, and justified his duplicity at least in the eyes of God.

But Father Domenicus, though not by any means a foolish man, did not realise that he was only the means whereby the warring factions, each led by men considerably his intellectual superior, achieved their own ends. For the Corps Commander and Walter von Langenburg each used the priest to carry information to the other, information that each was extremely anxious the other should have, without their recourse to the direct communication that would offend the elementary tenets and principles of war. When, for example, von Langenburg proposed to cleanse the mountain of its partisans he saw to it that the details of his plan first reached the priest so that the latter might at once inform the Corps Commander and the partisans depose themselves as customarily.

When they had vanished into the fastness of the mountain the Corps Commander informed the priest so that the information reached the garrison in good time to save its commander's face: where there is no enemy, who but a fool launches an attack? As becomes a good, if reluctant, Prussian, von Langenburg saw to it that the system operated equally well in reverse. When the Corps Commander had perfected with his staff a plan for breaking through the ring of mines and steel and men that so efficiently surrounded the mountain, he consulted Father Domenicus so that von Langenburg might bring an overwhelming superiority of men and weapons to bear upon the point at which the partisans threatened to make their break for freedom; as soon as the troops were in position the priest passed the vital report to the partisans by the usual means.

'We are betrayed again,' said Luca Pugnini, greatly relieved. None but an idiot attacks superior strength without at least the advantage of surprise. In any case, in the unlikely event of the attack being successful, what would they do with their freedom? Where would they go? It takes a long time to adapt yourself to such a phenomenon, Luca Pugnini pointed out; freedom was desirable only when you were free to pursue it. The Corps Commander smiled and said nothing.

The attack, naturally, was never carried out. And it was in this final respect, as the Divisional Commander said, that the system had its supreme, a metaphysical, advantage; that the attack retained to itself its own integrity. Eleven men and women had contributed to its genesis, each giving of himself according to his means. Now it existed beyond them, outside them, independently and without their future interference. It lived in time and in space, in all the qualities of existence, in fact, except substance. And it came, in the course of inchoation, to have a character of its own, its own insistent ego. Far from submitting meekly to the authority of its creators, it began to exercise an influence upon them, an influence sometimes malign and menacing, sometimes benevolent, sometimes terrifying, according to the nature of the individual and his reaction to the prospect of the sudden freedom it might bring. The personality of the attacks, for there were several in existence, was no more to be ignored than was that of the Corps Commander, for example, or any of his staff. Each found it increasingly difficult to regard the attacks objectively, since each had contributed to them and was therefore a part of them; nor yet quite subjectively, because there was always too much of the others in them. They accepted the attacks because they must. Indeed, as the months slipped past they came to have a curious affection for them; as Luca Pugnini emphasised, an attack once made no longer existed, and it was a pity to destroy them like that. As plans of attack they had a certain beauty, not to mention the possibility of success; as operations of war they were no more than ugly brawls. All the plans were similar, of course, in at least one respect—that each had as its motive the freedom of the attackers; the staff was now, however, working on an operation of a rather different kind. This was to be merely mischievous, its object being to cause the maximum of inconvenience to the enemy. It was to be an attack on the reservoir with the object of blowing up or opening the dam so that the entire valley might be flooded, much

27

damage done to the enemy's communications, and the peoples of the cities of the plain taught a very salutary lesson for omissions best known to themselves. It promised to be a most interesting attack, having many uncommon aspects.

'If a little sterile,' Luca Pugnini whispered to the Chief of Staff during the Commander's opening address on the subject, 'a trifle lacking in aesthetic values.'

The Corps Commander repeated his address in several languages. It had been through this happy facility with tongues other than his own that, during the early days on the mountain, the Commander had been able to control his quarrelsome juniors. There had been scarcely two of the first six or seven who spoke the same tongue and so the exchange of abuse and occasionally ideas was limited to such as the Commander chose to translate for them. As the headquarters expanded, however, and new recruits arrived, they built up between them a common language comprising a little English for Crosby; a little French for Pierre, the Breton fisherman who had escaped from a labour camp in Breslau; German for Hans, the elderly deserter; some Croatian for Otto and Slobadov; and Italian for the Divisional Commander and Roberto, the professional footballer. Now they could converse, on the whole, with comparative ease. At the same time their gradual submission to the will of the Corps Commander more than atoned for the loss in discipline that resulted from the growth of direct intercourse; formalities and restrictions in any case were slight in the headquarters.

It was probably because nobody knew him well that the Commander was so well respected. They were acquainted with a little of his history, but no more than he had cared to let fall in the course of conversation. He had lived, they knew, in Paris and in various English cities; as an actor of mediocre ability—his own adjective—he had toured parts of Europe and the United States of America. He had been a journalist and a soldier (it was believed he had fought in the Gran Chaco war) and at some time in his remarkable career had been a sailor. He was extremely tall and walked with a marked limp, his left leg having been damaged at the knee in some action or accident to which he never referred. He was still immensely powerful, but now his belly was straining somewhat at the broad black belt he wore about his middle, and the sandy hair grew sparsely on the crown of his head and grey about his ears. He spoke seldom, softly and as though tired, without emotion; the grey eyes watched the listener absently. It was always difficult to talk to him, he responded so seldom; a question about himself met with a slightly derisive wrinkling of the eyes, and silence. In the mornings he would often tour the defences, the minefields serving as well, he once said, to keep the enemy out as to keep the heretics in; he would go alone on a horse, the boney, knock-kneed mare he seemed to cherish. He was no horseman; he sat the wretched animal like a sack of potatoes.

They had been surrounded and cut off very soon after their arrival on the mountain to set up a headquarters and establish a recruiting office for the area. Their first raid, however, a sordid foray in search of office furniture and a few mattresses and cooking utensils, had prompted immediate retaliation by the enemy and the entire mountain was surrounded. They were fairly trapped. Von Langenburg set up his headquarters in Ronc, encircled the mountain with mines and wire and artfully-placed machine-gun posts, organised a system of armoured patrols, and made himself as comfortable as he could for the duration of hostilities. He had had enough, not that he admitted as much even to himself, but the comfort in which he now lived was unique in his life and he was reluctant to disturb it. He had fought in Italy and Russia and, as the result of the loss of an arm, had been posted for duty on the line of communications. His troops were elderly and sluggish, but numerous. From time to time, as von Langenburg was well aware, partisan sympathisers broke into the ring he had drawn, but none to his certain knowledge had ever broken out. Indeed, he issued particular orders that nobody was to be discouraged from entering; it was to be hoped they would, in large numbers; to have all his enemies in front and none behind was very much to his taste. He could then devote himself to the reports of his activities without a thought for the stab in the back. His reports, in consequence, were masterly.

In the early evening of the day the aircraft reconnoitred the plateau, Father Domenicus, following a disagreeable interview with von Langenburg during which the Prussian had been more than usually bellicose, took the key of the belfry from its hook behind the kitchen door of the vicarage, and went out.

The sun was setting then and the shadows were long and thin across the quiet street. The soldier leaning against the door of the hostel watched the priest incuriously. The skitter of brats playing about the fountain in the square grew suddenly silent at his approach and whispering withdrew to the other side of the fountain and busied themselves about the tap there. He changed his direction to pass among them and pat their heads with a wintry smile. They fled and he went on silently towards the church. In the belfry he removed his coat and rolled up the sleeves of his long woollen vest and pinned to the beam through which hung the greasy ropes a scrap of paper. He flicked the drop from the end of his nose and grasped the ropes.

The brazen clangour gushed from the belfry over the startled village, flowed across the land from which the night was already rising to the serene sky as the sun slipped down below the distant hills, blew with the evening breeze down the village street and into every room and closet and hirsute ear, into the place where von Langenburg warmed his buttocks at the fire and contemplated the trollop on the couch, into the back room of the bar where the mayor was preparing the table for the N.C.O.s this evening, into a little copse beyond the toll-gate where the boy and the girl lay among the rabbits, and slowly, ebbing and flowing, up the long green slopes and over the wood to the hamlet on the shoulder of the plateau. In Ronc none knew why the bells rang at that time; Father Domenicus was always somewhat erratic in the matter. Only two men acknowledged their summons. One of these was old Gregory who, drunk then as always, set down his beaker of wine firmly on the table, waited till the last iron note had faded, then struggled to his feet and staggered from the taproom, rebounding from wall to wall along the dark passage to the street. The soldier in the doorway picked his teeth meticulously and watched Gregory go, teetering like a leaf in a high wind, across the square towards the church. He was met at the great door by the priest. Fearful sometimes of the wrath of God and terrified always of the censure of Father Domenicus, Gregory dropped on his knees in the gravel and pulled the cap from his head.

' Father,' he said thickly. ' Is it Sunday?' Father . . .'

' It is always Sunday,' the priest said. He regarded the slovenly figure with cold wet eyes. ' God has no hours of business.' He swept past the man on his knees in the gravel.

And the other who listened to the bells was Pierre, the Intelligence Officer of the Corps Headquarters. He was sitting on the bank of the stream above the bridge fishing. There were no fish in the stream, that he knew well enough, but it made him feel better to fish again. He watched the float bobbing in the clear water and felt the tug of the swift current on his finger. There would be many fish, he thought, in the reservoir. When they attacked and captured the reservoir he would build a little boat and sail

31

about and fish till his back ached and the bottom of the craft was alive with the panting silver bellies and the dull flip of the tails against the hot dry wood. They would be coming into Concarneau now, he thought, with the great brown sails against the pale sky and the smocks they wore faded pink and blue moving to and fro on the decks and their feet too swollen for sabots after all day on the hot deckboards. The ships would be deep in the water, clear green water, rounding the walls of the Old Town squatting there in the middle of the harbour with washing hanging out to dry on the battlements. When they had off-loaded the catch and the ship was clean and the nets spread for repair and to dry on the broad, sandy quayside, then they would go home and the girl would show him where the new barrel was and he would drink deep from the barrel of red wine and raise his head for breath now and then, shaking the wine off his nose and then down again with nose and mouth buried in it till he had had enough and threw back his head to bring up the air he had swallowed with it. . . . Slobadov, the sentry, who leaned against the parapet of the bridge with the bayonet worn smooth (with chopping wood) against his leathery cheek, raised his eyebrows in their expression of perpetual surprise and called to him,

' No fish to-day?'

The dream was broken. He drew a deep breath and stared at the flashing water.

He raised his head only when he heard the bells. He pulled in the line and got to his feet and listened, the wind stirring the short black hair that overhung his forehead. He listened. When the tenuous reverberation was no longer in the air he packed up his line and went along the track, the weeds that grew from between the buried cobbles whispering about his ankles. Maria Pugnini, the Divisional Commander's wife, who was preparing the supper with

32

Roberto and Paula in the kitchen of the cottage whose outer wall had long ago crumbled to dust, raised her brown eyes to him and smiled their customary promise. The round arms were white with flour. Little Josef, her son, left his mother's side and followed the Breton along the track towards the Command Post. Josef followed anything that moved; it was impossible to circulate in the camp without little Josef following silently on his dusty bare feet. If you spoke to him and told him for God's sake to leave you alone and go away and stop haunting you, he would fix his vacant black eyes on some nearby object and stare at it till you shrugged your shoulders and went on; then he followed. Now they passed Otto, who was mixing paints on a bench outside his quarters; the pots stood in a row on the ground and Otto mixed the colours in a great earthenware bowl on the bench. He turned when Pierre passed him and bade him gravely good evening, the gouts of red and yellow paint standing out among the hairs of the forearms, the sloe amber eyes narrowed against the glare of the setting sun. Pierre nodded briefly, never wholly sure of Otto, and went on towards the Command Post.

He pulled aside the blanket and entered. The Commander was sitting on a box with a sheet about his neck, and Crosby was cutting his hair.

' A message, sir,' Pierre said, ' from the priest.'

The Commander did not speak.

' He says the enemy is contemplating a purge following the reconnaisance by that aeroplane to-day.'

The Commander's voice, muffled by the sheet, told him, ' Tell the Chief of Staff I'd like to see him.'

Pierre nodded and went out. Little Josef was waiting for him and followed him along the track towards the mill.

' Trouble, Crosby,' the Commander said briefly.

' Yes, sir.' He stood back and narrowed his eyes, the better to judge his handiwork. Then he went on, gingerly.

The Commander closed his eyes under the opiate of the clippers and the scissors and the comb. The box was confoundedly uncomfortable.

'You were your company barber once, Crosby, didn't you tell me?'

'That's right.' He crouched over the neck.

'And before the war?'

'Machine minder. Bretts',' he added, 'domestic appliances,' seeing in his mind's eye the chimneys against the low grey clouds in the late afternoon and the plumes of white smoke riding the wind. 'Big company,' he said.

'You'll go back there.'

'No.'

'What, then?'

'Anything, only not that.'

'And your wife?'

'She's all right.' He pressed the head with the tips of his fingers. 'Left a bit.'

'I suppose you're a bit bored with this . . . this sort of life.'

'Yes and no, yes and no.'

'Nothing much happens, does it?'

'No, sir, not much.'

'Pleasant, though, I sometimes think, to have nothing happening.'

'Makes a change.' He felt he was being drawn and fought against it instinctively, considering his replies carefully before giving voice to them.

'When will you try another trip into the forest?'

Crosby said, 'Had enough of that.'

'Why did you try it once, anyway?'

'Damned if I know, to tell the truth.' And it was the truth. 'Seemed to be quite a pastime. Thought I'd have a go, too. Funny business.'

'Very funny.'

'Right a bit.' He pressed the head to the right.

'What d'you suggest we do, Crosby?'

'In what way? Jerry, you mean? What about the reservoir? We're always talking about it. Let's have a go at the damn thing. That's what's wrong with this place, too much talk. Shave the neck? So damn busy talking we never have time to do anything.'

'You speak frankly, Crosby.'

''Course.'

'You'll be able to make up for lost time when you get home.'

'Maybe.'

His homecoming was not as he had expected. He wanted to run away when he reached the corner of the narrow street in which they lived and there was a constriction in his heart; he could hear it beating in his ears like the throb of distant guns and the wound across his left groin ached along its whole length. He felt sick and faint and people passing stared at him when he leaned against the wall to let the mist clear from before his eyes. Then he started forward again, lugging the bag up on to his back and cursing fluently when the things he had bought for her in Cairo and Tunis and Catania and Naples and Rome and everywhere, that he found still with his things in the battalion luggage-wagon when he was released from the mountain and returned to his unit, slipped from his shoulder. He could feel the way the street rocked under his feet and nothing had changed, nothing, absolutely nothing, everything was exactly as he thought it would be all the time, with the afternoon sunshine throwing the shadows of the chimneys evenly across the warm road where he had pressed the tar bubbles with his thumb all his life and all the windows open and plants with white wooden labels growing in the gardens and the air foul with cooking. But what he felt then was not love and gladness and a hard lump in his throat; it was

35

nausea—loathing, horror, revulsion from its hideous familiarity and the nostalgia that swilled about in his belly was not for home but for the desert and especially for the mountain. He began to run forward, the kitbag swaying and bouncing ponderously on his back. He saw her a long way away standing at the door waiting and when he came nearer he saw that she was shivering as though it was cold that day, her face as white as the step on which she stood. He slowed his pace to a walk, breathless and with a fluttering in his knees like the approach of fever.

'Jim,' she said in a high flat voice.

He looked at her over the gate, breathing heavily. Her hair was arranged differently, being also longer than he remembered it, and she was a little heavier; the dress was drawn tight over the big breasts. He could not speak and waited for her to speak again.

'You're back,' she said.

'Yes—' he cleared his throat, ' yes, I'm back.'

He looked at her over the gate, waiting for her to come to him, but she did not. He knew there was something wrong then. He became aware of the silence in the street and of the eyes and ears at all the windows.

'You've caught the sun,' she said.

'Yes.'

'Your face is quite brown.'

'Yes.'

Then he said, ' What's the matter?'

The child cried in the house and in a moment came to her on the step and clung to her skirt and he saw how very small and young it was.

'Jim.' Her voice rose and quavered.

He waited, looking at her.

'I'm glad you're back,' she said shrilly.

'Yes.'

'Everything's ready for you,' she said.

36

' Whose kid is that?'

' Your tea's ready,' she said.

' Whose kid is that?' His voice soared suddenly.

' Jim.'

' Answer me, damn it.'

' Jim, listen . . .'

Then he shouted at her. She was weeping now and the doors of the dwellings on either side of his own opened and people came out into the street from every house as though they had all been waiting for this moment, and stood listening, arms akimbo.

' Well?'

' Mine, Jim. Jim . . .' She was weeping piteously.

' And who else's?'

' Don't, Jim, the neighbours. Jim, stop it.' She put her hands over her face and the tears ran down the trembling fingers and the child at her side began to cry uneasily.

' Who else's, I said.'

' A soldier, Jim.'

His voice went up again. ' What soldier?'

' It was only once, Jim. I swear it, I swear it.' She stumbled down the little tiled path to the gate and took hold of the bars and shook the gate. ' You've got to believe me, Jim, you've got to. In all the time, only once.'

He put out a hand to steady himself and she caught it and kissed it many times, leaving tears on the blunt fingers, saying over again, ' Only once, only once . . .'

He pulled his hand free. ' I want to know who it was.'

' I don't know,' she said. ' A soldier, Jim, an American soldier. I don't know who it was. Jim, it doesn't matter, it doesn't make any difference . . .' She wept uncontrollably. ' I had to have it, Jim. Jim, it was years and years ago.'

He picked up the kitbag and swung it on to his back and went away up the street unsteadily and people he knew were calling greetings to him but he did not hear them and one or two tried to stop him but he brushed them aside. Iris was running beside him, weeping and tugging at his arm, and behind her the child ran and fell and cried purposefully. 'I could've had an abortion, Jim,' she was saying, 'I could've got rid of it, it would of been easy, there's a woman in Ashgrove Road been doing them for everybody, ten pounds, it would have been easy, Jim. Jim!' She screamed, 'Jim, I could've done it and never told you . . . Jim.' He threw her off and a man came out in his shirtsleeves to pick her up. He heard her screaming as he went away up the street. Afterwards he remembered the deep relief he felt then, the fine full satisfaction it gave him to defy the suffocating familiarity of the street and the houses and the odour of cooking and the seedy little plants with their labels all reaching out to close about his back and hold him there. He felt a profound gaiety; the bitter fury was only partly true. He felt himself starting the long journey back to the mountain, with everything settled and finished behind him. He saw the great peak in the sky, high, higher than the sun. The screams receded.

'When I get home,' he said to the Corps Commander, 'there's a lot of things I got to fix.'

'What's the matter with them?'

'They're all wrong, all wrong, all . . .' he cursed his own inarticulacy.

'And then, what? When you've fixed everything, what then, Crosby?'

The soldier frowned. 'It'll take a bit of time,' he said, 'afterwards we'll see.'

'You know what you want?'

'Yes, I know what I want.'

'You don't, Crosby. You only know what you don't want. Not enough.'

'It's a start anyway.'

The Corps Commander did not reply. He wondered

38

where Erica was now and what she was doing. He had not seen her for a day or two. Paula would be trailing her about, he supposed, with the mute wide-eyed adoration of a china doll, or Pierre, bored at last with the Divisional Commander's wife, or Otto, seeking inspiration from her fathomless character, or Slobadov or Hans or any of them; they all wanted her, loved her, he supposed, each in his way. His thoughts wandered to the message Father Domenicus had sent. Von Langenburg had taken the initiative again . . . must be an enterprising fellow, he had often thought he would like to meet the German. They would have to strike camp again and move elsewhere on the mountain so that the priest might report their exodus to the enemy and Von Langenburg would not launch his sweep and write his absurd reports about how the partisans had fled again. To-night, or maybe to-morrow night, Father Domenicus would come toiling up the mountain, looking like a great vulture in his hooded cape, to see that all was well and they were indeed preparing to move. The touch of the scissors on his temple soothed and satisfied his nerves and he yawned, the jowl beneath his chin ridiculously like an abbreviated bib on his chest. He watched the small sandy hairs rolling down the sheet.

A little before one o'clock of the following morning a bomber came out of the south and circled the plateau at an altitude of about two thousand feet. It flew off almost at once and when it returned it was flying very low indeed. Only Otto saw it the first time, a great black bird between himself and the stars. The second time Erica saw it. A small white flower blossomed in its wake.

WHEN he struck the earth he was calling a name and his mother was singing tipsily and his father smiled and told first Miss Quentin and then Adrian to take her upstairs and the thin screams hung above the road like a telegraph wire rising and falling from pole to pole. *With an alpaca frock and a green scarf shawl, a white straw bonnet and a pink parasol,* and he was at that moment a part of everything, of every blade of grass on the mountainside as though he had exploded and now was spread over the earth in everything there was, living and dead, grass, trees, rocks, the roots of the grass and the trees and the insects he could hear beneath his head stirring in the earth. He knew about everything, everything except maybe the way the harness unbuckled and he sat up at last and fumbled with it. The screams receded and the pain in his left shoulder grew. He discovered that he was weeping petulantly, tugging at the straps. Then it came undone. He looked over his shoulder and the parachute came into focus, like a pool of milk on the black earth. He got to his feet and fell again at once, his ears singing. He tried again and this time remained on his feet and he began to move unsteadily towards the parachute. He gathered it patiently into a pile and, taking it in his arms, went slowly up the slope towards the fringe of the forest whose tree-tops he could see against the moon, with the ropes trailing in the grass between his legs and behind him; twice he fell headlong over them, burying his face in the cold silk. Above the trees he could see now a mountain, a peak from whose apex a cloud streamed like white smoke from a tall chimney, giving the mountain the effect of movement towards him. He watched it warily. He left the parachute in the undergrowth beneath the trees on the edge of the forest and took the barrel and butt of the gun from his belt and pieced them together, standing in the shade and talking to himself as he did so, telling himself that everything was all right, but to be quick. For God's sake, hurry, Bullivant. I feel as sick as a dog, he told himself aloud. He remembered his glasses and felt in his pockets for the case and put them on. That was better, much much better. Now then. He patted his pockets : ammunition, chocolate, the map, compass, the money, the Palgrave, the pocketbook with the photograph of Judith in the celluloid frame. He looked at it, but there was nothing but the reflection of the sky in it; she was beyond. Anyway he was complete. He gathered himself together, into one place, one piece, and looked about him.

It was then that he saw the woman, standing quite still down the smooth slope about two hundred yards from where he stood. He was in the shade, but he knew she had seen him. The hair was white in the moonlight and he thought at first it was an old woman and raised the gun. He had heard something of women partisans and how they were inclined to shoot first and ask afterwards and of their monstrous cruelty and one thing or another. She came towards him and when she was close he saw that she was young and beautiful; pretty was the word he used to himself; beauty always embarassed him.

She stopped and set her arms loosely akimbo. He waited.

' You'd better come out,' she called at last in a clear high voice.

He felt somewhat foolish and stepped out of the shadow.

' You dropped from the aeroplane,' she said.

' Yes.' He cleared his voice. She spoke in English; maybe they expected him after all.

' Who are you?' he asked.

She did not move. He repeated the question.

' You're an allied officer,' she said.

He was irritated that she should find it necessary to tell him what he was and whence he came.

' Yes.'

' You'd better go back,' she said. ' We don't want any allied officers.'

For this he was prepared. ' The headquarters of the Twenty-Third Corps are somewhere near here, I believe.'

' You're wasting your time,' she told him.

He was mildly amused. ' It's one thing to jump from an aeroplane, it's quite another to jump back into it. Now take me to your commander, please.'

He went towards her and she watched him steadily. His glasses threw twin circles of light into her eyes and she could see nothing of his face but its outer contour. He was very tall and thin and stooped a little. ' Which way is it?' he said.

She swung about and he followed her down the long slope, looking at her furtively from the corner of his eye. The high cheekbones were edged with light. She evidently sensed his close regard for she quickened her pace and he fell behind and followed her watching the play of light on the hair that hung down her back and the movement of the narrow hips and the swing of the arms. He lengthened his stride again and came up alongside her.

' You're not quite the sort of person I expected to meet on a mountain at this time of night.'

She did not speak.

' This is my first assignment,' he told her.

He saw her smile, but she did not speak.

' My name's Bullivant,' he said, ' Adrian Bullivant.' He waited. ' You're a partisan, I suppose?'

'Yes.' She watched his long blunt shadow on the turf beside her own.

'I gather I wasn't expected,' he ventured in a minute.

'No.'

'You never got the message?'

'Message?' She looked him in the face. 'We never receive messages.' She shook her head. 'We're surrounded.'

He frowned. 'Surrounded? How d'you mean? Not by the enemy?'

'Yes.'

'Oh, Christ.' He stopped short, but she paid no heed to his stupefaction and went on alone through the grass. He caught her up. 'Completely surrounded?'

'Completely.'

'Then we'll have to break out, that's all.'

'Of course,' she said gravely.

'I have a job to do.'

'I understand.'

He fell silent, deeply shocked by the news she had imparted so casually. They went on down the long hills, knee-deep in the vapour that swept with the wind across the plain; the dull roar of the cataract grew louder. Adrian Bullivant's shoulder ached and his head spun giddily on the spirals of nausea that rose from his stomach. Surrounded! To drop into a trap like this on his first assignment, before he had even begun the work he had been sent to do! And it was urgent, urgent work. It was really very amusing, he supposed, when you came to think of it; that is, if the story were wholly true. Maybe she was pulling his leg. Certainly her attitude was one neither of welcome nor friendship. Downright hostile, in fact. He was puzzled and unhappy. He liked to understand what people did and said and why; a trifling eccentricity was comprehensible enough; but this was no time for joking.

43

He raised his voice above the rumble of the fall. 'If it's not a rude question,' he began, 'what's a woman like you doing here?'

'It's a rude question,' she said.

They went on down towards the ravine. He was very tired and swayed a good deal as he walked and stumbled repeatedly over the rocks that lay hidden in the long grass and the ground mist. They went up on to the northern cliff to avoid the marsh that lay across their path. The wind veered to and fro. She called to him there to keep close behind her and not stray towards the edge. He glanced into the chasm as he followed her and saw the great painting on the southern wall and then, as the mist shifted on the wind, the cradle on the end of the rope far beneath. He touched the woman's arm and pointed with the muzzle of the gun towards the minute black figure who would not have been visible at all but for the fact that at that time he happened to be working in yellow; against the broad belt of colour the artist looked like a spider on a wall.

'Who's that, for God's sake?'

'Otto,' she called, 'an artist.'

'What's he painting?'

'What?'

He shouted above the clamour, 'I said what's he painting?'

'A mural.'

'Good heavens,' he muttered, and shouted to her, 'Of what? What's the subject?'

'Life.'

The glimpse he had had, fleeting but strangely lingering, was of obscenity. He did not understand why he should have received such an impression; he had seen nothing to confirm the effect the monstrous work had upon him; but he was repelled and at the same time attracted and felt an urge to experience the thing, to see it and know and under-

44

stand every detail. The vast and sweeping areas of colour shone glassily in the moonlight.

' Why so big?' he called to the woman. ' What does he hope to gain by that?'

' Immortality.'

And, thinking it over, he was certain she was laughing at him, making a fool of him, and so he forebore to ask her why the artist painted at night; he was curiously aware that she knew a great deal about the painting. He did not speak.

The mist bellied on the caprice of the wind and obscured the man in the chasm and soon they bore away from the cliff and the din of the fall subsided somewhat. Fatigue dragged at his eyelids, for with the decreasing altitude the air grew warmer and heavier and he was already tired with the strain of the jump. He had it on his tongue to ask her if the artist was mad, surely the man was a lunatic, for his personal reassurance, but as he thought about the question he could not remember whether he had already asked it or not. They walked a long way; to him it seemed many miles. He heard the thin bright screaming in his ears again again and his father's voice, pitiless and like velvet, saying, ' Adrian, take your mother to her room, boy,' with a gesture of deprecation to the four men with glasses in their hands. But the screaming was Judith, he reminded himself, not his mother. It was his mother who was singing all the time.

They crossed the stream at the bridge and Hans, the elderly deserter, stirred and drew up his short legs so that they might pass across the hump of the bridge. The woman spoke to him in German and he said he thought the Commander was in conference with Father Domenicus, who had walked up from Ronc shortly after sunset; the luminous eyes watched them as they stepped past him and went down the little incline to the white track. The dust

45

deadened the sound of their feet as they walked between the eyeless dwellings. There was a thin bar of light across the track that came from one of the doors, and there she stopped.

'Wait here,' she told him.

She left him. He felt for a moment a flush of resentment at the peremptory instruction; he should assert himself. That was what his father was always telling him. He should assert himself more. He had a position to maintain and a job to do and should not allow himself to be treated in this way. Next time, he would. He would show them. He leaned against the wall and in a moment closed his eyes as the head nodded. He slipped slowly down the wall until he sat in the warm dry dust with his back to the rotting bricks. His mother was singing softly to herself as he led her up the wide staircase with the soft cool flesh of her arm between his fingers to steady her. *My mother said that I never should, play with the gypsies in the wood.* Her breath smelled strongly of port. The voice rose querulously and fell to a whisper. *For if I did then she would say, oh, you naughty little girl for to disobey.* She laughed breathlessly. Then she began again, *With an alpaca frock and a green scarf shawl, a white straw bonnet and a pink parasol.* Then she said she wanted to go back to Birmingham, back to Birmingham, with a long wail. And in the library Jonathan Bullivant went on talking with his husky velvet voice to the guests, Prendergast and Henderson the builder and Gough the borough surveyor and the loud ironic Heath, editor of Miss Cribbage's *Weekly Gazette.* For they were celebrating the opening of the Garden City that Bullivant had built for his workers and others and Mrs. Elizabeth Bullivant had cut the tape and planted the tree and one thing or another and she had been uproariously drunk.

Adrian Bullivant had not attended the ceremony, contrary to his father's wishes. Instead, he had sat in front of

46

the fire in his father's study reading and had fallen asleep. Quinnie was the first to return. Miss Quentin was one of his father's secretaries, the most private of them all, a lean grey woman who wore rubber heels on all her shoes; her movements had the stealthiness of a hunting animal. She had returned early to prepare the study for the special guests Mr. Jonathan had invited. Adrian heard her moving about the dark room silently, and then laying out the glasses and the decanters on the cabinet. If she saw him she gave no sign that she had done so; he was deep in the great high-backed chair at the fire. Then she went out and he dozed and when he awoke again his mother was already in the room singing to herself and weeping absently as a child weeps when it has forgotten the cause of its grief. She was carrying a posy of cornflowers and roses. He heard her go to the cabinet and uncork the decanter and then the liquid running into the glass. She said aloud, 'Blast the veil,' petulantly, fumbling with the glass and the posy and the veil. Then she drank and sighed deeply and filled the glass again. She began to sing, *a pink parasol, a pink parasol*, but when she saw Quinnie standing in the door she stopped abruptly.

'Is there anything you require, madam?'

She said shrilly, 'Why the hell don't you knock? . . . standing there staring. You're always sneaking about the place.' The voice shook. 'Well?'

'This is Mr. Jonathan's private study, madam.'

'What if it is? Well? What if it is?'

'Are you looking for something?'

'Spying, spying, spying. Leave me alone, can't you? Who told the servants to go through my wardrobe? You?'

'There were one or two empty bottles in your wardrobe, madam. Naturally the servants removed them.'

'Tell 'em to mind their own business, then.' The veil fell across her eyes. 'Damn the veil.' She fumbled with it.

47

The posy fell from her hand and Quinnie crossed the room silently to retrieve it.

'Shall I have them put in water, madam?'

'No.' She snatched the bunch of flowers from Quinnie's hand. 'Give'm' to me. Li'le girl gave'm' to me, at the ceremony, such a pretty li'le girl, so pretty.' She smiled and the tears ran from her eyes. 'Cornflowers, see? Smell.' She extended the posy to Miss Quentin, who leaned forward a little way. 'Smell, can't you?' She thrust the flowers into the woman's face; Quinnie recoiled. 'Li'le girl with a curtsy gave'm to me. With a curtsy. . . .' she essayed a cursty and lost her balance and put out a hand to the cabinet to steady herself and the glass fell to the floor, where it exploded musically. 'Now look what I've gone and done. Oh, dear. . . .' she began to weep, stooping to pick up the fragments, and Quinnie bent down at the same time for the same purpose and their heads met. Liza Bullivant giggled. 'Oh dear,' she said, 'oh dear, oh dear. Poor old Quinnie.' The woman's face was expressionless. 'I made such a mess of it this afternoon, didn't I? I spoiled everything, didn't I? Ruined it. Yes, I did.' The voice rose to the edge of hysteria. 'Don't tell me I didn't, because I did. I ruined it, ruined it. Now everybody's angry with me again. The whole world. Everybody. Yes, they are. And it was so lovely and sad with all those people clapping and the flags and the band and the li'le girl and everything.' She wept ceaselessly. 'I never wanted to do the damned old ceremony. I always said I'd do it wrong, I always knew. Well, I was right.' She struggled with the veil to get the handkerchief beneath to quench the flow of tears and the hat fell askew on the petrified curls and the tears made little purple tracks through the powder on the face.

Miss Quentin rose from the floor with the fragments of glass in the palm of her hand. 'The guests will be here in a moment, madam.'

' I never wanted to cut the damned old tape.'

' Perhaps you should go to your room.'

' I shan't.' She ceased to weep suddenly and peered at the secretary. ' I know what's the matter with you,' she said.

' Madam?'

' You're jealous.'

Quinnie held herself stiff and still. ' Jealous?'

' Yes. Jealous, aren't you? You always have been, haven't you? Eh?'

' What have I to be jealous of, madam?'

' Me.' She narrowed her already swollen eyes at the secretary.

Quinnie did not answer. She regarded Liza Bullivant with steady, hostile eyes.

' Me.' The voice rose shrilly. ' Yes, me. Don't tell me you're not. And if you want to know why . . . because I'm his wife, that's why. That's why, isn't it? You're his secretary and you know all about the things he does and he relies on you for everything and you've got it all . . . except his name.'

' I'll have coffee sent to your room, madam.' The voice was shaking.

' . . . and the name is mine.'

The woman turned on her heel and left the room without a word. In a minute Liza Bullivant began to sing to herself and then to dance clumsily, lifting her skirts a little the better to watch the ponderous movements of her feet.

Later, Adrian Bullivant heard how she had cut the tape too soon and had fallen over the little tree she was planting and crushed it flat and the crowd laughed tremendously and there were catcalls and she had wept thereafter throughout the proceedings, copiously, generously, noisily. Her husband's face, they said, was a proper study.

It was all very near and the taste still lingered in his

mouth when he entered the Command Post, on the mountain. The woman had been standing over him and had stirred his leg with her foot.

'The Corps Commander will see you now,' she said. He looked at her in the shadow.

'That's very nice of him,' Adrian Bullivant said sarcastically, 'very.'

He struggled to his feet, dusting his backside. She held aside the blanket that hung over the door and he entered, knocking his head against the jamb; he was very tall when he stood upright; but the blow brought him to his wits. He stood inside the little room with the crown of his head brushing the ceiling, and looking around him, blinking in the light, though it was not strong. Their faces showed curiosity, even hostility; but no friendship. Though there were not more than four or five people in the tiny place, it appeared at first glance painfully crowded, for the candles on the table were low and the shadows on the walls many and the air was thick with the odour of mice and wine. It was round the table that they were seated, or grouped, for there were not seats for all, the Chief of Staff and Luca Pugnini and Pierre and Father Domenicus; the woman leaned against the wall behind him. Only the Commander, who was seated at the table, seemed uninterested; he rested his chin on his hand and regarded the officer with flat grey eyes that flickered with the movement of the candle-flames in the draught. Nobody spoke.

'Commander of the Twenty Third Corps, please?'

'I am,' the Corps Commander said.

'I've been sent by the allies,' Adrian Bullivant said formally. 'My name is Bullivant, Adrian Bullivant, captain. My credentials.' He held out the bundle of papers.

The Commander waved them away with a slight movement of the hand.

'What is it you want?' the Chief of Staff demanded at

once. He was exceedingly irritated.

Adrian Bullivant looked at the man in surprise.

' Be silent,' the Commander told the Chief of Staff. He turned to the officer. ' I'm glad to see you, Captain Bullivant.' He held out his hand between the candles and the young man shook it. ' Let me introduce you. This is my Chief of Staff . . . this, General Pugnini, one of my divisional commanders . . . Pierre, the Intelligence Officer of the headquarters, and Father Domenicus, our agent in Ronc, who also attends to our spiritual welfare.' The Commander's face was expressionless; only the voice was a little dry. ' Erica, you have already met.'

Adrian Bullivant turned to the woman and smiled.

' And now, captain?'

He had a feeling suddenly that their attention was elsewhere, that it had wandered. He watched the glistening eyes; when they were aware of his regard they met his; when his were elsewhere, so also were theirs. There was a current in the air whose nature he did not recognise. Only the Chief of Staff, grey and dapper, watched him malevolently.

' You didn't expect me, I gather.'

' No.'

' A message was sent to you two or three weeks ago telling you to look out for me to-night if the weather was favourable. We rather hoped you'd light a few flares or something. . . .' He cleared his throat in the silence. ' Perhaps your Intelligence Officer . . .' he glanced at the Breton, but his dark eyes were elsewhere; it was exasperating. He looked over his shoulder, but only the tall flaxen woman was there, leaning against the wall with her arms folded across her slight bosom.

' No, I'm afraid we didn't receive the message.'

' Well . . .' he smiled. ' I don't suppose it matters, since I've arrived all right.' The smile did not engage.

51

'We are surrounded,' the Corps Commander said, 'we've received no messages for months.'

'No radio?'

'The batteries are flat.'

'It was sent by other means as well.'

The Commander shook his head. 'It never arrived, Captain Bullivant.'

'Oh.' It was very close in the little room, he wished they would open a window, but the only window, he saw, was a small aperture high in the wall that looked as though it had not been opened for many years. 'How many men have you?' he asked politely.

'Eleven men and women, and a boy.'

'How many?'

'Eleven.'

'Eleven men.' He laughed suddenly. 'I mean in the whole corps.'

There was no answering smile in the broad heavy face. 'Eleven, Captain Bullivant. With yourself, twelve.'

Suddenly the woman behind him lifted the blanket and was gone. And at once he understood the nature of the current he had sensed since the moment of entering the place, for he felt the concentration of interest turn upon himself. It was something of a relief.

'When do you propose to leave?' the Chief of Staff snapped.

'The officer has a charming little gun.' It was the first time Luca Pugnini had spoken.

'We don't want the man here at all,' the Chief of Staff said testily, 'bossing everybody about.' The pince-nez shook on his nose when he spoke.

'I'm not bossing everybody about,' Bullivant retorted.

'I wasn't speaking to you,' the Chief of Staff told him.

'If you'll allow me. . . .' the Commander began.

'We shall have to break out immediately,' Bullivant said. 'I have a job to do.'

'We are a headquarters only,' the Commander said softly. 'I command the corps. General Pugnini commands a division. All we lack are the men.'

'Then we have no choice but to break out.' They were silent. 'I may as well explain,' he went on, 'I have been sent here by the allies to assist in the organisation of partisan resistance in this area.'

They looked at him in silence and Father Domenicus flicked the drop from the end of his nose. 'My son,' he began, 'your enthusiasm does the greatest credit to your cause. In God's good time it will doubtless prosper. Meanwhile I, as agent of this headquarters in the village of Ronc, am fully informed as to the strength and dispositions of the enemy; there is no more chance of your breaking out of the cordon by which you are surrounded than of the rich entering heaven. And to attempt such an enterprise would be a very criminal folly.' He tapped on the desk with his fingernail as he spoke. The candlelight played joyously over the lines of his cadaverous face and shone in the water in which the pale eyes swam. 'Place your faith in the Almighty, my son, and have patience.'

Adrian Bullivant looked from one to the other, his head bowed beneath the ceiling, the eyes huge beyond the thick lenses. Luca Pugnini smiled gaily when he met the young man's regard.

'You'd probably like a glass of wine,' the Corps Commander said. 'Pierre, is there a clean mug?' The Breton shoved himself away from the wall and tinkered with the mugs on the floor by the great flask that stood in the corner.

'The boot,' the priest said, 'is, in fact, on the other foot. The very purpose of my visit to-night is to inform the Commander of the enemy's intention to sweep the mountain during the next day or two, as a direct result, young man, of the visit of an aircraft to this vicinity to-day. You were doubtless aware of that visit. I will not dwell on the fact that you are to blame. Let it suffice that resistance is out of the question.' He spoke with great force and unction and again the finger-nail tapped drily on the table. He gathered the cassock about his legs. 'The camp must be evacuated.'

It seemed that the priest was a power in the head-quarters, and was not accustomed to contradiction.

'We shall do whatever is best militarily,' Adrian Bulli-vant said with a touch of asperity.

The priest looked at him sharply.

'There's another allied soldier here,' the Chief of Staff said, 'called Crosby. He has, of course, placed himself under the orders of the Commander and myself.'

Adrian Bullivant was interested. 'Crosby? A soldier?'

'Escaped.'

'Good. I'd like to see him. Meanwhile,' he addressed them all but especially the Commander, 'I've been sent here to do a certain job and a good deal depends on it. It can't be done without your help. If I could do it alone, I would, but it just isn't possible.' It was curious how the little ring of faces advanced and receded with the flicker-ing light. 'It's a particular operation,' he said, 'we'll have to get on with it immediately.' He sipped the wine from the mug, bending at the knees so that he might tip back his head.

The Corps Commander drew a deep breath. 'You'll find life a bit difficult,' he said presently, 'here on the mountain. I urge you for your own peace of mind to accept it, to adapt yourself to it as soon as may be, captain. We shall naturally do all we can to help you.'

He guessed accurately enough at the doubt and loneli-ness in Adrian Bullivant, and the sense of duty without

54

which he would be nothing. He would cling to his obligations with the desperation of a young man who knows instinctively, because he has very little else, that if he should abandon them, if he should forgo his allegiance, he would collapse like a litre of wine divested suddenly of its bottle, an incoherent fatuity to be swept along by the first brush to come his way. Outside himself in his world he had found nothing worthy and inside himself had found only this, this small but rigid sense of duty, and to this he adhered and would adhere at all costs, secure in the knowledge that, in the event of his actions leading to catastrophe, he might at least face himself and find mitigation in having done what he believed to be right and to be expected of him, whatever its consequences for himself and for his neighbour. It rendered him singularly characterless and arid. You felt the force but not the will, the singleness of mind—what evil it had to answer for, this monstrosity!— but not of heart. He looked up at the face beneath the ceiling.

He said gravely, 'After you have been cut off from the war for a long time, Captain Bullivant, as we have, it becomes an oddly local affair in which you can interest yourself or not, as you please, and how and in such respects as you prefer. The business of taking sides ceases to be very important. We like to associate ourselves with everything. It takes time, of course, practice. . . .' the quiet voice trailed into silence.

'I don't know much about all that,' Adrian Bullivant said slowly, 'all I know is that I have orders to see that a certain job of work is done in this area.'

Luca Pugnini, behind him in the shadow to which he had crept while the Commander was speaking, said, 'This really is a most pleasant little gun.' He was holding Bullivant's gun in his hands with the awed tenderness a child will sometimes show for another's doll. 'What kind is it?'

'Sub Thompson,' the young man replied irritably. He was anxious to dispel some of the illusions the headquarters of the Corps seemed to have about themselves and their obligations. 'You cannot disassociate yourself from this kind of war,' he said to the Commander. He wished Luca Pugnini would leave the gun alone. 'Doesn't work,' he said, 'not in practice.'

'Crude, perhaps, but having a certain beauty.' The general carried the gun to the candles and bent over the lock. 'Ah no, not as crude as I thought, not by any means.' He was short and stout, Adrian Bullivant saw. The round bald head was bridged from left to right by a sliver of black hair that shone like ebony in the candlelight; it was faintly scented. 'I'd like to fire it,' he said.

'I'm afraid I haven't enough ammunition,' Adrian Bullivant told him sharply, 'I have really awfully little.'

'Crosby must have been here nine or ten months now,' the Commander said.

'An exemplary partisan,' Father Domenicus added.

'And a tolerable barber.'

'Exquisitely finished,' Luca Pugnini murmured.

Adrian Bullivant said, 'I haven't enough ammunition,' patiently but firmly.

'A little more wine?' Pierre looked up at him with dark eyes. The black hair tumbled down his forehead. He filled the mug till it overflowed and the bitter red liquor ran across the map pinned to the table and dripped from the edge on to the floor. The priest watched it absently.

'Crosby is a radical, I would say.'

'Listen—'

'By nature, I think, rather than conviction.'

'The lethal power of such a lovely weapon must be incalculable,' the stout general muttered.

'Crosby, one might say, would be radical in paradise.'

'We all have a job to do,' Adrian Bullivant said with

56

intense conviction, 'irrespective of personal considerations. All this metaphysical nonsense . . .'

'He will have to be got rid of,' the Chief of Staff barked suddenly, 'that is plain.'

'The peace of God must be kept, my sons.'

Pierre touched his shoulder. 'You have blood on your face, captain, you must have hurt yourself when you landed.'

'As satisfying, æsthetically, as a Tintoretto.'

'Listen, I haven't enough ammunition. I shall need it all, all, d'you hear? That's final.' The ceiling bore down on his head and the shadows thronged the walls about him; he was a little feverish, he thought, and the air was like soft warm cloth.

'We have quite an armoury,' Luca Pugnini told him, 'to-morrow you must tell us what you think of it. Mostly enemy equipment, of course, but very representative.' He removed the magazine from the gun.

'Damn it, haven't I told you I need that ammunition?' He stood suddenly upright in his vexation and his head struck the ceiling and the plaster broke and fell in a shower about his head and shoulders. Pierre laughed abruptly.

'You're easily amused,' Adrian Bullivant told him.

'There are more important matters than war, Captain Bullivant,' the quiet voice was saying, 'influences at work on the destiny of mankind in the light of which neither war nor peace is of more than local and transient significance.'

'I have a job to do,' the young man said clearly, 'and after that another one, and then others, and to the best of my ability I shall do them. So have you also, and you don't seem to have done very much about it yet, if I may say so.' He brushed the plaster from his sleeves and was faintly surprised to see that his fingers were trembling. The shadows on the walls drew closer. Even the candles cowered beneath the weight of the shadows.

'It is possible that von Langenburg may not be satisfied with a token withdrawal from the camp,' Father Domenicus was saying, 'and he may send troops to see that you have indeed moved out. This young man, in that event, may cause trouble.'

'There is no accommodation,' the Chief of Staff said.

'Nevertheless, you must show us how to fire it tomorrow,' Luca Pugnini told him pleasantly, the gold teeth flashing between his beautiful lips. 'We would all like to fire it, a few rounds each. We appreciate good weapons.' He patted the officer's arm. 'You must be patient with us.' He peered along the sights.

'There are no more mattresses,' the Chief of Staff cried triumphantly.

'Give it to me.' He reached out and laid his hands on the gun, but the plump white fingers did not relax their hold. 'God damn it, man, give me that gun!' He tried to wrench it free.

Pierre stood behind him and stuck his sharp fingers into the young man's ribs so that he stood upright suddenly to avoid the agony and lost his hold on the gun; his head struck the ceiling again and the ancient plaster fell on to the wine on the map and the dust clung to the lenses of his glasses and the drying blood on his face. He swung about furiously with clenched fist, but the Breton was not there, he was on the other side of the table, smiling naughtily at the officer.

'If there is no alternative and you must stay,' the Chief of Staff told him tartly, 'then you will have to consider yourself under the orders of senior officers.'

'I'm an allied officer.' He heard his voice from a great distance. 'I have my own orders.'

58

The Commander asked him, ' Are you a married man, Captain Bullivant?'

' Yes.' One of the candles wilted and the flame rose bright and high from the pool of wax. The wick staggered and then the flame went out. ' My wife is at present in a home.' He was surprised at himself, for he had never spoken of her to anybody. It came from him easily. ' In a home.' He was calm and pleased with himself.

' Then you have nothing left but your duty.'

' Kindly instruct General Pugnini to return that gun.'

' You must forgive him the collector's avidity, captain. His appreciation leads him badly astray from time to time. I have told him already that to appreciate æsthetically is to acknowledge material values, but without much effect.'

' I beg you, Commander . . .'

' Tell me, what particular operation was it the allies had in mind when they sent you here?'

They were silent then. Father Domenicus roused and nodded. ' A good question,' he murmured.

Adrian Bullivant said, ' An attack . . . an attack . . .' he hesitated, frowning.

' Yes?' General Pugnini looked up from the gun he was stripping and Pierre leaned across the table.

' Yes?'

' An attack . . .'

' The enemy is too strong, my son.'

' On what?' the Chief of Staff demanded irritably.

' On . . .' It was no use; he had forgotten. He looked down at the ring of expectant faces, smiling foolishly in his dismay.

' You said, an attack. On anything particular?'

' Yes.'

' Well, what might it be?'

He gritted his teeth and drove the tips of his fingers into his thigh in the effort to remember. O God, help me. The sweat trickled down his long face. The muscles ached in the set grin he kept there. 'Damn silly . . .' he muttered.

'We have a choice of several,' the Commander said politely, 'they are at your disposal naturally.'

Now it was coming.

'Only God is strong,' the priest whispered.

'The reservoir,' he cried. He laughed breathlessly. 'Damn silly of me to forget, wasn't it?' He laughed again in the great tide of relief that flowed over him. 'There's a big reservoir in the vicinity, isn't there? An attack on the reservoir with a view to blowing the dam and flooding the valley.'

4

THE CORPS COMMANDER rode slowly out of the camp and turned the mare's head towards the mountain. The sun shone with a clear hard brilliance that morning and the white hood the mountain wore tugged excitedly at the summit as the wind came shouting down from the north across the ancient land bearing the scent of snow on its breath. It was cold and the man's eyes streamed and his teeth ached when he opened his lips to utter little blandishments to the animal he rode so gracelessly. The ugly creature cocked its ears and listened, grey mane and tail flying bravely in the breeze, staggering now and then under the great weight of the rider and the thrust and parry of the wind. On the edge of the ridge he swung the head towards the reservoir whose northern reaches were visible beyond the shoulder of the distant spur.

They watched him go, Crosby and Adrian Bullivant, warming themselves by the mill above the bridge, their backs to the beams and the sun aslant their faces. Soon the horse and the rider were lost in the vast green uplands of the plain.

Crosby had been very pleased indeed to see the officer. Both were pleased, with the ridiculous warmth of two men who, having nothing else in common, yet speak the same tongue in a foreign land. They talked a great deal, Adrian Bullivant with the reserve that he felt was expected of him after the first over-friendly greetings, Crosby with the reserve of inarticulacy. But he described his life on the mountain with curious warmth and detachment.

'Nothing, sir. That's what we do. Nothing. Sweet fanny adams. Ought to get fed up to the back teeth with it, just hanging about all day waiting. The feeling of waiting's there all right. You don't know what you're waiting for, that's all. First you think things are going to hum, what with all the talk there is about attacks and one thing or another, then you know it's all my eye and they're just fooling themselves. The state of mind's about all they worry about. So damn busy acting and looking and thinking like partisans they never have a minute to do anything about it. They talk, I cut hair, that's all I do, a bloody barber. Yet all the time you know it's not so bad, you know damn well you ought to be glad you're here. Bit of peace once in a while. Funny, isn't it? with the other fellows sweating their guts out somewhere south there. You get to know after you've been here a bit that it's just the job, just what you've always been hankering after in a way. Just want the wife with you and everything would be all right, piece of cake, and maybe you'd settle down and the way things are back home would stop nagging at you day in day out. You know you'll want to come back the minute you've left, it's like the old desert, only better, yet you can't stop wanting to get home and see if everything's the same as you know damn well it is. That would be the thing to do, of course, just get home so you can see everything once and pick up a few things and get back here leaving nothing you'd ever miss. You know perfectly well everything's lousy at home but you just got to go and see and make sure . . . and then spend the rest of your life wishing to God you'd never been such a b.f.' He narrowed his eyes into the sun. 'They're a crazy lot of bastards, you'll find that, but they leave you alone.'

He seldom spoke so much. He glanced at the young officer, already half-regretting his verbosity.

'We have a job to do, Crosby,' Adrian Bullivant said.

'Oh, sure.'

'It's not going to be easy.' He was vaguely alarmed at the spirit of resignation that shone through the soldier's words; it had infected Crosby also, he thought. No, it was not going to be as simple as he had thought: a nice, clear-cut job of blowing up a dam. First he must convince them that it was their duty to assist, and that maybe would be most difficult of all. 'Somehow we've got to get these people moving. That's what I've been sent here for.'

'You've got a job on, I'll tell you.'

'I didn't imagine it would be easy.'

'Jerry's damn smart, sir. Lot of old dugouts, but smart as ever. Let's you in all right, but you try getting out.'

'Who's the woman, Crosby, the one with the flaxen hair?'

The soldier looked up at the face above him, white and earnest. The sun cast the shadows of the dust on the glasses down across the taut skin and the eyes were great blue lakes beyond the lenses. 'Erica,' he said. 'Don't know much about her myself, don't think anybody does. Not my cup of tea in any case, though half the others have got their tongues hanging out after her.'

'Very pretty, isn't she?'

'So they say.' He scratched his chin reflectively. 'Bit on the scraggy side, for my taste. Prefer a bit of flesh, myself . . . all those bones sticking into you.'

'I was thinking rather of the influence she might have in the camp, Crosby.'

'Oh, bags of that. Though the chap who seems to run things around here is the reverend from the village, him and the Commander.'

'Yes. I haven't quite placed the Commander yet.'

'No, sir. Takes a bit of cottoning on to.'

'And the priest . . . wouldn't do any harm to get him on our side, either.'

63

Crosby drew in his lips. 'If I was you, sir,' he said slowly, 'I wouldn't think much of my chances of fighting my way out, with or without help.'

'We shall have to.' He was aware of the slight stiffening in the soldier's attitude. 'It depends. That's the job we have to do . . .' he nodded towards the reservoir glittering in the morning sun. 'Blow the reservoir—or open the lock, doesn't matter which.'

Crosby said, 'The Boche won't let you within a mile of it, sir.'

'Those are the orders.'

'They must think we're a couple of armoured brigades, then. Same old story.'

'We have about ten days. Or less. Nine.'

'Better knock off one or two of those. We'll have to get out for a bit to-morrow or the day after, Jerry's making a sweep.'

'Yes, that's another thing. I'm not at all sure I like this idea of getting out and letting him have it all his own way. The place ought to be defended.'

'Who by?'

'There are ten or a dozen people here, presumably trained in guerilla tactics. We could catch him on the hop, specially if he's expecting a cakewalk, as he will be. Let him think we've gone and get a bit careless, then we'd hit him. We'd have time to get out long before he could deploy, or get his mortars up.'

'It's a nice idea, sir.'

'You mean you think it's lousy.'

'Try it on the reverend. Or the Commander. Or any of them.'

'And you?' He waited, staring at the distant reservoir.

'Me? I have to do as I'm bloody told.'

'Half a dozen men could hold this place for a couple of days against small arms. Plenty of automatic weapons here, aren't there?'

For he had already visited the armoury. Early that morning he had been awakened by the liquid spatter of a Sub Thompson on the hillside beyond the window under which he lay. It was his own gun; he remembered the Divisional Commander's envy of the weapon. He sat up on the mattress they had found for him; the gun was not where he had left it, on the floor beside the pillow. He pulled on his boots and ran out of the cottage into the track. The thin white sunshine brought tears to his sensitive eyes for a moment and he was aware only of the pain and the scent of the wind. Then he dodged between the houses and out on to the soft green turf where the little crowd of men had set the empty tin in the grass fifty yards away up the slope and were firing at it. The bullets splashed in the thick turf about the tin. He shouted and ran towards them.

Luca Pugnini ceased firing and turned, as did they all, his smile shining prettily in the sun.

' Ho,' he called, and waved. ' A wonderful weapon . . . wonderful!'

Adrian Bullivant came up to the group. ' Give me that gun.' He snatched the weapon from the man's hands. ' I thought I told you I hadn't enough ammunition?'

' But one little magazine, captain . . .' he spread his hands in a vast gesture of deprecation. The rest looked at the officer curiously. He recognised Pierre, grinning at him mischievously; the rest, Hans, Slobadov and Roberto he did not know.

' I shall need it all, every round.'

' For what, pray?'

So Adrian Bullivant, drawing breath told him. ' To fight with,' he said, ' odd as it must seem to you. To defend your camp with, among other things. You people are going to get the surprise of your lives any moment now. You'll be surprised at what you'll do. You're living in a glorified fool's paradise. Now kindly leave my gun alone.'

'But there are plenty of other weapons, Captain Bullivant,' Luca Pugnini told him, 'plenty, more than you can ever use. And sufficient ammunition for a major engagement. Let me show you. Come.' He shouldered his way out of the circle. 'Roberto,' he called. 'This way, my dear fellow,' he said to the officer. Adrian Bullivant, angry, dishevelled, but interested, followed him, and the man called Roberto fell in behind, adjusting the set of the small pearl grey trilby he wore and fastening the buttons of his jacket; it was a thought too tight for him, as though he had recently put on weight, and the shining patent leather shoes appeared to be too small, for he turned in the pointed toes and walked with a peculiarly mincing gait, elevating the bony shoulders and swinging his arms across his body, his face bland but otherwise expressionless.

'Roberto is my assistant in the armoury,' Luca Pugnini whispered to Bullivant as they walked through the village towards the mill. 'At one time a professional footballer, hardly above mediocre, I believe, though I never saw him play. But as an armourer—a treasure, a treasure, my dear chap. Curious, isn't it? One meets all sorts in the partisan movement.'

They entered the mill, Roberto followed briskly. The place smelled strongly of mould. The worn stone troughs, the millstones one upon the other lay as they had been left by the miller, the lichen now wandering freely over the broken surfaces. Ivy clung to the beams overhead and to the narrow staircase that led to the loft. The stream sang among the blades of the wheel and the sun, thrown up by the dancing water, flickered among the webs and crevices in the walls. With the smell of mould there was now the odour of oil and the millstones were stained with it; and the scent that followed the plump general mingled with them both impartially.

Luca Pugnini stood inside the door and swept his arm

66

across his body in a gesture that embraced the whole remarkable achievement. From floor to ceiling the rifles stood solidly in their home-made racks against the wall, glistening with oil. Beyond the millstones there were machine guns, standing in ranks on the floor; to the right, mortars, mines and bayonets. All were clean and obviously in good repair.

'Well?' Luca Pugnini smiled. 'Help yourself.'

Roberto drifted to the bench and began to tinker with the rifles. Thereafter he paid little attention to the officer and his escort. The child Josef stood in the doorway, unblinking, and watched them.

'Well, my dear fellow? If there's anything that takes your fancy, it's yours.'

He was evidently well pleased to exhibit his collection. The dark eyes smiled and flashed and he assumed an air of pride and complacency that was nearly childish, slightly smug and certainly, to Adrian Bullivant who felt his annoyance over the firing of his gun to have been somewhat premature, irritating.

'And the ammunition?' he asked.

'There is a cellar beneath. A trifle damp and not very spacious, but enough for ordinary purposes. For every type of weapon we have, naturally.' He ran the tips of his fingers over the arc of hair that spanned the shining crown. 'In the loft we keep the revolvers, traps and other novelties.'

'Extraordinary.'

'Would you care to examine a few, captain? Or perhaps fire a few rounds yourself?'

Bullivant flushed. 'Thank you, no.'

'There are some very beautiful items in the collection, captain . . . you'll forgive the connoisseur's pride, I hope, a shade overwheening at times . . . very lovely indeed. Lethal capacity varies from weapon to weapon, of course, that is to be expected. And it is the lethal capacity to which we must give precedence . . . æsthetically, you understand, for its effect upon oneself. A woman, for example, taking a revolver into her hand, will usually experience a slight sense of nausea, a tremor, a little shudder; she may even shrink from the touch of a gun. In ourselves the immediate revulsion is lost in habit, we feel . . . what? a little throb of power in the palm of the hand? . . . until the nerve is acutely sensitised, as it is in the true connoisseur. And then we begin to appreciate it much as we thrill to a work of art. We learn to assess a weapon by its effect not upon the enemy, but upon ourselves.' He laughed gaily. ' It comes to have a meaning greater than death. Take a Bellini, for example, a very obvious example, but it will do : it is not a Bellini unless it moves you not only to admiration for the skill of the artist, my dear fellow, which is after all a very commonplace and easy escape, but to a deeper appreciation of the meaning of the painting. A bad Madonna, if I may so put it, leaves you cold. A Bellini is God.'

' You have no armoured vehicles?'

Somewhat crestfallen, Luca Pugnini's face straightened and he raised his shoulders. ' Alas, no, a catchpenny enemy . . . the price is beyond our present means.'

' Pity.'

' I have longed for an armoured vehicle, I confess.'

Adrian Bullivant frowned. ' Price? What price? How were all these obtained?' He indicated the stacks of rifles. ' All these . . . didn't you have to fight for them?'

General Pugnini cleared his throat. ' We found it more expeditious to obtain them by other, more sordid but more peaceful, means.' The mobile face cleared. ' But we have them and that is the main thing, isn't it?' He smiled at the young man's puzzlement. ' We arm ourselves, feed ourselves and amuse ourselves, all by the same means, a small affair of business that Roberto and I have developed.'

The man looked up and nodded and smiled pertly. ' I have promised Roberto a football.'

Adrian Bullivant did not know what to say. He felt acutely embarassed and did not know why. ' You seem to have done pretty well, at all events,' he said at last. ' What's the system? How does it work?'

Diffidently at first and with the exercise of all the charm of which he was capable, aware of the young man's principles and ironclad integrity but uncertain of his sense of humour, later wholly carried away by his own powers of description and narrative and in any case too appreciative of his own part in the affair to gloss the smallest detail, Luca Pugnini explained the system. It depended, he said, primarily on the goodwill of the people of Ronc, their generosity, their gullibility and their fear of the devil they knew not; particularly, and to an unhealthy extent, its continued success depended upon the sense of duty of Father Domenicus to his parish and his God. The people, during the early days of the partisan movement, were extremely proud of their proximity to the heart of things and were prone to speak of the little band on the mountain as theirs, possessively, jealously and on occasion with considerable emotion; it was Our partisans, Our resistance movement, Our corps. When the headquarters marched in triumph through the village to be blessed by Father Domenicus and to encourage recruitment, as they normally had done on Sunday mornings, the entire population, with the orchestra, would throng the square to welcome them, to cheer the Commander on his mare, to wine them and feed them generously and without stint at the public expense; these, they said, belong to Ronc. In the course of a few months, however, during which the village was occupied by the enemy, their interest in the men and women who lived above them on the mountain began to pall; to feed them was dangerous, expensive and it went on too long.

The consignments of food which one or other of the villagers had been used to collect from the rest and drag up the mountain on the mayor's ass sank to half their former abundance and finally ceased altogether. The Corps headquarters experienced hunger.

'Very fortunately,' Luca Pugnini continued, 'at about that time Father Domenicus paid us one of his periodic visits, and we felt compelled to enlighten him as to the possible consequences of the villagers' paltry behaviour. We would have no course but to attack the village with all our strength and thus raise the curtain on a period of unbridled banditry and destruction, in which none would suffer more than the villagers of Ronc themselves, for we would take off them what we wanted and the enemy would take reprisals. We left the matter in his hands.'

Father Domenicus, it appeared, was impressed by the argument and agreed to enlighten the villagers of Ronc in the matter. Three nights later he himself delivered the first of the consignments of food which had not ceased since.

Adrian Bullivant was astonished and somewhat shocked. 'Damn it, that's nothing short of blackmail,' he protested.

'Thus are all armies maintained,' the general replied gravely.

It was about this time, he went on, that Roberto had bought a rifle from a needy German soldier. The pawning of weapons is of course a crime in the German, or indeed any other, army, but it occasionally happens there as elsewhere that the common soldier, feeling no particular affection or need for the cumbersome contraption with which he is burdened, sells it for money, which is easier to carry and more useful. There are plenty more, he tells himself, where that came from. The professional footballer was the only member of the staff with money, at any rate on his arrival on the mountain, and so was able to pay the sum demanded by the rascally soldier. His toy was the object of much admiration and envy in the camp; Luca Pugnini also wanted one. And why one only? he asked himself. He laid the matter before Father Domenicus. It was little use for the village to feed its partisans, he pointed out, unless the latter were equipped to defend themselves. Unarmed they served no purpose at all. A small toll, or tax, levied weekly, he said, would remedy the defect.

The priest, obsessed by the necessity for the maintenance of peace in his parish, arrived on his next visit to the camp with a considerable sum of money in the pocket of his cassock. With it the partisans bought arms from the enemy, the transactions taking place at night at a spot near the reservoir where by an oversight there was a gap in the wire and fewer mines than elsewhere. It was very simple. Von Langenburg's administrative staff was surprised at the sudden increase in the number of weapons lost and stolen and von Langenburg wrote a forceful circular to his subordinates, a copy of which was pinned to all notice-boards. He did not seem to care greatly, however; as long as the losses could be dealt with in the usual manner he was not unduly disturbed; indeed the occasional indents he signed for armament replacements tallied nicely with the details he included in his reports. The vendors, the soldiers themselves, after the first enthusiasm, were intelligent enough not to overdo it, preferring rather to steal the weapons of other units and careless individuals on evening leave in the cities of the plain than to sell always their own.

It was an abominable story and Adrian Bullivant was deeply shocked. As a record of base treachery, blackmail and amorality he had seldom known its like. Were these the people whom he must lead into action? The thought sickened him.

And now, scarcely an hour later, he detected in the one man upon whom he had thought to rely the same disquieting lack of integrity, of moral fibre, of honour. It was

71

difficult to describe such a state of mind, it was too resilient and evasive. Faced with itself, it side-stepped, slipped away with a sly grin, dodged the issue. 'All men are rogues before breakfast,' Luca Pugnini had told him, 'even the best of us.' He shrugged his shoulders.

Adrian Bullivant felt the first wave of despair, an inexplicable inclination to self-pity and tears and with it, a bitter determination to root out the evil and destroy it. He would show them.

'We shall defend the camp,' he said abruptly, 'and we shall attack the reservoir.'

He did not wait for Crosby's reply, if indeed the soldier replied at all, and swung about and left him. He went down the grassy bank to the track and slowly along it towards the Command Post. In the sun, in the doorway of her billet, he saw the woman who had met him on the mountainside in the night. He nodded and spoke.

'Good morning,' he said.

When she looked up he noticed for the first time that her eyes were different colours, the one blue, the other blue shot with grey. The mouth was thin but wide and humorous and the forehead above the level white brows was smooth and high. The bones of the cheeks also were high and this gave the strange face a Mongolian air, so that it was at once attractive and repellent.

'Mind if I talk to you?'

'Not at all.'

'Let's walk a little way.'

She stood away from the wall, very tall and straight. He noticed her hands then, for it was difficult not to notice them, they were so big. They were like pendula, having broad spatulate fingers, the hands of a man, of a painter or a pianist. She thrust them casually into the pockets of the slacks she wore as she fell in at his side and went with him along the track towards the bridge.

Well?'

He hesitated, feeling once again that she was laughing at him. He swung round and vented his irritation on the child who followed them. 'Go away,' he shouted.

Little Josef came to a standstill and his vacant blue eyes fixed themselves on the fragment of glass that shone in the dust by his foot.

'D'you hear? Go away.'

He went on down the track at the woman's side. The child followed. They crossed the bridge and walked over the soft turf.

'I have a job to do here,' he began. It was always a good gambit, a little solid ground from which he could attack, to which he could always withdraw in case of emergency.

'Yes?'

'Yes. You have a lot of influence in the camp, haven't you?'

'Very little,' she said.

'You could have, I mean, if you wanted.'

She smiled faintly. 'What is it you want me to do?'

'Jolt these people into action. They're all asleep. Help me to get them moving. It's important, Miss. . . .'

'Erica.'

'Miss Erica.' He smiled.

'Why didn't they send somebody older than you?' she asked him suddenly. She laughed. 'I feel sorry for you, you're not enjoying yourself much, are you?'

He compressed his lips. 'If they want anything they've damn well got to help to get it.'

'That's the point,' she said, 'I don't think they want anything.'

He sniffed. 'Attitudinising, that's all that is.'

'Oh, I don't know.'

73

'Well, I do.' He turned on the child. 'For God's sake go away, will you?'

'Take no notice,' she said, 'that's the best way.'

He drew breath. 'Don't you want anything yourself? What are you doing here if you don't believe in what you're doing?'

'I was bored,' she said.

'I don't believe that.'

'Very well.'

'But don't you want anything? A decent home? A bit of time to look about?'

'Oh, I suppose so.'

He gritted his teeth against the laughter at the corners of her eyes. 'You don't seem very keen.'

'I'm not.'

He asked her irritably, 'Is there something specially funny about me?'

'No, no, not specially.' She touched his arm. 'If I were you, captain, I'd give up the idea of saving humanity and let it go its own way for a time.'

'I'm going to do what I've been sent to do, ' he said doggedly. 'Come what may.'

She looked up at the narrow earnest face. 'You feel everybody ought to want something . . . what is it that you want?'

Well, what did he want? That was simple enough. He wanted the end of the war. That was easy. After that, after the end of the war . . . then he would help to clear up the mess and go home and get on with his life. That was what he wanted. He wanted to wear a pair of flannels on Saturday morning and get a bit of exercise on Saturday afternoon, football or something, and maybe go to church on Sunday mornings, not because he believed a word of it any more, he told himself, but because it left him easy in his mind afterwards. He wanted to be able to go home in the early evening and maybe go to the cinema with Judith and enjoy the soporific boredom of the organ recital and listen to a lot of other people making fools of themselves singing to the beat of a little white ball that bounced from word to word across the screen about how it was all over now and we were back again with our loved ones . . . lot of eyewash, of course, but good eyewash, like Kipling and Rupert Brooke and old thingummy's speeches in the House. Sailing a yacht on the river, that was another thing. And doing what he wanted to do instead of what he was told perpetually. All sorts of things, ordinary things. It was difficult to say just what you wanted, like that. Damfool question really, when you came to think of it. Of course you knew what you wanted . . . why ask? The first thing he had to do, of course, was to get Judith out of that awful asylum and get her well again, fresh air and one thing or another, and look after the girl. Then there was his mother; something must be done about that; she could not go on drinking port in her bedroom and wanting to go back to Birmingham, not indefinitely. His father should do something. His father. Well, his father. Yes. Oh, Lord. His father, he had discovered only recently, was a They, one of those misty omnipresent personalities who had been telling him and everybody else what to do for a long time now, really one of the swine who had led us into the holocaust. Well, They had done it for the last time, absolutely the last. He, Adrian Bullivant, and a lot of other chaps, would see to that. And now his father expected him to take over the multiple businesses he had built up, but he would not, he was damned if he would, they were stinking lousy rotten through and through and he would have nothing to do with it. Yes, there were many things he had to do, much he wanted. And later on, maybe, he would have a shot at politics and get himself elected to the House, it set a sort of coping-stone on a fellow's career. Adrian

75

Bullivant, M.P. And damn well see to it there would be no more wars. And do a good job of work, helping to keep the country going generally. With everybody having what they wanted, except, of course, the mischief-makers.

'The first thing to do,' he told her, 'is this job I've been sent here for.'

'And then?'

'The rest will follow.'

She nodded. 'It usually does.'

'But I can't do this job alone.'

'How d'you suppose I can help you?'

'I don't know. Throwing your weight in. Persuasion. It may have to be unconventional.'

She smiled. 'You've no respect for the sanctity of womanhood.'

'I didn't mean that,' he said. 'I mean generally.'

'You're a great liar, captain,' she told him. 'You've come to me because I'm a woman.'

'No, not a woman,' he said, '—woman.'

She looked at him sharply with raised eyebrows, but he seemed unaware of any particular significance in his words. She shook her head.

'You may count on my complete neutrality,' she told him.

'That's all, is it?'

'Much.'

'I don't understand you people,' he said at last.

'It's quite simple. We like being here, on the whole. Where do we go if we do break out?'

'Well, where were you before?' he asked, as if that were the place to which she would naturally return.

The physical, the circumstantial, answer, was the one he presumably expected: Greenwich Village or Florence or Bloomsbury or Budapest; and if they were destroyed or occupied or otherwise unattainable just now he would solemnly suggest some other place. What a fool the man was! Before what, anyway? He, of course, would return to the junction at which he had left the main, the dear familiar road; not to the same spot exactly . . . a few yards further along, she thought, to allow for the passage of the intervening years, those spent in pursuance of orders; he would allow the war to change him as little as possible, would endeavour to ignore the apocalypse. *Chacun* is not *responsable de tout devant tous,* he would say very loudly, being, with perfect justification, embarrassed to speak French and in any case a little afraid of the quotation. The war had been forced on him by somebody else, by clumsy leadership, by a megalomaniac, by a set of circumstances entirely outside his control. The best thing to do was to forget it as a very unpleasant business. He would return to the main road and kick the mud from his heels and continue precisely as before.

But it was an alarming question, in all conscience. In his terms, then, where was she before? Everywhere. Cities, in the cities, where she belonged. Never more than a few months in one place, perpetually itinerant. Her mother had been French, a Parisienne, an actress of considerable renown in her time, and her father a Polish surgeon. She had been educated in fifty schools, and by nearly as many governesses. She was trained, at her mother's instigation, as a dancer, and to act a little. She matured very quickly and at the age of seventeen was unusually beautiful. Her father, the Polish doctor, had disappeared then, none knew where, and her mother, aware of the girl's beauty and jealous of it, busy about her own affairs and much pre-occupied with the wrinkles about her eyes, decided that the contrast was now too much for her, and married her daughter to an Austrian of ancient family and some wealth. He was also a sadist, however, and addicted to the use of a whip. Disgusted and terrified, the girl left him within three

77

weeks of her marriage and went back to her mother who, infuriated by the girl's unexpected return and wholly unable to accept the flimsy reasons she gave for it, used her influence, still considerable, to obtain for her daughter employment in a company of dancers. The company left Vienna almost immediately and Erica never saw her mother alive again, for she was found drowned in the Danube a few months after, whether by her own hand or by that of a murderer was never established; it was believed that the Austrian nobleman to whom she had married her daughter was involved in some way, but his alibi was flawless. She left her daughter a little money. Convinced now that she would never succeed as a dancer, on account of her hands if nothing else—their size and gracelessness was a continual embarrassment—she left the company. In fact, as she came to understand later, she was not at all a bad dancer; it was that she would never be more than not at all bad. She began to study music, and then sculpture. Eclecticism, she found, was to her taste. And then at the age of twenty-two she found herself suddenly quite rich, for her husband, of whom she had seen nothing for several years, died of an obscure disease of the brain, intestate. She could do anything, materially, that took her fancy. And to begin with, she did nothing very singular. She took a number of lovers, not because she was naturally promiscuous—she enjoyed their company rather better than their love—but rather because the mental stimulus their proximity afforded her had become necessary. The kind of men to whom she gave herself was usually the artist, the artist in the fullest and truest sense, the painter and the writer certainly, but not less the artist in finance or statescraft or even industry; the creator, in a word. She did not understand then, though it became clear enough in the course of time, that she was seeking only self-expression. All the direct media, the more obvious ones, she tried herself, reached a certain level of

78

technical skill and then stopped, aware of something approaching genius in herself and totally incapable of giving it expression. Once or twice, in the composition of somewhat erotic verse, of which she published a book in Paris, she felt she had at last found articulacy, perhaps because the making of poetry is as nearly a physical effort as an intellectual exercise; she pursued it and it fled in the conscious effort. It was not for several years that she began to appreciate her relationship with the men who loved her. She had believed that the taking was all hers and that she gave nothing more than any other woman of intelligence might give; with detachment and enjoyment. It was in fact she who gave and they who took, for she began to see herself too often in their work. The artist is sometimes inspired because of a woman, but to be inspired by a woman is another matter, and very rare. In the first the inspiration is already within and only dormant; in the second the artist is only the means by which the woman expresses herself, or the *geist* within her. And when she understood this, she changed her whole attitude; now it was deliberate. She picked out the fledgling. She sought, and put to her own use, the promising nonentity. When they had served their purpose, when she had used them as a means of self-expression, she let them go and found others. Some fell at once and thought their failure ascribable to her callous treatment of them, some held the ground they had gained, and a few reached the heights. None acknowledged her, but of that she was well content; it proved her case.

She walked slowly back to the camp with Adrian Bullivant. The wind thrust at their backs and laid flat the tall grasses and the clouds hurried anxiously across the sky. The mountain sailed serenely among them, white-tipped like a finger dipped in cream.

' Seems to bear down on you all the time, doesn't it ?' he said.

79

' Yes.'

' Has it a name?'

' I never heard of one.'

' Can you get to the foot of it?'

She shrugged her shoulders. ' You'd better try.'

' Have you tried?'

' I got lost in the forest.'

' It doesn't look awfully difficult. You just walk up through the forest?'

' That's all.'

One day, he told himself, if he had time, he would walk up through the forest to the foot of the peak. They went on towards the camp, the woman's hair streaming forward on either side of her face in the wind. They were nearly at the bridge when they saw Paula. She called and ran towards them, her dark fluffy hair bouncing as she ran. She took the older woman's arm and looked up into her face, laughing breathlessly. Then she looked at Adrian Bullivant with hatred.

5

SO YOU INTEND to do nothing, he would say bitterly, and with contempt. Nothing. You intend to stand aside and let the others do the chores. To hell with everything and everybody . . . that's your attitude, isn't it? Well, he would continue, it is not mine. I'll do it myself, if I must, and damn the consequences; with uncommon emphasis. He would defend the camp and blow the dam and they could look on or participate, as pleased them. But, he would add darkly, let me tell you this : if and when the dam goes up, all will pay, every man jack. Did they understand that? Or were they too deeply immersed in their own abominable apathy? A splendid speech, a fine, resounding speech. The German, he would tell them, would take it out of them . . . of them, not him alone. So they could either help him or they could sit on their backsides and watch, but in any case they would pay. The Boche will clean out this mountainside, he would tell them, till there is scarcely one stone standing upon another, let alone a school of idiot children yawning away the war a few hundred yards from the headquarters of a stiff-bellied Prussian. The camp would be defended. He would repeat that : this camp will be defended. I shall defend it. He had approached every member of the staff in turn and there was not one of them prepared to do a hand's turn to help. Partisans, he would say, partisans indeed! He would tell them about the men and women who had been fighting the enemy for four years all over Europe, in France, in Italy, Russia, Norway. . . . while they, they did less than nothing, and fed themselves on the basest variety of blackmail. Peace-time partisans, he would call them. Rats that came out of their holes and scavenged the battlefields only when the fight was over, flaunting their paltry honour while the women and children cheered. The world would be infested with their kind. Beetles.

' If the enemy took it into his head, Captain Bullivant,' the Corps Commander told him, ' he could destroy this camp and every man in it without the slightest difficulty.' He looked at the pale, earnest face across the table; the size of the eyes beyond the glasses rendered them strangely ingenuous. ' I understand your feelings perfectly, and to a certain extent share them. Nevertheless, owing allegiance to none and therefore having no obligations to fulfil, I will not order this handful of people to attack an objective they have not the smallest chance of reaching, let alone destroying, so that you may tell yourself you have fulfilled yours. For the same reason we shall not defend the camp. If we happened to hold the camp very dear, that would be another matter. We don't; it's uncomfortable, insanitary and wet. We are doing very well by pinning down some three or four hundred middle-aged soldiers in this vicinity. They are happy to stay there, thank God, and we shall not disturb their rest. If and when they move away, then we shall venture into the valley and make ourselves a nuisance till they come back.'

' The Allies are launching an offensive during the next week or so,' Adrian Bullivant said, ' with the object of destroying, preferably by capture, the German armies on this front. My orders are to blow up the dam and flood the valley so that their withdrawal is hindered, if not impossible. I must do it.'

' A secondary consideration is,' the Commander continued, calmly, ' that we have no faith. Not in the military prowess of the Allies, but in what they and, if you like, we, are busy fighting for. We don't feel inclined to lift a finger to accelerate the process of evolution as advertised.'

Adrian Bullivant stared at him. The Commander's face was brown and the heavy chin bristled with many little points of light, for he had not shaved that morning and the sandy hairs shone in the arrow of sunlight that fell across the desk from the dusty window high up in the wall behind him. The grey eyes were wholly expressionless, narrowed a little against the bright light.

'I'm very sorry you had to drop on this particular bit of country, Captain Bullivant,' he said gently, 'it must be very discouraging. Nobody wanted you, you or your obligations or your doctrine or really anything about you. Since you are here and there's no going back, I earnestly counsel you to accept it as you find it. You may even get to like it in time. Is it your duty to your superior officer that worries you, or your duty to yourself? Your ideas, perhaps?'

Adrian Bullivant said stubbornly, 'Your duty and mine happen to coincide in this particular. I shall do my part of it. I'm asking that you do yours also.'

'But I don't feel it a duty.'

'I'm trying to tell you that it is a duty.' He was arguing now for the sake of argument. He wished he could get closer to the man opposite him. He knew that within five minutes of leaving the Command Post he would not be able to recall even the face. The man's personality was altogether nebulous and remote: you felt yourself in the presence of a power, but you never touched it; there was nothing you remembered, nothing you recognised immediately as human, no frailty, no strength. Oh, damn it all, there must be a chord somewhere that he might strike; he would have to canvass the whole staff, one by one, like some commercial traveller, selling an idea. 'And the others?' he said.

'It may be,' the Commander answered, 'that you will

83

find one or two of them willing to help you, though I doubt it. If they do, I shall raise no objections. Every man here is himself quite capable of deciding for himself. I shall issue no orders for or against. Have you tried Crosby?'

'Crosby will obey orders.'

'He might, he might.'

'He will.'

'Possibly.'

'Crosby's a soldier.'

'I would put it to him as an idea, if I were you, rather than an order. He's something of an idealist, I think.'

'You could order the rest of them into action if you chose.'

The Commander moved his shoulders in the old leather jacket he wore. 'I'd hesitate to jeopardise my vanity to that extent.'

'But I don't see the point,' Adrian Bullivant persisted. 'What are you doing here if you won't fight? I don't see what good you're doing, to yourself or anybody else. What's the idea behind it? Is it getting you anywhere?'

'Not everybody wants to go anywhere, Captain Bullivant.'

'Well.' This was rank silliness.

'Does it seem amoral to you?'

'Immoral. You know perfectly well what you're doing.'

'I fear we shall never see eye to eye, Captain Bullivant. We both have much to learn.'

'Nothing, that is what you're doing, nothing at all.'

'Very true. I can understand that it shocks you a good deal. I'm simply living. I believe in nothing that you believe in. As far as you're concerned, I'm living without beliefs. Just living. Take it or leave it, Captain Bullivant, I'm not forcing it on you, which alone is something of a novelty, isn't it? . . . or even being unduly fractious about it. But by the same token you really can't expect me to

84

plunge headlong into catastrophe on behalf of a flatulent ideology in which I no longer have the least faith.' The wrinkles about his eyes were very pronounced as he looked at the young man. 'It may come as a surprise to you to know that there are quite a lot of ordinary, decent, intelligent folk who believe that the tenets of your political cult are no wit less evil in effect than those of any other, rather more so, if anything, since they want only my body —speaking for myself—and you are after my soul. As an Anglo-American export, Captain Bullivant, your democracy rings smug and false in every note and I for one will not raise a hand to further it. As an idea it may once have reached the stars; between you, you have made a dunghill of it which, with a little judicious manipulation, is transformable, as the occasion presents itself, into anything from an altar to a sound commercial proposition, from a pulpit to a commercial traveller's intrigue, according as whether you are buying it or selling it. I'm sorry if I offend you. I'm aware that the alternative is starvation and personally, all things considered, I prefer it. If there is to be no freedom, I'll choose my own form of slavery.'

Adrian Bullivant, already angry, said, 'I haven't tried to sell you anything.'

'Only because you assume I already want to buy it. You are quite mistaken. I accept the fullest responsibility for my odious attitude. Indeed, I accept the responsibility for everything, every little beastliness there ever was or ever will be, by whatever name it goes. Good and bad, it's all one, the expression of one personality. We like to think it's God. Pity is dead in us and so we look elsewhere.'

Bullivant felt a slow flush of embarrassment rising to his cheeks; the mention of the Almighty in conversation was always unnecessary, he found. The Commander scratched his genitals.

'The God-hunters of Christendom have dug up a handful of pious catchwords and they are so far about the limit of their success. They're busy scratching about for the answer without knowing exactly what the question is.'

'You, I suppose, do know?'

'I know nothing, except that you can't fiddle about trying to separate good from evil, so that you can attribute the one to God and the other to the devil. They both come from the same place and I see no difference between them. It's all one. This . . .' he flicked the corner of the map pinned to the table, 'and this . . .' he rolled the pencil between his fingers, 'your little gun that Luca Pugnini's so fond of. Buonaparte and Hitler and St. Francis of Assisi . . . lots of little expressions of a personality. You. And me. I accept the responsibilty for the whole frightful mess, Captain Bullivant, and I need nobody to tell me what a culpable fellow I am.'

'I'm afraid I don't understand what you're after.' He passed a hand over his face.

'Humility, Captain Bullivant, and love and courage and pity, all applied to the ordinary business of living.' He smiled suddenly, showing his big white teeth.

'How can you apply them. . . .'

'If you really think you should defend the camp,' the Commander told him a little wearily, 'then by all means do. I won't hinder you. Remember only that you take the responsibility for the lives of all the people in the headquarters. That it may be your duty will perhaps help you in your own eyes, but not in theirs. For the German will certainly destroy you, the village, and root out the rest of us from our holes in the mountain. So, in effect, we shall all defend the place: if we pay the penalty we commit also the crime.'

'I have a wife,' Adrian Bullivant said slowly, 'to whom I would like to return with a clear conscience.' He saw Judith's face in his mind suddenly and felt in his pocket

86

for the wallet in which her photograph lay; it was still there. 'She has lost her reason, temporarily. She's very highly-strung and the air-raids upset her a great deal.'

'Yes?'

'Yes. It's very important to me to do my job.'

'And to her?'

'She doesn't recognise me—or didn't the last time I visited her—except as the cause of her illness.'

The Commander watched the flow of expressions across the young man's face as he groped for the idea. 'And so?'

'I don't want to lose both . . . you understand?'

Now she was coming towards him down the long corridor again, with the nurse. It was a clear, hard picture. The walls were tiled brown and buff and there was a long fibre mat on the concrete floor. The rain drummed softly on the windows; beyond them there was a courtyard and then shining roofs and then the tall chimneys from which a trickle of smoke fled to the flat grey sky. The nurse who held her arm as she would have held the stem of a tall flower was elderly and her hair was iron grey and artfully arranged in two or three symmetrical hoops that peeped beneath the napkin she wore about her head and on her wizened lips there was a gentle, proprietary smile. He could see her coming beyond the doors, many doors all glass-panelled one beyond the other, her face weaving and writhing through the bad glass as though seen through clear, deep water, and sometimes it was his wife and sometimes the lovely face was that of a stranger, the eyes wide with excitement and the approach of terror. They had pinned a ribbon to her hair, a great blue bow that he hated and longed to whip from her head; the wings rose and fell like those of a bird as she moved. They were a long time in the corridor, for the doors had handles only on his side and on hers there were keyholes into which the nurse inserted the keys, one by one, closing the doors carefully behind her.

87

His heart was beating in his throat. When she was close he saw that the lips were drawn back and the teeth bared slightly.

He whispered her name.

The nurse shook the arm she held. 'Say something, dear,' she said, 'it's your husband.'

He waited. The wide eyes were fixed on the bright buttons of his uniform.

'It's the air-raids, dear,' the nurse told him. 'Just the air-raids.'

'I don't think she recognises me.'

'A bit high-strung, that's all,' the nurse told him, 'soon be all right again.' She shook the arm gently. 'Won't you, dear?'

Then the girl uttered a thin, high scream and threw herself at him, thrusting off the nurse who tried to restrain her. The nurse lost her balance and sat down heavily on her broad backside, the napkin slipping over her eyes and one of the loops of hair protruding like a horn from beneath. He put up his arms to protect his face but she reached over them and ripped open the smooth skin of his forehead with her nails till the blood ran down into his eyes and his glasses fell off and he felt them under his foot. The nurse struggled to her feet and came between them ineffectually saying, 'Ssh, ssh, dear,' and he thought what a futile thing it was to say, 'Ssh, dear, now, dear, it's all right, it's all right,' and trying to silence the screaming and hold her from him. Then the others came running down the corridor, fumbling clumsily with the doors, one after the other; and took her firmly by the arms while she struggled to get at him. They held her still while the cries subsided. Then she went with them unresisting through the doors, the blue ribbon clinging to a wisp of hair on her neck. When the psychiatrist came at last in response to his request to see somebody in authority, the man was extremely vexed. 'You should not have come. I advised you most strongly not to come.' And when Adrian Bullivant said he was going overseas on the following day: ' And to come in that uniform. You really ought to have had more sense.' She was screaming again in the distance, the taut, frail sound drifting about in the great building as though seeking the way out, out into the open air and the rain. ' It's quite impossible, at this stage, to say whether she will make a complete recovery or not.' ' No, we're very busy, very busy. The air-raids.' And finally, ' You'd better call in at the first-aid post and get some antiseptic on your face. And you've broken your glasses.'

Maybe she would be all right, he told the Commander, by the time he got home. The Commander said yes, he expected she would be.

6

OF THOSE to whom an appeal for help might be made there remained only the priest. Father Domenicus would not leave Ronc and attempt the ascent to the camp except during the hours of darkness. (He was on excellent terms with Walter von Langenburg, but he knew better than to trifle with the Prussian in matters of military procedure; to walk out of the village and up the hill in broad daylight would invite and most certainly merit a bullet in the back.) With what patience he had, and in despair there is little, Adrian Bullivant waited for nightfall. It was, he thought, a fair assumption that the priest would visit the camp that night, all things considered; he remembered with an inward smile the anxiety in the unlovely countenance of the priest when he had spoken of blowing the dam. The smooth flow of discouragement had not concealed but emphasised his apprehension. In any case it was Friday, and he had been told that it was normally on Friday that Father Domenicus delivered the supplies for the following week. Adrian Bullivant wondered idly if tobacco were available; and pulled himself up hastily . . . to condone the intolerable for the sake of a minor personal convenience was unthinkable.

He filled his pipe from the all-but-empty pouch and sat on the sill of a window of the scabrous ruin that faced his billet. Behind him the grey rubble littered the floor and a cloud of mosquitoes hung in the still yellow sunlight. He watched the slow, tranquil life of the camp and knew suddenly, without becoming fully conscious of the thought, that he would look back upon his few days here with a certain affection. You did that wherever you were, of course, but he had been running for a long time now, years, towards something or away from something, and it was not unpleasant to slow to a walk. Pierre ambled past him, hands in pockets and eyes on the ground, and then Roberto, going in the opposite direction, with quick neat steps. Neither greeted him; he might not have been there. He asked himself idly what the consequences would be if he did nothing, as they would have him do, if he abandoned his duties and slid gently down the hill to resignation. He might stay here for ever, forgetting and forgotten as were the rest of them, and he would be assumed dead and Judith would marry again (he winced at the thought of another man's arms about her) and his father would have to do without his successor; he would have to do without in any case, of course, but it was interesting to think of. The Allied armies would sweep across the valley and the birds would be flown and the intelligence people would be livid, absolutely livid, and the general philosophical, as became him. Then he would sink into a sweet torpor of aimlessness and infinite leisure and maybe fall in love with Erica or one of the other women, he was a man after all, he told himself, and lie on the warm earth with her and feel the life in his arms and the life in the earth and forget all else. Maria Pugnini, the Divisional Commander's wife, passed him and smiled and dropped the heavy black lashes over her eyes. He had never been unfaithful to Judith; sometimes he thought there must be something amiss with him, for nobody else he knew was so scrupulous; several times he had been on the brink of letting himself go, and each time he had checked himself. Oh well. He drowsed in the sun. In a moment he would go and have a look at the mill with a view to its defence. The mill would certainly be the best place . . . not to defend it to the inevitable end; as a token only, a gesture of disrespect for the enemy and for the Commander, as a fillip to his own vanity. There would be a fair chance of getting away up the bed of the stream towards the chasm. It would surprise them all right. By God, he would give them a nasty surprise. There was always the possibility of capture or death, the former disagreeable, the latter . . . at least heroic. It was not a possibility that attracted him. No man dies deliberately, except maybe by his own hand. You carried your Golden Treasury about with you and a photograph of Judith and hoped for the best.

In the deep grass by the stream Pierre was holding the Divisional Commander's wife in his arms, kissing her with the ferocity of a lover whose mind is elsewhere. She lay supine and resilient beneath him, her arms about his neck and her eyes closed. Their love-making had all the indifference of ritual and much of its anæsthesia. Luca Pugnini slept at that time, on the mattress beneath the window of the room he shared with his wife and child. Certainly he was aware of his wife's perfidy, but until the matter became too flagrant for him decently to ignore, he was not disposed to interfere; he had no liking for scenes. The flies buzzed excitedly over his round, shining face. In the armoury, Roberto cleaned a rifle slowly, whistling to himself as he ran the tips of his fingers along the smooth brown stock. When he had finished the weapon he raised it to his shoulder and drew a bead on the pine that grew a fraction higher than the rest on the fringe of the forest and pressed the trigger on the empty chamber and clicked his tongue as he lowered it and adjusted the safety catch. Below the ridge, on the short, crisp turf, Slobadov and Hans were torturing with a rare disinterest the rabbit they had caught in Slobadov's trap. The animal lay still and only twitched sometimes and opened its maw as though stifling a yawn; no sound emerged. The men bent over it, their heads together. They were very angry when it died, and set the trap again for another. In the Command Post the Chief of Staff prepared the list of requirements he must produce this evening when Father Domenicus would come toiling up the hill. The small, neat handwriting danced decorously across the paper and his head swam with sleep; there was paint for Otto, chiefly gamboge this week, and the flour and polento and the meat and tobacco and a pair of socks for himself (not to be knitted by the mayor's wife) and the milk. What a mistake it was to have eaten the goats! Luca Pugnini needed oil for the armoury. And candles, they were getting short of candles. In the old days in the Ordnance somebody else wrote out the indents and you only signed them. His moist wrist clung to the flimsy paper and the flies wheeled about the small grey head.

In the billet she shared with Erica the small dark girl whose name was Paula sat on the edge of her mattress and bit her nails in her misery and loneliness. The setting sun shone through the dark, fluffy hair. She wept absently, scarcely knowing she wept at all, and watched the door for the shadow that must sooner or later fall across it. For she had seen Erica walk out of the village with Otto, in the direction of the Wall of the Oblique Death, and she had been away over three hours. Paula had been sitting on the mattress all afternoon, waiting, until now when the duck gathered secretly on the plain and prepared for the night; soon it would flood the warm earth and rise upwards to the sky. When it began to rise Erica returned.

The girl looked at her with inflamed and bitter eyes. ' Where have you been?' she said in a high voice.

Erica did not turn from the mirror, cracked and fly-blown, that hung on the wall between the windows. ' Ssh, ssh,' she murmured. She looked closely at herself and ran the tips of her fingers across the lids of her eyes once or twice.

'You've been with that artist.' The girl's voice trembled on the edge of hysteria.

'Be quiet, Paula.'

'Yes, you have. I saw you.'

Erica turned from the mirror and looked steadily at the girl on the mattress.

'I saw you.'

'Did you?'

'Yes. Four hours you've been gone.'

'Dry your eyes,' Erica told her, 'you look hideous.'

'Oh . . .' the girl dropped her face into her hands and sobbed brokenly.

'Here.' Erica threw a handkerchief on to the girl's knee. 'Blow your nose.'

'I wish I was dead.'

'Blow your nose, Paula.'

'Yes, I do.' She blew her nose on the handkerchief. 'I wish I was dead.'

'Don't be silly.'

'One day I'll kill myself and then you'll be sorry.'

'Dry your eyes and be a good girl.'

'I wish I'd never seen you.' She buried her face in the handkerchief and wailed tenuously. 'I wish I was dead.'

'For heaven's sake . . .'

'You don't care. I know you don't care.'

And in truth, at that moment Erica did not. She was not unmoved by the child's tears, but it was nearly as though she herself were enduring the pain and it was a strange sensation.

'Stop crying now,' she told Paula briefly.

'Oh, Erica, be nice to me, I'm so miserable.'

'There's nothing to be miserable about. Get up and dry your eyes, and stop it, for heaven's sake.'

'Say something nice.'

Erica would have done so, but nothing came to her mind;

94

irrelevancies and scraps of conversation; nothing coherent. She went to the door and leaned against it in the sun and wound her wristwatch absently. Behind her Paula whispered to herself.

' What did you say?'

' I said I'm going to kill myself,' the girl answered, ' now.'

' To-morrow,' Erica said, ' save it for to-morrow.'

' I'll throw myself off the Wall,' the girl said. She sobbed spasmodically. ' Where were you?'

' Sleeping.'

Paula looked at her. ' There's no need to lie.'

' Thank you.'

' I hate you.'

' Yes.'

' You were with that artist.'

' Yes.'

It had been dark nearly four hours when Father Domenicus arrived. He was leading a small grey donkey, the great paniers on either side of which were full; the unhappy animal was even more spent than the priest. He was welcomed warmly, however, by the staff, of which all but one or two were already gathered before the Command Post awaiting his arrival; in an otherwise barren week the arrival of the provisions was an event of some importance.

Father Domenicus raised his arm and blessed them breathlessly, handing the bridle of the ass to Luca Pugnini. Then he pushed his way through the little gathering about the paniers and found himself face to face with Adrian Bullivant.

' I want to talk to you,' the young man said softly.

The sharp voice of Luca Pugnini bade the people remove their inquisitive fingers from the paniers.

' I must talk to you before you go.'

The priest looked at the pale oval of the officer's face and the stars shining in the glasses. He did not reply. He

95

stepped to one side and entered the Command Post, Adrian Bullivant close on his heels, determined not to let the man out of his sight. The Corps Commander and the Chief of Staff looked up, their shadows huge across the ceiling. The priest wiped the drop from his nose and said without preamble,

'The enemy attacks to-morrow afternoon.'

There was no sound. The candles sputtered and threw out little sparks.

'Attacks?' the Commander muttered.

'This is all your fault,' the Chief of Staff barked at Adrian Bullivant. 'That infernal aircraft, I knew it, I knew it.'

'But . . . attacks?' the Commander repeated.

'He intends to send troops across the mountain,' the priest said. 'If they meet opposition they will attack. The camp will have to be evacuated.' He crossed himself and raised a lymphatic eye to the ceiling. 'God lend you wings.'

'It's highly irregular,' the Commander said.

'The last person they should find, I need hardly say,' Father Domenicus continued, 'is this young man, or any sign of him.'

'Captain Bullivant is aware of his responsibilities,' the Commander said.

The priest looked at the young man. He had already contemplated betraying the officer's presence on the mountain to the enemy. It would be very simple, a matter only of a word or two to Walter von Langenburg, and the rest would doubtless follow with smoothness and efficiency. But the Prussian might take it into his head to annihilate the little band on the ridge, and, once he had tasted blood, it was unlikely he would stop at so trifling a reprisal. Father Domenicus remembered with a shudder the hanging of the Perathoner family, father, mother, a son and daughter, for their defence of their property. There would be no more such scenes in Ronc, the priest decided. He would lie and cheat and betray, but on God's behalf these things were forgivable; there would be no bloodshed in his parish. The people would give their food to the partisans and their money to arm them, but starvation is the Lord's chastisement, and they would starve in peace.

He scrutinised the young man. 'I hope so,' he said, 'I hope so, indeed.'

Adrian Bullivant was aware of the priest's fear. It was something of a revelation. To turn it to his own advantage, however, was not a method of action, of forcing them into action, that he liked. But he felt, and this for the first time, a measure of power. He could at least talk to them, or at least to Father Domenicus, as man to man, levelly. He smiled.

'I hope so, too,' he said pleasantly.

'It needs only an example, you know,' he told the priest when they left the Command Post. 'Your example. You and I could do it . . . set the whole country ablaze from end to end and kick the bastards out neck and crop.' The idea glowed in his mind. 'These people know how to fight when they want, they've been fighting for hundreds of years. All they need is a spark, one little light to set them moving. To defend this camp to-morrow would do it, more than do it. They'd follow.'

They stood facing one another in the dark. The donkey thrust its head between them for warmth and company. Beneath the bridge the stream murmured and now, as the moon hove up beyond the peak, shone softly in the light it gave. The faces of the two men were luminous and the eyes of the animal between them, when it threw back its head to nuzzle their shoulders, glowed with an irridescent orange flame. Somewhere in the camp a man was playing a harmonica carefully and the sound was extremely moving at that moment; the wandering music jammed fast in the

97

throat. And as the moon, still red in the mist, struck upwards to the brittle stars, the stream raised its voice and sang a shriller note and the wind stirred restlessly in the distant forest and the grass and the weeds about the parapets of the bridge fluttered excitedly and the creatures of the night came out to feed, the rabbits, the moles, the bats about the window where the light shone; the earth broke into life.

'There is victory only in God, my son,' the priest said. 'Don't persist with this fantastic notion. There is enough suffering.'

'Then I'm afraid I shall have to force the issue.'

'Listen, boy.' The priest spoke now with asperity, his breath heavy with the odour of mould breaking in little gusts across Adrian Bullivant's face. 'It has taken me a great deal of time and trouble to keep the peace in this neighbourhood. I have a duty to the Heavenly Father and to my parish. To myself I have none. I will not stand helpless and watch you destroy the labour of years.' The drop beneath his nose glittered in the moonlight. He turned about and dragged at the bridle of the donkey. The animal followed him down the hill and soon they were at one with the night.

Adrian Bullivant walked slowly along the pale track. He found Crosby squatting on a heap of rubble.

'That you, Crosby?'

'Me, sir.'

He sank on to the stones beside the soldier. 'How about having a go at a few Germans to-morrow afternoon?'

'Me, sir?'

'You and me.'

'Cause a lot of trouble.'

'The whole affair's a lot of trouble, Crosby.'

'Upset things round here, I mean.'

'They need it.'

98

'Oh, I don't know. Might be worse.'

'Got to be done, I'm afraid.'

'Supposing I say no, sir—I mean, just supposing—what then?'

'I don't think you'd be such a fool, would you?'

'I'd be that anyway.'

'I could make it an order.'

'Better make it an order.'

'I hate to have to do that, Crosby.'

'I'm no chicken, myself.'

'All right. You and I will defend the camp to-morrow.'

'Yes, sir. Very good, sir.'

Bullivant got to his feet. 'I'm going to bed,' he said. 'Goodnight, Crosby.'

''Night, sir.' He rose from the stones.

'Don't get up.'

He sat down again and blew into the harmonica to clear it. He shook the instrument. Then he began to play, sounding first a few chords. In a moment he stopped and patted his pocket to see if the gun was there all right. He began to play again, the toe of his boot tapping the dust gently. The sad, frail music drifted away on the air.

'Things will change, Jim.'

'With you here to see they bloody don't.'

Chubb drew breath and let it out slowly through his teeth. 'You get my goat, Jim, sometimes.'

'Drink your tea.'

'You can't go on like this.'

'Can't I?'

'It's just leading to trouble.'

'No good, Chubby, you're on one side now and I'm on the other. No good talking.'

'You're not a criminal, Jim. The policeman ran his big fingers through his hair wearily. 'It's no use trying to pretend you are.'

99

'I'm a criminal to the people you work for, Chubb, that's what you don't understand.'

'That's for the law to say, not them.'

'Christ. They are the law.'

'I've got my opinion, Jim,' the policeman said stubbornly.

'You, you never had an opinion of your own in your life, so don't talk cock.'

'I don't know, Jim, I don't know. You didn't used to be like this, before. In the army, I mean. You were always one of the chaps.'

'I still am. Only you're not.'

'You always talked like this, but it was different. It was human talk. Now it's something else. Now I don't know what it is. It's bad, that's all I know. Bad, Jim.' He shook his head. 'It's not so much the talk that's changed, it's you.'

'Make up your mind.'

'Where's your old mouth-organ.'

'That? God alone knows.' And then he thought suddenly about the night he had sat alone on the mountainside in the moonlight and played the harmonica for two hours and twenty minutes, solid, everything he could remember. Oh, Jesus, that was a long time ago. Just about the time they tried to defend the old headquarters, with the mountain high up there all the time, watching, listening, with the cloud on the summit.

'What makes you keep thinking you're a criminal, Jim?'

'I don't belong here.'

'That doesn't put you in prison.'

'Who said it did?'

'Having a gun is the only thing that puts you on the wrong side of the law, Jim.'

'That damned gun.'

When he got stiffly to his feet and put the instrument in his pocket and walked slowly towards his billet, he saw the woman with long white hair standing in the doorway of the place she lived in, watching him. She did not move. She must have been listening all the time, he thought. He went on to the house.

This night, none heard the approach of the aircraft. It was very late and they were all asleep when it passed over the village.

7

THEY COULD scarcely leave the equipment where it lay, scattered about the camp for all to see and steal, but, since the only means of transport was the Commander's mare, and this he would ride himself—on his damaged leg he could move neither fast nor far—to burden themselves with it would be no less imprudent. Fortunately the cellar of the mill was sufficiently capacious to hold it; it was also deep, well below the level of the earth, and the only entrance was under the wheel. So the contents of the armoury were transferred to the cellar; in such room as was left the cooking utensils were stored, and the mattresses, and Otto's pots of paint. For the rest, their own property, they did as they might, shoving each small hoarding of clothing and necessaries beneath the rotten floorboards and under the ancient moulds of rubble that lay about the village.

Adrian Bullivant and Crosby watched the preparations with a certain sardonic interest; there was considerable excitement, much gesticulation and calling to one another across the village street and up and down its length. There was no sun that morning. The clouds were low and heavy and dark and the lonely peak was no longer visible; it was a presence only, a sensation in the deep mists. Later it would rain, they thought.

' We shall hang about in the rear of the column,' Adrian Bullivant told the soldier. ' Follow them out of the camp, and then we'll drop off a bit later, when they scatter.' For the Chief of Staff had already addressed the remainder of the party on the necessity for dispersal; certainly they would carry arms, he had said, but they would fight, if it became necessary, alone. ' Let them get well ahead.'

The air was still and lifeless and small sounds carried far. Now and then a breath of wind came lightly from the west and raised the sluggish dust in little spirals that careered about the street and sped between the dwellings and there subsided. Little Josef trotted purposefully after them, and after the men and women who moved about the village; there was much to follow. A shred of mist stalked along the track and in the valley the clouds clung to the wet land.

They gathered outside the Command Post somewhat reluctantly, with many backward glances to their billets lest there might be something they had forgotten, hitching the burdens a fraction higher on the shoulders, attending to one another's sacks and rucksacks and blanket-rolls. Roberto adjusted the set of his trilby and polished the tips of each dusty shoe against the other leg and skipped once or twice and flicked a dainty pass with his foot to make sure his bundles set well upon his back. Slobadov leered at Erica, who stood alone and quiet against the wall, with Paula at a little distance glancing up into the cold, impassive face and nervously wringing her hands. For some trifling omission Luca Pugnini rated his wife and she stood with eyes downcast and the trace of a smile on her full red lips, occasionally easing the weight on her back with a hitching forward of the shoulders and an absent frown. Pierre leaned on his rifle and listened, sometimes turning his head towards them, sometimes with a glance at Erica, more often staring beyond them all at the great rents in the clouds through which, beneath, lay the valley. Sometimes a small plume of white dust moved along the roads there.

The Chief of Staff adjusted his spectacles and announced the order of march. Scant heed was paid to the detail of his instructions, but they shuffled into a ragged line. Adrian Bullivant and Crosby interested themselves in the Commander's mare; the animal shifted its weight from one leg to the other, and its gaunt head hung almost to the ground. When the Commander limped from his office they moved away, but his eyes followed them. Slobadov and Hans hoisted the Commander on to the mare's back; there was no saddle, he rode bareback, but they got him up at last. He swung the animal about and ran his eyes over the patient staff. Then he nodded and turned again and kicked the mare into movement; it appeared to be blind in the left eye, for with its head on one side it watched the ground carefully with the right. The staff picked up their bundles and fell into line behind the horse and Adrian Bullivant and the soldier shouldered their weapons and followed them. As the column moved the sun broke through a narrow fissure in the clouds above and the pool of light hurried across the plain.

'You never know whether to laugh or bloody cry when this lot gets going,' Crosby said.

Adrian Bullivant did not answer.

His responsibility sat heavily astride his neck. If only they were not so damned pathetic! He hated them for their wretched pathos. They were doing it deliberately. It was an affront, a challenge. But it would not have the desired effect, he told himself; they could make fools of themselves or not as they pleased, it would move him from his purpose not a wit. He had a job to do and he would do it and had no intention whatever of being diverted from his aim by a scurrilous appeal to the emotions. If he gave in to them, if he surrendered to his own paltry senti-mentality, he would never be able to look himself in the face again, or them. He ground his teeth and kept his eyes on the heels of Otto's rope-soled sandals in the dust, and then in the short green turf, and finally among the weeds and rocks and the nameless undergrowth of the plain. The column opened out and soon there was as much as fifty yards between each man, or couple, walking with heads down and backs bent to the incline, soundlessly, the rising wind catching every loose end and skirt and scarf and the long grey tail of the mare and tugging at them. They went into the decline on the southern side of the Wall.

' Slow up a bit,' Adrian Bullivant said.

They shortened their stride. Otto did not turn. In a few minutes they saw the bright red head vanish beyond the great hump of the hill and they were alone.

' Fine. Come on.'

They stopped and turned about. Little Josef stopped also and looked at them steadily. He stood about twenty yards away, down the slope.

' Damn,' Adrian Bullivant said. He looked at the child. He motioned to the child then to pass and follow the column into the dale. Josef did not move. The officer repeated the gesture with greater emphasis, but the boy only stared. ' This is going to be difficult,' Adrian Bullivant said.

' What about trying going down anyway,' Crosby suggested, ' and seeing if the little bastard follows?'

Adrian Bullivant shook his head. He bent forward and held out his hand to the child and snapped his fingers and uttered coaxing sounds with his lips. Josef watched him with a mild but dispassionate curiosity.

' Come on, then, we'll try going down.'

They set off down the slope with a careless swinging gait, passed the child and went on. They turned. Little Josef was following them.

' Oh, God.'

Arms akimbo they looked with loathing at the child.

' Go back,' Adrian Bullivant shouted. He gestured in the direction of the dale.

' Go away,' shouted Crosby. 'Go on, clear off, can't you?'

They went on down the hill and the boy followed them.

They stopped again. 'Can't take a child with us on a show like this,' Adrian Bullivant said. 'Out of the question. Fantastic.'

'Wouldn't stand a chance,' Crosby said.

'Not a chance.'

Adrian Bullivant sank on to a rock at the side of the track the little column had made and lit a cigarette. Crosby sat down also.

'Cigarette?'

'Got used to not smoking, sir. Better not start again.' He looked at the motionless child twenty yards away. 'We could beat the hell out of him,' he said, 'but that wouldn't do much good.'

'Damn it, you ought to know how to shake him off, you've been here long enough.'

'Keep still, that's the only way I know.'

'Well, we are doing, aren't we?'

'Yes, sir.'

'The thing's perfectly absurd. We can't sit here indefinitely, just because of an idiot child.'

'No, sir.'

'Bloody ridiculous.'

'Only one thing to do, sir, far as I can see.'

'What's that?'

'Take him with us. Let him lump it. Serve him right if he does stop a packet. Learn him not to.'

'We'd never get away with a brat to haul about.'

'Or give up the idea altogether.'

Adrian Bullivant looked at him sharply. 'None of that.'

'Well, sir.'

'We might tie him up and leave him here.'

'Probably starve to death.'

'I would sincerely hope so.'

'Wonder what makes him follow people about.'

'Yes.'

' Must be some kink.'

' Yes.'

They were silent. At last Adrian Bullivant rose and threw away the cigarette. ' Hell,' he said, ' we'll simply have to risk it, that's all. I won't be baulked by a half-witted infant. Come on.'

They set off again down the bleak hillside towards the village whose broken outlines were already soft in the gathering mist. Little Josef followed them amiably. ' Let's try running a bit,' Bullivant said suddenly, ' we might shake him off that way.'

They broke into a run. They ran a long way, until the child was far out of sight behind them. ' Down here,' the officer shouted. They threw themselves into the undergrowth and lay heaving in the nettles and raw yellow dandelions.

' How long do we lie here?' Crosby asked him when he had regained his breath.

' Ssh. Quiet.'

They lay still and listened. There was no sound but the whisper of the wind in the weeds. After three minutes Bullivant raised his head cautiously above the level of the undergrowth and looked about him. Little Josef, a few yards away, watched him curiously.

' It's very humiliating indeed,' Adrian Bullivant said.

They got to their feet slowly and picked the verdure from their clothes.

' I'd like to know what the kid's mother thinks she's doing,' Crosby muttered.

They ignored the child and set off down the incline to the hamlet. The mist was thick now and it had begun to rain a little, a loose light rain under which the empty dwellings cowered sad and grey and lifeless. They went past the Command Post and on down the street towards the mill. The fire glowed still in the kitchen. The great door of the mill was open and they entered and looked about them; the odour of oil clung to the stones and there were oil stains on the dry floor, but all the weapons had gone; even the racks were dismantled. They set about preparing the place. They would need a couple of light machine-guns, Adrian Bullivant said, from the cellar, and belts of ammunition. Nothing heavy : they would snipe only, a few bursts of fire, and then they would have to run—through the window and the wheel and down into the bed of the stream beneath. The banks were relatively high, at least four feet on both sides, he thought, from the bed of the stream to the level ground, and the course of the stream was devious. They reconnoitred the mill very thoroughly, and the ground it covered. To the north the plain fell away in a long concave slope towards the spur of land that formed the southern side of the reservoir at its lower reaches; there was no cover on the plain; a magnificent field of fire, at least a thousand yards, he thought, though it would vary with the density of the mist. To the south, however, and to the west, there was too much cover; indeed there would be time for perhaps one burst each before the enemy would be upon them, coming up fast from the dead ground below the bridge, or through the dwellings along the village street, if they decided to attack from the south.

'Let's hope they come across the plain.'

Crosby said nothing.

They did what they could to fortify the mill. Crosby broke into the cellar and brought up two machine-guns and belts of ammunition. Adrian Bullivant climbed the ladder to the loft, but the walls above were of wood and gave scant protection; they would stay where they were. They set the light machine-guns in the windows and fed the tongues of the belts into the locks, the one pointing across the plain to the north, the other having its narrow snout projecting through the casement that gave on to the bridge and the village street. Little Josef watched them all the time, standing in the rain a few feet from the open door. Crosby examined his revolver.

'Where did you find that?' Bullivant asked him.

'My little souvenir.'

The rain fell steadily. Breaths of mist trailed across the plain and the doors of empty houses banged in the wind. The stream broke noisily over the blades of the wheel. It was ten minutes past two o'clock when Adrian Bullivant looked at his watch. 'Better settle down,' he said. He motioned to the child to enter, but Josef did not move until the officer made as though to push the door to; then he entered and remained at a distance.

'We'll take one gun with us,' Bullivant said. 'And drop the other into the stream.'

Crosby did not reply.

They took their posts, Bullivant at the window facing north across the open country, Crosby at the other, dragging lumber to the window so that they might sit more comfortably. They fell silent in a little while. A rat scuffled among the litter in the loft above. Crosby examined the belt in his gun.

Adrian Bullivant began to hum softly to himself, till the words of the song formed themselves on his lips. *My mother said that I never should, play with the gypsies in the wood*. He stopped abruptly. A pool of rain was forming slowly on the sill of the casement; he watched an ant cross the stone to the water and stop there and turn back and meet another ant marching to the pool. He was cold, he remembered, and hungry. *For if I did then she would say, oh, you naughty little girl for to disobey.*

'I'm sorry about this, Crosby.'

Crosby raised his head from the gun.

'We've no choice, you know, not really.'

Crosby did not speak.

'We'll get away all right, you'll see.'

And then, 'No option.'

Crosby cleared his throat but did not speak.

'Cold, isn't it?'

He was cold inside, deep in his vitals, frozen, horrified by his own uncertainty. No argument, and there were many, all sound, was convincing enough to overcome the doubt in his own mind. And the arguments for the other side were not easily ignored. If they failed to surprise the enemy and did not get away they would be shot, killed, or at best taken prisoner and the blowing of the reservoir, still his primary task, would never be carried out; to incite the people of the valley, of Ronc, of the headquarters of the Twenty Third Corps to resistance was only a means to an end and the end was the reservoir and if he, the instigator, were killed . . . if he could blow the dam himself, then the preliminaries might be dispensed with altogether. And supposing we are successful now? he asked himself, and we kill or wound a handful of elderly German soldiers, then what? The consequences might be disastrous; at best the headquarters would be eliminated; at worst the enemy might well make of Ronc an example that would never be forgotten, the threat of repetition of which would cow the people of the valley into utter submission rather than incite them to vengeance, and his own liberty, with whatever satisfaction he might derive from his futile gesture, would be no more than a burden to him. Maybe he should turn to Crosby now and say, 'This is downright idiocy, come on, let's get out of here,' and they would put the guns back where they had found them and the child would follow and there would be no harm done. There was still time. He looked at his watch. It was all but three o'clock. They would be coming now, somewhere out of sight in the mist, grey bulks plodding up the hill. Why don't I get up and go and take Crosby with me? and the stupid child for whose death I shall be directly responsible? He found no answer and felt the panic wind itself about his heart and the faint sweat break out on his brow. There was an answer, there must be an answer. He would not do this for no reason at all. There must be some unanswerable instinct that might not be gainsaid. Only to identify it! To produce it for himself with a flourish of triumph and say, There, there it is, that is the reason and it is worth my life, Crosby's, the life of an idiot child and of all the people of the headquarters and the valley. That is the reason, the thing for which I do this and drag the rest with me. That is why I have said I would do it, and that is why I am true to myself, and away with the rest.

'Don't you wish we was back in the old desert?' Crosby said suddenly.

Bullivant turned his eyes from the plain and looked at the soldier. 'Yes, sometimes I do,' he said.

'All right, wasn't it?'

'Yes.'

Wherever you were though, Crosby thought, that was never where you wanted to be. The present was always the worst; there was always something better in your memory, something more promising in the future. The present ought to stand still sometimes, he thought; maybe it ought always to be the present, all one, and then you could see the whole thing and know where you stood. If you could see what was going to happen to you, though, my God, you'd never move another inch. But you could see, that was the trouble. It was in you, down in your guts, all of it, you only recognised it afterwards and said to yourself, you knew that, you knew what was coming to you, all the time; you saw it, felt it, knew it, and ignored it. The old desert was pretty quiet at this time of day, hot, but quiet, and you'd be brewing up and having a shave and a little later the sun would go down fast and your shadow would stretch for miles across the sand like a bit of ribbon to the end of the earth which was the sea. It was so damned simple there. You dug a hole and lived in it and got to know it, all its contours, the way the sand would trickle in from that corner when they started chucking stuff, and one another; till it became home, and then you went a bit further, or back a bit sometimes, and dug another and every place you stopped was always the lousiest place you'd ever stopped in till you got used to it and then you hated to leave it. Just getting killed or not getting killed, that was about all it was. And somewhere ahead of you there was a state of mind called Tunis and beyond that, so far away it no longer existed at all, was another called home and Iris and a pair of sheets and one thing or another. But here, here on this mountain, you seemed to know that this was the place you had always been hankering after, that so far everything had been leading to it and afterwards everything would look back to it; this was the top, the climax, the middle; you were happy here and wanted to stay and would always want to return; you would always be here.

'I could do with a drop of tea,' he said.

'So could I.' Adrian Bullivant drew the back of his hand across his mouth, his eyes fixed on the plain. In his mind he listened to Gough, the Borough Surveyor, telling Heath how the ceremony should be reported in the *Gazette*, warning him to be careful of his handling of the tears of the benefactor's wife, and Heath replying with a certain splendour of manner, 'Marcus, I accept orders from no man. The press is free. All I know is which side my bread is buttered.'

And then, rhetorically, 'Was the lady drunk? Was she? certainly not. Every eye but mine says yes, the lady was drunk, wondrously, ineffably drunk, but mine is the eye of the press, mine is what the newspapers say. Drunk? Drunk, Marcus? She was her sweet and gracious self in pale blue organdie with a bunch of flowers, playing her part in that distinguished gathering with the poise, elegance and charm to be expected of so great a lady. Drunk? Perish the thought.'

'And the Mayor. Take the Mayor. I give you the Mayor, gentlemen, that paragon of civic virtue, Woody Jones. I remember him when he was so high and all the world was golden, a loathsome little brat covered with wood shavings and a running nose. Woody Jones. What a speech he made! What a peroration! A river in flood, gentlemen, a mad Mississippi, a cataract of noble sentiments to stir the seediest heart. In that speech, gentlemen, if you were able to recognise it, there was an indifference to the principles of grammar and the language of Shakespeare such as bespeaks a mind as great and unfettered as that of the bard himself. Lesser men can only wonder. Subject and verb, subject and verb, following each other from those chiselled lips with the profusion of stars across the vault of heaven. And the predicate, the poor bloody predicate, stretched to all infinity. Toll, bells, for the predicate, for Woody Jones is Mayor. His worship, Woody Jones. No, gentlemen, forgive me, no. Democracy should stop somewhere short of Woody Jones.'

And Henderson: 'You're a bitter, cynical fellow, Heath. Never content.'

'I weep, Councillor, for the passing of truth. I mourn it. All I see revolts me and I see all and none more clearly than Adam Heath, editor of that great and impotent organ of the people, that phallus, the *Gazette,* circulation eleven thousand weekly. My bread is buttered, but my stomach refuses food. No, Councillor, I am not content.'

And Prendergast: 'My wife, by the way, asked me to speak to you . . .'

'A photograph, I know, I know, I know. Rest assured, my dear Prendergast, she shall be there in all her divinity,

113

slap across the middle of the middle page, reading from left to right. How old does the lady wish to look? Thirty? Forty? So. A little touch, no more . . . *pour réparer des ans l'irréparable outrage.'*

And then Jonathan Bullivant entered at last and Quinnie followed him silently. The picture he kept in his mind of his father was always clear: short, swarthy, grey at the temples, having a great charm of manner; a hard, dynamic little man, wearing a black velvet smoking jacket. He spoke hardly above a murmur.

'Adrian, re-charge the glasses, please,' raising his soft voice at the end of each sentence.

'Gentlemen, we began Bricker's Hill Garden City eight years ago, we six . . . Henderson, the old man of bricks and mortar, Gough, the sage, the critic, Heath, the voice, the rod for all our backs, Quinnie, the whip. My son . . .' the small firm hand fell on the boy's shoulder, 'it came to manhood with you and with you it will mature. And I? What am I?' He smiled round the little circle of smiling faces. 'The ringmaster? A toast, then, to . . .'

'I am strangely moved,' said Heath, 'in taking it upon myself to reply to your toast, Mr. Bullivant, and I must ask you to overlook the tear in my voice. I have followed your spectacular career, sir, from its infancy; indeed we are something of an age. And therein, I fear, lies our only similarity. For you, you have always been the doer, the maker, the giver; I the spectator, the dilettante. You the great industrialist, philanthropist, benefactor; I the complainer, the cynic, drifting along in your wake, happy, occasionally, to report some great new work, another masterstroke of industrial or philanthropic genius. I ask you, gentlemen, where would Bricker's Hill be without this fountain of generosity in its midst? Where would any of us be? Where would this country be without its Bullivants, its . . .'

Then Liza Bullivant entered timidly.

'Don't mind me,' she said a little roguishly, 'go on just as if I wasn't here.'

'Liza, I'm very busy just now,' Jonathan Bullivant said sharply.

'I won't make a sound, really. Promise.'

'My wife is unwell,' Jonathan Bullivant said to the silent men. 'The strain of the ceremony . . .'

There were murmurs of sympathy.

'I'm all right,' she said, surprised. 'There's nothing at all wrong with me. I feel absolutely wonderful.'

'My dear.' The voice rose sharply.

But she had moved away and was going round the circle shaking their hands and saying, 'How d'you do? How d'you do? So glad you were able to come. So nice. Delighted, I'm sure. Would you like a cup of tea? I've told them to put the kettle on.'

To her son she said, 'How d'you do? You're my li'l boy, aren't you? Your father's always talking about you.' And passing on to Quinnie, 'And poor old jealous Quinnie. Don't mind about me, really,' she addressed them all, 'just pretend I'm not here.' She had had more to drink, Adrian thought.

'Adrian, take your mother to her room.' It was strange the way the rising voice carried its threat.

'But I don't want to go to my room,' she said petulantly, 'why should I go to my room?'

'Adrian will take you upstairs.' The face was inscrutable.

She began to weep. 'I don't want to go upstairs. I want to go back to Birmingham.'

'Adrian.'

He went to his mother's side. 'Mother, please come now.'

She swung about, her face set. 'You're all angry with

me, aren't you? You're all mad because I spoiled the ceremony, because I ruined it and fell on the tree and everybody laughed.' Her eyes flashed between their swollen lids and for a moment she had an obscure dignity. 'Blasted ceremony. I hated it. I hate the estate. I never wanted to go. I always said I didn't want to do it, and you made me. . . .' the dignity dissolved in tears. 'I knew what would happen, I always knew. I told you I'd do it wrong, I knew all the time.' And with spite, 'Well, you made me do it and it serves you damn well right.'

Jonathan Bullivant said, 'I didn't make you do it, Liza. And there was nothing wrong with the ceremony. You were very good, d'you hear? Very good. You did it very well.'

She looked at him searchingly. 'No, I wasn't. You're telling lies. I was awful.'

He said again softly, 'I say you did it very well, Liza. You will see what the newspaper says.'

'I was dreadful, so it's no good saying anything else. I know perfectly well I was.'

'You will see.' He looked at Adrian.

Adrian took her arm and led her to the door. 'I ruined it, ruined it!' Her voice rose. 'Let go!' She shook off the hand on her arm. 'I spoiled the ceremony and it's no use saying I didn't when I did. I didn't want to spoil it. I tried, Johnny, I tried for you, I always try to do what you want and help you, Johnny. . . .'

He led her out of the room and up the wide staircase. She began to sing querulously, *with an alpaca frock and a green scarf shawl,* and then fell to whispering to herself, she was going back to Birmingham, going back to Birmingham.

The grey bundles in the mist floated suddenly into focus and moved towards him. 'Here they come,' he said.

Crosby left his gun and crossed the floor to narrow his

116

eyes over the officer's shoulder. He nodded and went back to his post to swing the gun across the aperture till he could cover the bridge. They were still a long way away, Adrian Bullivant thought, though it was difficult to say accurately; maybe six or seven hundred yards, jutting through the mist and the slanting rain with their heads lowered against it. He pulled the gun into his shoulder and laid his cheek along the cold stock and sighted on the nearest. He would give them another hundred yards, at most, and then let them have it, sweeping to the left. He felt for the trigger. His heart was beating in his throat. The man on the sights plodded up the long slope and listened to the dainty patter of the rain on his helmet. He looked up and saw the broken outline of the mill against the sky on the crest of the ridge.

Father Domenicus flung himself against the door and it swung back with a bitter cry. He told the officer to stand away from the machine-gun. There was a shrill menace in the voice and Adrian Bullivant turned and saw the priest in the doorway with the revolver in his trembling hand. The man was breathless and his clothes were sodden and the taut skin on the face was mottled unbeautifully. But Father Domenicus had not seen Crosby. The soldier was behind the door at his post and when Adrian Bullivant rose slowly to his feet and the priest stepped into the granary, Crosby's shoulder struck him in the small of the back and the man pitched forward on to his face with the soldier on top of him. Adrian Bullivant prised the gun from the cold hand on the floor.

' Let him up,' he said, ' quickly.'

Crosby rose and the priest drew down his outstretched arms till he could rest his forehead on the wrists; he lay face down on the dusty floor and retched feebly. Little Josef stared from one to the other of the three men.

' Did you hurt him?' Adrian Bullivant stooped over the prostrate figure.

Crosby shook his head. 'Winded, that's all.'

The priest stirred and belched hollowly, but made no effort to rise.

It was at that moment that they heard the armoured car. At first it was no more than a thread of sound above the bustle of the stream, but it was sufficient. Adrian Bullivant caught the soldier's eye and went to the window. They were barely three hundred yards away now, and converging on the bridge. In the van of the troops there was a small armoured vehicle in whose turret a head swayed to and fro with the pitch and toss of the car over the rough ground.

He left the window. 'Too late,' he said, 'they're here.' He looked at the child and then at the priest heaving on the floor. The man struggled to his knees.

'Get up there,' Adrian Bullivant ordered him, pointing to the ladder that led to the loft. 'Look sharp.' The priest crossed himself and closed his eyes and broke into prayer.

'I said get up there.'

Father Domenicus prayed hoarsely.

Adrian Bullivant took him by the shoulders and hoiked him to his feet. 'Listen,' he said, 'if you don't go by yourself, I shall kick you up.' He raised his voice above the babble of the priest. 'There'll be no fighting. You've mucked it all right. You've got your way. Now get up there and do as you're told.'

The priest fell on his knees and prayed fervently. Bullivant lugged the man to his feet again and propelled him towards the ladder where Crosby set him on the rungs and, putting his shoulder beneath the backside, lifted him bodily. The priest ascended. But the child would not be caught. With a solemn face Josef dodged behind the millstones and then beneath their outstretched arms. In the corner they trapped him and carried him to the ladder. Crosby dragged him upwards while the officer retrieved

118

the guns and, carrying them on his shoulder, followed the kicking child into the loft. They lowered the trapdoor.

' Quiet!' Adrian Bullivant raised his finger.

They listened. There was no sound but the clatter of the rain on the broken tiles above. They sat on the floor and waited. Adrian Bullivant did not know what they would do if they were discovered and only a fool could fail to see that the mill had been vacated by human beings barely a moment before; there were even the wet imprints of their feet on the rungs of the ladder, the naked evidence of a scuffle in the dust of the floor. Perhaps they could cope with one man; and then they would die ignominiously by a casual burst of automatic fire through the rotten floorboards of the loft. But he knew there was a smile on his face. And the priest was smiling, a distortion, you might call it, of the thin lips. Even Crosby, crossing his legs and squatting uncomfortably above the trap in the floor, was hugging to himself some private pleasure. Little Josef sat still with the officer's arm on his shoulder. The priest's lips moved, but no sound issued from them.

They heard the armoured vehicle cross the bridge and roll down the little slope to a standstill at the bottom; the engine hummed. Then there was a voice shouting and the trudge of tired feet through the mud. A man called briefly to Fritzi to wait for him and then those listening in the loft heard the rattle of light accoutrements as the heavy footsteps approached the mill. They held their breath and Crosby raised his revolver and Adrian Bullivant tightened his hold on the child's shoulder. The priest raised his face and closed his eyes.

But the man was not seeking them, and if he saw traces of their occupation of the loft he ignored them. They heard him close against the millstones, whistling to himself between his teeth. Then he was stamping his feet in the dust. He went out and they heard him shouting to Fritzi.

8

THE MARE steamed in the rain and the black stains, beginning at the crest of the gaunt spine, spread slowly down the flanks. The Commander stared into the valley and pulled forward his shoulders against the drops that fell heavily about his head from the branches above. Pine trees afforded little shelter from rain. He listened absently to the tapping of the woodpecker somewhere to his right among the tall trees, hearing the sound clearly, but yet unaware of it. He peered into the mist. Below him, where he had allowed the tired beast to drop its head to the cool, sweet turf, the enemy moved across the plain. They were visible only when the mist shifted or thinned, small, shapeless bulks against the pallid void beyond, sometimes in groups, sometimes each man alone, weaving one upon the other as they moved across the sodden earth towards the empty hamlet. He waited for the rattle of the guns, for he knew that Adrian Bullivant and Crosby were there, somewhere. The enemy would not climb higher, of that the Commander was certain; they would content themselves with adherence to the letter of Von Langenburg's plan . . . a sweep, a token expurgation, an exercise in the rain. The woodpecker paused and then began again. The Commander raised his eyes and looked into the dark forest, but the bird was not visible; he had not really expected that it would be. And then it occurred to him, lightly, that such a bird at such an altitude would be rare indeed; and pine was not the tree it was said to favour. He listened more carefully. He tugged the mare's head about and touched the brittle ribs with his heels and rode among the trees along the edge of the forest towards the sound, fumbling beneath the cape he wore for the revolver at his waist.

He had left the staff among the litter of great rocks they sometimes called the Town, since in their formation and design they resembled somewhat a huddle of simple dwellings. Here they had parted from one another and gone their ways singly or in pairs to the burrows they had scraped on other occasions beneath the rocks and the towering walls. When the Chief of Staff reported the absence of Captain Bullivant and Crosby there had been almost a flight; only the Corps Commander seemed undisturbed. What did they expect? he asked with a shrug of the shoulders. The Chief of Staff gritted his teeth and looked to the valley as if half inclined to start after them. The rest, preoccupied with fatigue and the rain that was seeping steadily into their clothes, took their cue with some relief from the Commander since it involved no action on their part. Maria Pugnini cried out for little Josef and began a feverish search among the rocks. She was easily comforted, however, and was in any case accustomed to the child's frequent disappearances. Little Josef, they told her, would return, inevitably. The Commander left them and drove the mare between the rocks towards the forest.

Now he drew in the reins again and listened, for the sound was closer, almost at hand. He cocked the action of the gun. The tapping was in some way familiar and yet its identity evaded him. It went on during a few moments, and stopped, then spurted excitedly, and stopped again. In the dry metallic patter he heard the high sweet sound of a small bell.

The man was huddled beneath his parachute, two cords of which he had wound about the tree-trunk he sat against so that it made a kind of tent, crude and shapeless, but effective enough, the Commander supposed, as a shelter

121

from the rain. His head was buried in the silken folds and between his knees in the grass there was a small typewriter.

Conscious at last of another presence or perhaps disturbed by the cropping of the mare, the man beneath the silk raised it from his head and peered from beneath the fringe at the motionless horseman. He nodded and grinned and let the silk fall about his neck.

' *Ciao,* ' he said.

The Commander looked down at him.

' I represent the Transatlantic Press Service,' he said. ' Slater, the name.' He grinned again. ' That gun loaded?'

The Commander lowered the revolver and then returned it to its holster beneath the cloak. He cleared his throat.

' Where did you come from?'

Slater raised his small blue eyes and pointed a finger to the sky. ' Heaven,' he said. ' When's it happening?'

' When is what happening?'

' The attack.'

' Attack?'

' On the reservoir, man.'

The Corps Commander dismounted slowly. He stood in the grass and leaned against the horse and drew the back of his hand across his mouth. ' Are there any more of you?' he asked at last.

' None, I hope,' Slater said. He grinned all the time, showing his sharp brown teeth.

' You'd better explain yourself,' the Commander told him.

' My story's getting wet,' the journalist said. ' Come into the parlour.' He raised the parachute on his arm. ' Come on, come on,' he said impatiently when the Commander made no move, ' no use all three of us getting wet.'

' Three?'

' You, me, my story. Come on, for God's sake, if you're coming.'

It was difficult to deny the simple logic. Reluctantly the Commander swung the bridle about the trunk of the tree and knotted it. He lowered himself to the ground and pulled the silk over his head. The rain drummed lightly on the taut tissue and the light beneath was soft and milky. He eased his leg into a more comfortable position and looked more closely at the journalist, at the pale face and tight mouth and the evasive blue eyes. There was an ugly red spot on the man's cheek and the nails of his fingers, when he raised his hand to finger the spot, were bitten to the quick.

'Quite a story,' Slater said, raising the sheet of paper in the machine, 'damned good stuff.'

'Where d'you come from?' the Commander said softly.

'Aircraft,' Slater said, 'parachute. My first jump. Just jotting down how it feels—' he flipped the page again, '—before I forget. I landed last night. Didn't you hear the plane? Heard there was a bit of a party on here and got the pilot to bring me up, same pilot that brought the other fellow. Bullivant. Is he about?'

'Yes, he's about. Won't that get the pilot into trouble?'

'Doubt it. I'm T.P.'

'T.P.?'

'Transatlantic Press,' he said with a touch of impatience.

'Oh yes, of course. Forgive me.'

'Bit of chocolate?' He broke off a square of the chocolate he was eating and offered it to the Commander. 'No?'

'No. You landed last night?'

'Just before dawn. Never had a parachute on before. Quite an experience. Been written dead, of course, nothing new in it. No story. About the attack . . .'

'How did you know there was to be an attack?' the Commander asked him.

Slater frowned. 'Can't ask a journalist for his source of

123

information, old boy. You ought to know that.'

'True. I forgot.' He felt a little ashamed.

'Where did you learn English, by the way? You're one of these partisan jerks, I suppose?'

'Yes,' The Commander was uneasily aware of his own timidity. 'I learned English in England and America . . .'

'Name? Age? Any relatives in the U.K. or U.S.?'

'No.'

'Don't worry, we'll fix you up with some. Where did you live?'

'Nowhere for long. I was an actor.'

'You don't say?' The journalist scribbled industriously on a scrap of paper he pulled from his pocket. 'Pittsburg and Wolverhampton. Present rank?'

'Corps Commander.'

Slater raised his head with a grin of incredulity. 'So I dropped on the king pin first time, eh? Good old Slater.' He wrote busily. The Commander noticed suddenly that when the young man smiled, and his mouth carried a grin nearly all the time, the small blue eyes showed neither humour nor pleasure. 'What are you fighting for?'

'I . . . I don't understand.' He eased the wet silk on the crown of his head. 'Fighting for?'

Slater said patiently, 'What are your war aims, Commander?'

'I haven't any. I'm not fighting.'

'Demccracy,' Slater said. 'That covers anything.'

'But I don't . . .'

'Public loves it,' Slater said, 'fairly laps it up. Anything else?' He scanned his notes. 'Divorced?'

'No.'

'Pity. You got a wife?'

'She's dead.'

'Blonde?'

The Commander raised the parachute with his arm.

'It's painfully hot in here.' He breathed deeply the cold moist air that swept into the little tent beneath the silk.

'Good.' The journalist thrust the scrap of paper into his pocket. 'I can make that into something all right.'

'That's very kind.'

'My job, old man. Now, what about communications?'

'Ways of transmitting—'

'Right. What's the form?' He flipped his fingers. 'Radio? Courier?'

With a satisfaction that he deplored in himself and strove to keep from his voice, the Commander said, 'There are none, Mr. Slater.'

Slater raised his restless eyes and they lit for a moment on the Commander's, steady and grey and without expression, and then shifted swiftly to the machine in the grass between his knees and then to the chocolate in his motionless hand and at last again to the Commander's face. 'None?'

'None at all.'

'You mean there are no communications of any kind?'

'Of any kind.' The Commander reached forward and selected a morsel of chocolate from the young man's open hand. 'We are surrounded by the enemy, Mr. Slater.'

The rain which had formed in a little pool on the silk above their heads began now to seep through the tissue and drip slowly upon the sheet of paper in the typewriter, the heavy drops exploding sonorously and spreading over the typescript.

'Surrounded,' Slater repeated, making a little circle with his finger, 'completely surrounded?'

'Quite completely.'

'Oh balls, old boy.' He threw off the notion with a sudden movement of the narrow shoulders. 'Can't be, can't possibly be.'

'Nevertheless it is so.'

'But how am I to get my stuff out?'

'That I couldn't say.'

'God damn it, it's important.'

'I appreciate your concern.'

The journalist leaned forward suddenly and whipped the sodden paper from the machine and screwed it into a ball in his hands. 'You wouldn't be fooling me, would you?' He glanced obliquely at the older man. He gripped the ball of paper till the knuckles shone white beneath the flesh.

'I tell the truth as often as possible,' the Commander said.

'You're too damned cryptic, by half.'

The Commander moved his shoulders under the cape.

'Listen,' Slater tapped him on the knee. 'If you think I've stuck my neck out to get this story and find I can't get a word of it back, you're wrong. Understand?' A faint flush had stolen into the pale cheeks and the lips met closely when the words ceased to flow from between them. 'The public's waiting for this stuff. They've got to have it. Nine hundred and thirty-seven newspapers, d'y'hear? Nine hundred and thirty seven. Damn it, this is the best break I ever had in my life and I'm not going to have it wrecked by a lot of toy soldiers, let me tell you that. Negligence, that's all it is, a deliberate interference with the flow of news.' He was very angry indeed, and grew even angrier as the enormity of the situation became clearer to him; the lash of his own words drove him to a white heat of indignation. 'The freedom of the press is threatened by this,' he barked.

'You might edit a little news-sheet here on the mountain,' the Commander suggested. 'we've needed something of the sort for a long time.'

'News-sheet. For Chris' sake. What's the circulation?'

'Eleven.'

'I'm not interested in thousands.'

' Nor I, Mr. Slater. Eleven, I said.' He leaned forward and selected another piece of chocolate from the packet at the young man's side. ' It's a longish time since I tasted chocolate,' he said.

' Eleven.'

' You will have to be patient,' the Commander told him. ' Your stay with us on the mountain will give you the time the public doubtless expects you to devote to your despatches.'

' The hell with the public. What about the city editor? What about my story?'

' Yes. But surely a month or two . . .'

' I'm going to get my stuff out of here at any cost,' the young man said quietly. ' I've a long way to go and I haven't that much time to spare.'

The Commander asked him, ' Where are you going?'

' When I've got my own chain of newspapers I'll tell you. International newspapers, that's me.' The bright blue eyes flickered over the Commander's face. ' Meanwhile, how the heck d'you eat if you're surrounded?'

' We are supplied by the villagers of Ronc.'

' Oh. Where's that?'

' Beyond the edge of the plateau.'

' You're in contact with them, then.'

' With the priest only.'

The journalist fingered the scarlet circle on his cheek. ' Then there must be movement to and from the village, eh? Communication of some sort. How does the village live? There must be people going to and from the place, right? There must be contact somewhere.'

' With whom?'

' With the armies, who else?' His voice rose. ' With the Allied armies, damn it. There are people passing through the lines all the time. They could carry it, couldn't they?' He laughed suddenly, briefly, triumphantly. ' That's it. By

God, that's it.' He threw back his head in a wide, sound-less laugh, and leaned far forward to smack the Commander on the shoulder, and the wet silk sagged unhappily between them so that they were obscured from one another. When he straightened his back the silk rose again. ' Easy. Easy. Where's the priest, in Ronc?'

' Usually.'

' We've got to get hold of him. Either that or . . .' he flipped the short blunt fingers again . . . ' or the attack.'

' If I were you, Mr. Slater—'

' Cripes, yes, the attack. Of course. That would be best of all, wouldn't it? That would get us out. The enemy holds the reservoir, doesn't he?'

' Firmly.'

' There you are, then. That would do it. But it's terrific, I tell you. It's a world-beater. I'd scoop the earth.' He laughed breathlessly and rocked himself to and fro on his heels and the silk rose and fell between their heads. ' See it? Behind the enemy lines? Date-line: enemy territory. With the partisans in action. Guerillas led by famous corre-spondent. Slater paves way for Allied advance . . .' he made small sounds in the back of his throat. ' That way we'd get it both ways, see? It's the biggest break of the war.' He fumbled in the haversack at his side and found paper and carbon and ran it into the rollers of the machine. He whispered to himself. The Commander watched him absently.

' What are you going to write?' he asked at length.

' The story of the attack.'

He began to type.

The Commander eyed him, faintly disturbed by the anger that murmured in his ears and set his fingers twitch-ing. He told himself severely he should be able to accept Slater with a dispassionate shrug of the shoulders, with no more than a passing interest such as one might show for an ugly street accident to learn the manner of the mishap rather than its effect upon the injured. The young man, he told himself, should no longer have the power to disturb him; he was above it, remote, impartial, able to witness the fantastic charade with an unjaundiced and unjudging eye and leave it to others more deeply involved to pass sentence or censure if they must. The challenge should leave him quite unmoved, the ebullient ruffianism scarcely amuse. And to a certain extent this was so; only inwardly, and very deep, was there anger. It was a warning: he had not progressed as far as he had thought. Oh, certainly there was Erica, but she was always there and he could control it; it was strong, his longing for her, but not strong enough. Now anger had come to join her, provoked by this ridiculous child within a few moments of its arrival. He wished the boy would go, go away and pursue his evil career somewhere else so that his existence might more decently be ignored, and more easily. It was unfair that he, the Commander, should be brought thus cruelly face to face with it and offered the choice of condoning or condemning. He must broaden his vision, that was all. There was always a third eye if you would but use it.

He coughed discreetly. 'When you have finished,' he said, 'and I presume you don't intend to stay here indefinitely, my headquarters is to be found straight down the plain on the edge of the plateau. A deserted village.'

'Right.' He went on working.

The Commander prepared to move. 'You should take care not to run into the enemy, by the way. He is liquidating us this afternoon.'

'Oh?' He looked up suddenly. 'Trouble?'

'A little. Captain Bullivant has threatened to defend us. So far there appears to have been no fighting, but there is time yet.'

'It would be just like the army to muck this up,' the

journalist remarked bitterly, ' just like them. Typical. The story of the whole war.' The hands hung over the keyboard, strangely like claws, the Commander thought, and then dropped and began to strike the keys again. The bell tinkled sweetly.

The Commander raised the silk from his head carefully and Slater looked up with a frown and put out a hand to protect the paper in the machine. The Commander struggled to his hands and knees and backed from the stifling place into the cold air, letting the silk fall again to the ground so that it might not impede the young man's work. He rose to his feet and stood upright in the rain, bracing his hand against the small of his back where it ached fiercely. The mare raised her melancholy head from the turf and waited. But he could not mount the animal without assistance; there was no choice but to walk. He untied the bridle and slung it over his shoulder and the horse followed him, the stringy neck arching to the pull of the reins. Among the trees he turned and looked again at the shapeless white heap beneath the pine and listened for a moment to the brittle chatter of the typewriter.

He called, ' Can you hear me?'

' Yes?' The typing ceased.

' How did you become a foreign correspondent?'

' Ever hear of the Bressard murders?'

' No.'

' Well, they were mine.' The typing began again.

The Commander turned slowly and limped away through the trees, the mare following him, head back and whites of eyes huge in the black head. The rain had dropped then to a steady drizzle and the mist was rising. Far away, once, down on the level country, he heard the hum of a motor, a wisp of sound on the uneasy air. He went on towards the Town, where he had left the others.

They were waiting for him, hardly troubling now to conceal themselves, standing in the open among the great square rocks. They gathered about him when he arrived. The enemy, they said, had undoubtedly gone now and there could be no acceptable reason why they should continue to invite pneumonia like this. Indeed, they were soaked to the skin. Only the Chief of Staff, watching the Commander narrowly, did not add to the clamour; there was something amiss. The Commander took him aside and motioned to the Divisional Commander to follow also.

' We have another recruit,' he told them briefly.

' I knew it, I knew it.' The Chief of Staff rammed his spectacles further on to the bridge of his nose. ' Who is it this time?'

' The press.'

They looked at him incredulously.

' The representative of the Transatlantic Press Service dropped by parachute last night.'

He left them abruptly and called for Hans and Slobadov to help him mount the mare. The remainder, huddled beneath the sacking on their heads, watched him in silence. They were to wait here, he told them, he would be back in a few minutes. He swung the animal about and forced it into a canter and they watched him go down the long slope, his cloak billowing in the wind. Then they turned to the Chief of Staff and the Divisional Commander, whose voices, raised now in argument, echoed to and from the towering rocks.

' I'm not interested in the least in public opinion,' the Chief of Staff was saying. He was evidently extremely vexed. Rain hung from the lenses of the glasses, fell, and ran down the smooth grey skin. ' I don't care what people think, or whether the press tells them what they think or the people tell the press or anything about it. We don't want the press here, interfering and bossing everybody about and writing it all down for people to read. There's nowhere for him to sleep.'

'It is a moral obligation,' Luca Pugnini said. The florid face peeped through the seam of the sack he wore on his head against the rain. 'We are morally obliged to place ourselves at his service. It is an obligation we have to ourselves, my dear fellow.' The golden teeth shone prettily between his lips. 'We have lived long enough alone. World opinion is a dimension we have lacked for some little time now. It is a frame, you must understand, a foil without which to live artistically is a poor sprawling business. The artist needs appreciation, and that is what the press will supply. No artist, not even the true genius, can continue without hope of understanding in some kind of world . . . it's part of the nature of genius. Take Otto there . . .' he pulled the Slav into the little circle . . . 'here is a man, an artist, perhaps a genius, who is apparently content to paint a mural nobody can see or ever will since the canvas is inaccessible except to an unusually nimble mountain goat, of which, since the Chief of Staff ordered their consumption, there are none remaining . . . a man who knows in his heart that he would not devote his life to such a work unless he thought that some day, in this world or the next, his mural will be appreciated by others. No, sir, for the artist the eye of God is insufficient. We need the press. Otto needs the press. I need it. We all do. We need its blame, its praise, its divine corruption.'

They regarded him wretchedly. Slobadov blew his nose with thumb and forefinger. The rest shifted from one foot to the other in the deep wet grass and hugged their soaking clothes about their shoulders.

Only the Chief of Staff replied. 'You're a clown,' he said, 'a clown, general,' in a paroxysm of irritation. 'We don't want the man here, and that's the end of it.'

The rain ceased after a little while and the clouds shifted

on the bitter wind that rose and swept gustily across the earth. A rod of yellow light dropped into the valley and moved across the invisible land. The forest shivered and sighed and the crows pursued an owl from tree to tree, shouting raucously, the brown weaving swiftly in and out the shining black among the lean branches. In the chasm the cataract muttered to itself.

The Commander was not long. They saw him far down the green slopes coming towards them at a cumbersome trot and they shouldered their bundles and prepared to move gladly. When he came up to them they formed a line. He would wait for them, the Commander said, on the shoulder of the ridge; he would go on ahead of them. In a few minutes they were strung out again and each alone on the mountainside, following the tracks the mare had made, first the Chief of Staff and then Maria Pugnini, Pierre, then the Divisional Commander, and then Erica and Paula, with Otto not far behind, his heavy eyes fixed on the rippling fair hair, and last of all Slobadov and Hans and Roberto, his shining shoes bubbling at the seams with every brisk step. It was a long walk and almost dark when the head of the column reached the village on the edge of the plateau.

Adrian Bullivant and Crosby watched the little cortège enter the village. The feelings of the officer were mixed. Watching them now, he felt somewhat ashamed of his attempt to drag these pitiful creatures into a battle which would surely have led to their immediate annihilation; but he was very sensitive to derision, and he had not done as he had said he would do; he had failed to fulfil either his duty or his word. He searched their eyes for contempt or mockery as they passed him, but only in those of the Chief of Staff was there more than a bleak unhappiness; in the glance the small grey man threw at him there was only hatred, and that did not disturb him at all. They were curious people, he thought, and felt a little surge of affection for them. He took the heavy bundle from Maria Pugnini's shoulder, and Erica's and Paula's, and carried them to the doors of their billets. When he returned, Crosby had gone, apparently unaffected by the awful pathos of the procession. They had all gone, he was alone in the empty street.

In the Command Post the Commander was on his knees, lighting a fire of twigs and paper at the open grate. He did not turn when Bullivant entered.

'Isn't there anyone else to do that?' he asked.

'Their feet are wet.'

The officer flushed and was silent. He wanted to say, Then let me do it, I will do it, gladly, but the gentle refusal was already in the set of the great shoulders bent over the hearth and so he did not speak.

'What happened?' the Commander said. He blew at the fire.

'The priest . . .'

'I thought he might.' He rose painfully from the fire and lowered himself on to the box by the desk.

'The priest is a very brave man.'

'Very.' He ran the back of his hand across his forehead.

'A bit of a fanatic.'

'In his way, yes.'

Adrian Bullivant cleared his throat. 'I'd like to say . . .' he began.

'No need.'

'I simply wanted to say that I'm glad nothing . . .'

The Commander raised his voice a little. 'I said there was no need, Captain Bullivant. Your conscience is clear.' He smiled, softening his voice. 'You did your best, of that I've no doubt whatever. You would not have foregone what you believed to be right unless the alternative was better still.'

134

'I'm sorry it was so near a thing.'

'We are pinned to the earth, my dear Bullivant, not by the evil in us, but by the good.' He stooped and began to untie the laces of his boots. 'And now, if you would be so kind as to help me off with my boot, I'd be very grateful.'

Adrian Bullivant eased the boot off the foot.

9

THE JOURNALIST arrived in the camp shortly before midnight. He was tired and angry, having wandered over the mountainside for several hours carrying his typewriter and haversack before dropping by chance over the ridge. He saw then the little cluster of dwellings in the deeper shadow below him and stumbled down the steep incline to the bridge.

Adrian Bullivant had gone to bed early but, unable to sleep, he had roused again and lit the candle with which the Chief of Staff had grudgingly supplied him and was reading his Golden Treasury in an effort to set his mind at rest and induce sleep. He heard the footsteps and voices outside and looked up as Crosby put his head round the door.

' You awake, sir?'

' What is it?'

' There's a fellow here looking for you. Newspaper reporter.'

' Go back to bed, Crosby.'

' He's outside, now.'

' Rubbish, man. Are you drunk?'

Slater had entered the first dwelling in which a light had been visible. The soldier looked up startled at the figure in the doorway, the razor, which he had been whetting, poised over the strop.

' This the partisan headquarters?'

' Yes.'

' Captain Bullivant about?'

' Who are you?' The man's features were indistinguishable in the light of the single candle and his clothes were nondescript.

'Transatlantic Press. Where is he?'

'How did you get here, for God's sake?'

'Never mind that. Where's Bullivant?' And when the soldier did not move, 'Come on, man, I can't wait here all bloody night.'

A slow flush rose from the neck to the face of the soldier on the mattress. 'You'll never get anything that way, mister,' he said.

'God damn it all, I've been wandering about this lousy hillside for the last five hours and I'm in no mood for argument. Who's your commanding officer?'

'Me.' He bent his head over the razor and applied it to the strop with slow liquid strokes. The blade flashed in the light.

'Listen.' The journalist stood fully in the doorway. 'I want to speak to Captain Bullivant or the priest, or both. Now just tell me where they are and I'll have you dealt with later. You're a soldier, aren't you?'

'Yes.'

'Escaped?'

'Yes.'

'Well, you seem to have forgotten one or two things. Meanwhile you're holding up the news, d'you see?'

'You can't touch me, mister, I'm too small.' He looked up, smiling faintly. 'Try asking me again, only nicer this time.'

Slater's voice trembled. 'Where is Captain Bullivant, please?'

'That's better. Now I'll take you along, if you'll just wait while I put my things away.'

He closed the razor carefully and wrapped it up in the towel with the clippers and the scissors. He got to his feet and stooped to blow out the candle. Then they went out into the cold starry night.

But Adrian Bullivant's reception of the journalist, after the first moment of utter incredulity, was somewhat less trenchant than Crosby's had been. He was put about, primarily, that Slater should have obtained with apparent ease detailed information of an operation supposedly most secret; he removed his glasses and polished them carefully on his handkerchief. Then he invited the journalist to seat himself on the foot of the mattress. Thereafter he showed considerable respect, not to say deference, for the newspaper man. Slater, for his part, was feeling a little better then and, encouraged and warmed by the flask of brandy which Adrian Bullivant offered him, of which he drank the major part, was prepared to dispel by simple cameraderie and charm the not unacceptable reverence that stole into the officer's voice. Crosby listened sourly to the slightly honeyed words, the deprecation with which the officer spoke of himself, the curious ingratiation of his manner. Evidently he was deeply impressed by Slater's identity and not a little flattered by the man's attention. Adrian Bullivant himself, wholly unconscious of his own change of manner, blessed the coincidence, with perhaps greater fervour than he in fact felt, that brought so powerful an ally to his side. Not only would the presence of the press bolster up his own morale, his own determination to blow the dam and flood the valley in spite of all obstacles, but, and rather more important, it would place the staff under an obligation to assist in the attack. The journalist had not come all this way, taking the gravest risks with so scant a regard for anything but the high principles of his trade, to potter about a mountainside and listen to a deal of poppycock being talked. The man had a job to do, and this the officer understood and respected. He would take the press, he decided at once, wholly and unreservedly into his confidence, so

138

that they might accomplish their several duties quickly and thoroughly. He wished only that Slater would cease to fumble with the pimple on his face and stop rocking himself to and fro on his haunches. The great shadow swept backwards and forwards across the ceiling.

'If there's anything not quite clear,' he told Slater, explaining the situation to him, 'don't hesitate to ask.' The journalist scribbled spasmodically on one of the scraps of paper with which his pockets appeared to be filled.

He paused, expecting appreciation at least, but Slater did not speak. It occurred suddenly to Adrian Bullivant that the journalist had not been listening—

'The armoured car . . .' he began again.

Slater said, 'Where's the priest?'

'In Ronc. The armoured car . . .'

'He'll have to do it.' And then viciously, 'I'll show the bastards, I'll show them something.'

The officer looked at him in surprise.

'The whole bloody world.' Slater muttered.

'What's that, old boy?'

'Just talking to myself.' He grinned and drew breath. 'Got anything to eat? I could eat a horse.'

'I'm afraid not. You might try the cookhouse. Everybody's in bed.'

'Mind if I do a bit of work in here?'

'In here?'

'Just a few flashes and a story. When does the priest show up again?'

'No idea. To-morrow, I imagine.'

'He'll have to send somebody through the lines. If I can get just a couple of takes away . . .' he spoke as much to himself as to the young man in the bed. 'How about the soldier?' he said suddenly. He looked at Crosby, motionless and hardly visible so far from the candle, standing in the doorway with arms folded across his chest. 'You like to take it?'

'Take what, and where?'

'My cables, back through the lines.'

'Me?'

'Why not? I'll make it worth your while.'

Crosby shook his head. 'Not me.'

'Why not?'

'Not interested. If there'd been a chance of getting out, I'd have been gone, months ago.'

'At night you could get through, couldn't you?' He turned to the officer. 'Couldn't he?'

'I don't know. In any case . . .'

'It's your duty to try and escape, isn't it?' His voice rose sharply. 'That's military law, isn't it?'

Adrian Bullivant interrupted. 'He has a job to do here.'

'But this is news I'm talking about. Millions of people are waiting for this stuff.'

'How do they know they're waiting?' Crosby asked quietly, 'all those people.'

'They're always waiting.'

'Then it won't do any harm to let 'em wait a bit longer, will it? Makes no odds whether they read it to-day or to-morrow.'

'D'you realise you're interfering with the free flow of news? It's liable to get you into a lot of trouble. People get angry about it, see?'

'But nothing's happened,' Adrian Bullivant said. He was surprised at the journalist's attitude. 'What news? News of what?'

'You'd be surprised,' Slater said, grinning. The tip of his tongue flickered between the brown teeth. 'This place is news. You're news. The public's been waiting a long time to know what goes on behind the enemy lines, how the partisans live and one thing and another.'

'Would a chap get through carrying stuff like that?' the officer said. 'Suppose the fellow's caught? He'd be shot on sight. Is it worth a man's life?'

Slater shrugged his shoulders. 'I'd make it worth his while. If he agrees to take it, then it's his own funeral, isn't it?'

'Out of your own pocket?' Crosby asked.

'Well, expenses.'

'I fully appreciate the necessity for getting the news back and so on, Mr. Slater, but really if we don't do this attack there won't be any news and our strength is feeble enough already without sending good soldiers chasing about the country with incriminating bits of paper in their pockets.' He was a little bewildered by the turn the matter had taken; it was getting out of control; and there was something else he wanted to say. 'Damn it all,' he muttered, 'it seems a bit . . .I don't know, a bit . . .'

'Needn't worry about the attack,' Slater said. 'I'll fix that. You get my stuff back, I'll do the rest.'

It was on the tip of Adrian Bullivant's tongue at that moment to tell the journalist that the attack might never materialise. But it must materialise, he told himself. 'How do you mean,' he said, 'look after the attack?'

'Leave it to me.'

He felt himself go cold. 'I don't quite follow.'

Slater had had no sleep now for two nights and the circumstances in which he presently found himself were not conducive to patience with dull-wittedness. He knew well enough that if he did not cable at least a part of his story to his head office soon it would not be worth sending at all. The Allied armies had all but completed their preparations for another offensive whose initial momentum would carry them at least as far as the mountain, if not well beyond it, and with the armies would come the rest of the pack, the correspondents of the daily and afternoon newspapers, of the broadcasting companies, the magazines and the other agencies. He knew them. Unscrupulous bunch of hacks, he muttered to himself; Dilling and Woronski and Hendrick and Mary and Dicky Willis and Percy Demetz and Old Melton Mowbray and Brenda Phillips and the rest, scores of them, hot on the scent. Indeed, it was not improbable that they were already on his heels for, once the lone wolf dropped behind to sneak away and follow a trail of his own, the rest must follow lest he find prey of which they knew nothing. The object was not so much to keep your victim to yourself as to see that the other man did not keep his. Already they would have noticed his absence and would be sniffing about for his tracks. There was not a moment to spare. By some means he had yet to discover, either through this simple-minded officer with the long lean face and the thick glasses, or through the priest whom he had still to unearth, he must send off a few preliminary flashes and a colour story to establish fairly his ownership of the carcass; if thereafter the meat must be shared, then at least the bones would be his. When the attack would take place, as it soon must and the sooner the better, then, by virtue of having his alternative stories already written—success and victory or defeat suitably tempered by gallantry—he could quickly despatch the one or the other by the best available means, and of those, once the German cordon were broken, there would surely be many. He thought of sending his alternative stories now, at once, so that the city editor might hold them pending a cable telling him which to use. He had tried this method of overcoming difficulties before, however, and the head office had taken exception to the double cable charges.

' All right,' he said briefly. It was no use pressing further at present. Only the first alternative was written—he had completed it after the Commander had left him, on the edge of the forest—and the second would take time. He would use pressure later. ' Forget it,' he said.

He opened the typewriter and set it upon its lid between his knees. ' Mind if I borrow that candle?' He did not wait for the answer. He set the candle in a pool of its own grease on the frame of the machine.

' You're going to work now?'

' I am.'

He began to work. The candle shook with the force with which the short blunt fingers struck the keys and the shadows on the walls trembled with the trembling light. Adrian Bullivant opened his Golden Treasury and brought the print close to his eyes so that he might see. The machine drummed loudly on its lid and the bell tinkled sharply from time to time. The soldier in the doorway turned without a sound and went out.

In his billet Crosby lit the candle and dropped on to the mattress. The drab familiar fury took hold of him, returning with the venom of a jilted mistress, till the dim red mist dropped down over his eyes and he took his head in the vice of his clenched fists and stared at the floor. He realised with a shock that he was shaking from head to foot and told himself not to be such a fool, this is the way things are, the way they were meant to be; but he had never believed it and did not believe it now. God, give me only understanding of myself! For Slater he could see, Slater was easy, Slater must be obliterated and there was no problem; but himself . . . he shook his head between his fists. I will take it, give me the money. And then Iris and clean sheets and the weight of her big breasts on his shoulders and the love she had for him enfolding him. And then back into the pit, the tunnel whose end he never reached, chasing the answer to the question he did not know through an everlasting night. Or to stay here, here on the mountain, and forget it, all of it, and Slater's offer would slip from him like water on a duck's back. He would choke the man. It was a pretty sensation. He remembered it later, long after, nearly two years, the night he attacked Dollis on the common. Beating Dollis about the head and shoulders with the heavy stick, he remembered the journalist so well that he paused for a moment with the club in mid-air and looked at the writhing figure in the short grass beneath him to see who it was.

The assault was sudden enough, but ill-planned and childishly clumsy. Chubb, a few minutes later, recognised the victim as Dollis, the small humourless foreman who wore clothes always the same colour as his hair, which was the colour of pepper, and gaiters in winter and leather gloves always. Crosby had been placed under him at the works and had never forgiven the man his arrogance, his treatment of little Pettigrew, who had been released and re-employed with Crosby. Every night Dollis would take his dog, a spaniel, out on to the common for a few minutes before he went to bed, you could hear him sometimes whistling softly to the animal under the trees to encourage the inevitable. And that night Crosby had been waiting for him by the lake where the children sailed yachts on summer afternoons. Dollis screamed even before Crosby struck and the policeman on his beat heard the scream and broke into a run. When he reached the trees Dollis was down on his back in the shadows with Crosby standing astride him, beating him wildly with a stick while the dog whimpered in the grass, its eyes luminous in the light of the windows that were thrown open in the houses along the fringe of the common with people leaning out in their night-clothes calling to one another to know what the commotion was at this time of night. Crosby broke away cursing and flung the stick at the policeman and took to his heels. Chubb turned his flashlight on to the man in the grass, who was bleeding badly about the face and head but, deciding that he was not gravely injured, left him there and set off after

Crosby across the common. He knew it was Crosby without having seen him. In the bright windows people were shouting and the ducks on the lake muttered among themselves.

'Jim!' The policeman called to him many times. 'Jim!' But Crosby did not stop.

Then they were in the woodyard, having travelled right across the town, moving about in the darkness among the stacked timber; the wood smelled of resin and there were rats scuffling among the shavings with which the lanes between the tall stacks were littered. Now and then a car swung round the bend in the High Street, the lights catching the tallest timbers naked white against the sky. The policeman would stand very still among the shavings, listening, but then Crosby would stand still also and move only when he heard Chubb's boots among the dry slivers. Chubb might have blown his whistle at any time during the long pursuit, or now, to summon assistance, but he wanted to finish the business himself : it was a very personal matter.

He called softly, 'Jim.'

Crosby heard the voice but he did not answer.

'Jim.' The policeman raised his voice a shade.

'Leave me alone, Chubby.' He was close, to the left among the smaller piles in the darkness that was neither shadow nor substance. Chubb drew back his fist to strike and lumbered towards the place the voice had seemed to come from. There was nobody.

'I'm warning you, Chubb. Leave me alone.'

'Jim, listen. Can you hear me?'

He heard Crosby running.

He climbed laboriously to the summit of the stack to his left, slipping on the smooth wood and barking his shins. He stood upright on the crest and the whole stack swayed under his weight. Crosby saw him outlined against the stars, bulking big with arms akimbo.

Then Crosby was making all the noise there was in the

world, going fast over the loose timber on his hands and knees towards the wall by the gate and Chubb was coming down from the stack and trundling after the sounds Crosby made. The stack collapsed behind him with a rending of wood and a sharp crack like thunder. He tried to cross the loose stuff upright and fell heavily two or three times till his hands were lacerated with splinters. He caught sight of Crosby on the wall a moment before he jumped, thrusting away the ladder there. And he heard quite clearly the small cry of pain Crosby uttered when he landed in the road on the other side of the wall.

Crosby hurt his ankle. His left leg was always a little weak after the wound in the groin; it did not take the shock of the landing and he fell heavily across the ankle. Whether broken or sprained he did not then know, but the effect was the same, for it would no longer support him; he could move only on hands and knees or with the support of a rail or wall. It was swelling rapidly. He knew then that there was no further escape, that the thing must be decided now for good. And the realisation brought him at last a certain peace.

10

BUT ADRIAN BULLIVANT slept scarcely at all. The journalist worked until the sky in the east was a clear pale green and there was no sleep for either. When he had finished he borrowed a blanket from the officer's bed and lay down against the wall and fell asleep at once. Then Bullivant slept, but lightly and uneasily, waking with a start after an hour and ten minutes more drugged than refreshed and with anxiety in his mind. The cause of the malaise escaped him at first. He knew he could do nothing until he knew it and so sat on the edge of the mattress with his head in his hands and sought it deliberately. It came to him at last: the armoured car, to-day he must attend to the business of obtaining an armoured car. Relieved that it seemed so little, or at least, so material, he went out into the bright sunshine to find water in which to wash and shave; Maria Pugnini gave him a bowl which he filled at the stream. Later she supplied him with breakfast, bread and cold meat and a mug of milk. She watched him evasively, dropping her eyes and flushing prettily when he caught her watching him.

There was a hush in the camp, he noticed, an atmosphere of expectancy. He leaned against the kitchen wall and ate the bread and meat the woman had given him and watched them. Evidently they knew of the arrival of the journalist; they were gathered in little whispering groups; they walked almost on tiptoe; they watched the door of the officer's billet. As he passed down the street towards the mill he caught the drift of their conversations.

'As I believe I've told you before,' Hans, the elderly deserter, was saying to Slobadov somewhat peevishly, ' my motives in deserting the Wehrmacht were those of pure pacifism. I followed my own convictions. I have no further interest in the war whatever and certainly have no intention of sacrificing my integrity to provide the Anglo-American public with something to talk about at breakfast.'

' Them's big words,' Slobadov said simply. ' What 'as to be 'as to be.' But he was uneasy. ' Let's go and take another rabbit.'

A few yards further, in the doorway of her billet, Erica combed her hair and stared morosely at the glowing peak while Paula wept at her side and wrung her hands. ' Another man,' she cried, ' don't tell me you're not interested. It's a lie. I know, I know you're waiting for him. That's all you're thinking of, isn't it? . . . isn't it?' she insisted.

' Be quiet, Paula.'

' I won't, I won't. I'll kill myself, I swear I will . . .'

' For God's sake, go away.'

Adrian Bullivant was astonished. He was tempted to ask if there was anything he might do to help, but something in the manner of the older woman warned him against any such foolishness. He looked back, when he had passed, and heard the girl laughing hysterically.

He found Luca Pugnini on the other side of the track. The general was talking to his wife and Pierre, the Intelligence Officer. He joined them, with diffidence, though he had no intention of broaching the subject of the armoured car except to Luca Pugnini alone. He heard Pierre saying, as he approached,

' Let 'em whistle for it.'

' Your defiance, my dear Pierre, betrays your fears,' Luca Pugnini said smoothly, ' and well may you have them. As a matter of principle I could hardly agree with you more, but ethically your position is quite untenable. We shall do well to avoid any such discussion when the matter comes to a head.'

And Maria Pugnini looked demurely from her husband to her lover and back again to her husband as they argued, conscious now as always of the refinement in the one, the bawdy male in the other, loving each for his nature. For she was a woman with a great capacity for love and there were few men in whom she could not find something to appreciate. She brushed the flour from her arms with long slow movements and listened to them as though from a little distance. The relationship between the two was cool but not demonstrably hostile. Luca Pugnini nursed few illusions about his world and its people and did not deceive himself that the occasional pangs he suffered over his wife's dalliance with Pierre were more than those of outraged vanity and flouted ownership; she was a possession, pretty, diverting sometimes in her simplicity, an exquisite cook and the mother of his son—whose arrival had come as a great surprise to him and whom he suspected of small-wittedness —but little more. He well understood the attraction the sturdy Breton would hold for her and strove, as he believed mature and civilised, to ignore its effects. Sometimes he wished they might appreciate his restraint and moderate their behaviour, for it was not always discreet. Indeed, they seemed to delight in making the matter as difficult as they could for him, as though inviting his intervention, a possibility the thought of which filled him with horror. He had no stomach for bickering of that nature. No man looks such a fool, he told himself, as the jealous husband. And he was not jealous. The whole thing was uncommonly embarrassing for him.

'Can you spare a moment, general?' Adrian Bullivant touched his arm.

He swung about. 'Of course, of course, my dear chap, naturally.' He bowed to Pierre, momentarily forgetting his position—but then, was courtesy ever untoward?—and, thinking he might as well finish what he had begun, raised his wife's muscular hand and kissed it fervently. He excused himself with a flourish.

'Shall we go into the armoury?'

'I am entirely at your service.'

They walked along the track towards the mill. Already the sun was warm and the dew had dried from the dust. It rose about their feet and settled slowly.

'This journalist fellow,' Luca Pugnini began, 'tell me about him.' He knew no more, it appeared, than that Slater had arrived and was asleep in the officer's billet. 'Who is he? Where does the wretch come from?'

Adrian Bullivant told him. 'Quite a brave little man,' he concluded. 'Must have been, to jump in cold blood like that, armed with nothing but a typewriter.'

'But there you have it, my dear Bullivant,' the general exclaimed, 'in cold blood. That is the how and the why of it. It is a matter of mathematics for such creatures, a totting up of pros and cons. A credit balance, and jump . . .'

'Oh no, not when it comes to the point, not really.'

They paused at the door of the mill and Luca Pugnini stood aside so that the officer might precede him. They went into the cool oil-smelling place where Roberto was cleaning and re-stacking the weapons he had carried up from the vault below. The air was alive with the movement and the murmur of the stream. 'I like this place,' Adrian Bullivant said.

'It has age.'

'Well, let's come to the point.' He cleared his throat. 'Does he talk?' He nodded his head towards Roberto.

Luca Pugnini raised his shoulders with a slight smile.

'We all talk when we can no longer hold our tongues,' he said, 'but Roberto perhaps less than most.'

The footballer seemed busy enough about his rifles, oiling them and clicking the triggers and replacing them in the racks with geometrical exactitude. He raised his hat to the officer, and thereafter ignored him.

'I was in the camp yesterday,' Adrian Bullivant said, turning to General Pugnini, 'when the enemy marched through.'

'I believe so,' Luca Pugnini said.

'They have an armoured car.' He dropped his eyes to the pipe he was filling.

'Yes.'

'You knew?'

'Of course.'

He was discouraged. But he continued, 'Have you ever thought of adding it to your collection, General Pugnini?'

The general smiled. 'More than once.'

'Oh.' He paused, momentarily at a loss. His eyes followed the flight of a wasp that entered down the arrow of sunlight from the window and settled on the oil that spread across the millstones. 'Well . . .'

'I may say it has been something of a dream of mine,' Luca Pugnini said, 'for a long time. Every collector has in mind a piece without which his collection will never be truly complete. I would like an armoured car.'

'Seems a pity.'

'A tragedy, my dear Bullivant.' The general spread his hands, raised them, dropped them limply to his sides. 'We cannot afford it, that is all. We cannot pay the price they ask.'

'It's high?'

'Exorbitant. I have scraped and husbanded our resources like a needy peasant for a new plough. . . to no purpose at all. Every time I raise the necessary sum, the lily-

livered crew take fright and raise their figure.' He ran a
hand over the thong of shining black hair that ran from
right ear to left across his head. 'I fear the prize is not
for me, captain.'

'Ever thought of stealing it?'

'Of what? Stealing it?'

'Yes. A little raid.'

Luca Pugnini looked at him gravely. 'Are you serious?'

'Perfectly serious.'

'My dear Bullivant—'

'Why not? You'd like to have it?'

'Dearly. But a raid . . .'

'I have a little plan.'

'I don't even want to hear it.'

Having only the vaguest notion as to how such a raid
might be carried out, Adrian Bullivant was relieved. 'We
need an armoured car, general,' he said, 'badly. Raid or
no raid, we have to have it.'

Luca Pugnini looked up at the still blue pools beyond
the lenses. 'Your interest, I take it, is not wholly artistic?'

The young man said firmly, 'We need it to fight with.'

'I feared as much. The reservoir?'

'To fight with. Yesterday we didn't fight. Next time we
shall.'

'Yesterday I admired you for your restraint—'

'General, you really can't tell me all this . . .' he waved
a hand about the bristling granary . . . 'all these rifles
and machine-guns and mortars and mines were collected
at such pains for art's sake? I simply don't believe it. As
a joke of sorts, yes, I enjoy it as much as anybody. But
it's gone on long enough now. It's no longer amusing.
These things are to fight and kill with. Don't tell me you
started this collection for fun.'

'Once,' Luca Pugnini murmured, 'once we might have
been in earnest perhaps. That was a long time ago. I forget.'

His eyes wandered over the rows of weapons. ' Now . . .'
he raised his shoulders.

' An armoured car would look very well in here.'

' Not large enough. We'd have to build a special plinth
for such a piece.'

' How many have they, the enemy?'

' Oh, several. A whole platoon, I believe.'

' An attack supported by armour . . .'

Luca Pugnini interrupted gently, ' You have an unhealthy predilection for the offensive, captain, which I
deplore. Fabius, may I remind you, fought Hannibal by
avoiding battle.'

' We have to blow the dam.'

' By fighting?'

' There's no alternative.'

' Because you choose not to see it?'

Bullivant looked at the man reflectively. ' First we must
get ourselves an armoured car,' he said. ' There's no alternative to that anyway.' For he disliked alternatives. The
state of the armoury was proof enough, if needed, of the
efficacy of the alternative to fighting for weapons, and he
could scarcely deny it. Whether an armoured car might be
obtained by the same means or not, he did not yet know.
Having an innate revulsion for what he would dismiss as
jiggery-pokery he would have preferred to insist upon a
raid. But he would see. He felt himself in a most unpleasant position. To begin with, now, the press was looking
over his shoulder and he felt it encumbent upon him to
conduct himself with scruple and honour. Such, moreover,
was his own inclination, whether his actions were submitted
to public opinion or not. To haggle over the price of a
weapon with a German soldier was in bad taste in any
case; suppose the incident were reported in the press? The
system was nothing short of iniquitous—vicious, was perhaps a more accurate description—and, while he was no

plaster saint, as he frequently reassured himself, there were limits. To use such a method of obtaining arms himself, after his frank condemnation of it, was arrant hypocrisy and he wanted none of it. To use their scurvy system would imply his acceptance of the principles underlying it; to accept their help, in anything but the final fulfilment of his duty, would, to his mind, brand the cause for which he fought as mere opportunism. It was bad enough to have to accept their food in these circumstances and he felt the loss of caste very keenly indeed; further than that, he told himself firmly, he was damned if he would go. Now he was faced with the alternatives: either to forgo the armoured car and therefore the attack, for he was aware that to attempt such a task without armour would be to invite disaster, and was not far short of idiocy in any case, or, to set aside every law of decency and integrity and bargain with the enemy on the proceeds of a singularly base variety of blackmail. Such action would involve the press, since he would have to beg Slater not to report the matter, the church, since Father Domenicus would have to be prevailed upon to raise more money, and the unhappy people of Ronc, since they would have to find it. He thanked God only that it was his duty.

When he left the mill he saw the journalist walking down the track towards the Command Post. Little Josef, attracted by the sudden purposeful movement, followed at a trot; the rest of the staff followed with their eyes. When Slater saw the tall flaxen-haired woman standing in the doorway of her billet, he seemed to pause for a second, as though all the strength had suddenly left his legs. In the cottage Paula cried, ' Go on, go on, why don't you go to him? What are you waiting for?'

'IF YOU wish to talk to the priest yourself,' the Commander told Slater bluntly, 'then by all means do so. For my part there is nothing I can do to help you and I don't think Father Domenicus will be able to help you much either. No, I cannot say when he will be here again. This evening perhaps. In the meanwhile you'll have to wait, unless, of course, you feel the matter is worth your own time, in which case you can very easily walk down the hill and into the village. The road runs north and south.'

He was tracing the course of a river on the map that was pinned to the table at which he sat. He did not raise his eyes from the pencil.

'Isn't there a path through the minefield?' His voice assumed the edge which had so often cut through official stupidity in the past. 'How does the priest get through?'

'Yes, there's a path, I believe. But only Father Domenicus knows where it lies.'

'Seems quite a fellow, that priest.'

'Quite a fellow.'

Slater looked at the bent head. Somewhere in the Commander's resilience there was a core of hardness. He would like to find it and break it down. At the moment he was making no progress at all, and it was vastly irritating. He would wait till this evening, he decided, and talk to the priest himself. He ran a hand over his dishevelled hair. 'Now,' he said, 'about the attack on the reservoir.'

The Commander continued to trace the course of the river on the map. Slater experienced a little wave of helplessness. 'When does it take place?'

'Briefly, Mr. Slater, when there is a chance of such an enterprise succeeding. There is presently no such chance.' He raised his head and looked at the journalist. 'I hope this isn't too great a disappointment for you. Sooner or later you would have to be told. The attack on the reservoir is a dream you share with Captain Bullivant only.'

Slater shifted the box on which he sat a few inches closer to the table. He placed his elbows on the table and leaned over them towards the Commander. 'Why not?' he said quietly, 'why won't it take place?' The hair had fallen over his eyes; they were half closed.

'Our total strength is eleven, as I believe I told you yesterday. The enemy's strength is several hundreds. not very good soldiers perhaps, but many of them, and they have a squadron of armoured cars.'

'You know what the idea of blowing the dam is?'

'Yes.'

'We're trying to wipe out the German armies in the valley. To flood them out would help.'

'I quite understand.'

Slater leaned back. He said softly, 'Mister commander, you wouldn't do that attack anyway, would you?'

The Commander had often asked himself the same question, whether, with the necessary equipment and men, he would in fact attack the reservoir or anything else. It was not an easy question to answer. To imagine yourself in other circumstances was always a facile amusement and seldom led to anything but gross over-estimation of your own character. He replied now,

'I think so, I think so.'

'You wouldn't. But you will,' he said suddenly, raising his voice to lean forward and tap the table, 'you will.'

'I doubt it.'

'I'm telling you you'll bloody well have to, see?' He was beginning to lose his temper. 'A lot of people think they can get away with your sort of attitude. They never do. They always have to climb down in the end.'

' Why don't you just send off the story of the attack and leave it at that?' the Commander suggested.

' The attack must take place,' Slater said firmly.

' I advise you to have a talk with Captain Bullivant about it. His intentions were very similar to your own.'

' Captain Bullivant will do as he's told.'

' Will he?'

' There's such a thing as public opinion, and he knows it. You can leave Bullivant to me.' He stood up. ' I've a few things to do just now. We'll talk more about this later. But let me tell you this—' he leaned over the table and tapped the map with his knuckles—' you're going to do that job. Very soon, any minute. You'll save everybody a lot of trouble by resigning yourself to the idea right now. Why the hell should you get away with it while everybody else is sweating their guts out trying to do something? I'm not asking you any more—I'm telling you. Have I made myself clear?'

The Commander did not reply. The point of the pencil snapped suddenly on the map.

' Excuse me.' The journalist showed his teeth, like pen nibs, in a sudden grin. He turned and went out, springing on his toes as though the muscles of the instep were too strong for his weight. The Commander sharpened the pencil slowly.

They were waiting for him, not ostensibly, perhaps, but nevertheless waiting, and he was aware of it. They sat in the doorways of the dwellings like whores in a casbah, he thought. Beyond the village he saw Adrian Bullivant leaning over the parapet of the bridge watching the flow of water beneath him, the sunlight flashing on his glasses. Slater was not displeased with his conversation with the Commander, for now he knew where he stood—alone. They were hostile and that was sufficient. He walked along the street towards the bridge. He would show them.

He remembered the woman with the white-gold hair only when he saw her. But then it occurred to him that she had never in fact left his mind, that she had been there all the time he had been with the Commander, as a nameless unease, a distraction, something he must deal with soon. He slowed his pace and went towards her where she stood in the doorway of the cottage waiting.

He nodded. ' Speak English?'

She raised her eyes. ' I speak English.'

He put out a hand to the wall and leaned against it, his eyes roving lightly over her body.

' Ever been told you're beautiful?'

She returned his regard levelly, critically. She looked at the untidy sandy hair and then the crimson blot on his cheek, the restless eyes and the sharp pointed chin. She saw, or sensed, his inward uncertainty and the intensity of determination of which he was capable.

' Wasting your time here, aren't you?'

She was silent.

' I need a shave,' he said suddenly, running his hand over his chin.

' You're a foreign correspondent?' she said at last.

' Right.' The naughty grin split his face. ' War correspondent. Same thing, more or less. There's a war on, so I'm war; when it's over and the squabbling begins, I'm foreign.' He offered her a packet of misshapen cigarettes. ' Smoke?'

' Thank you, no.'

' Bit lofty, aren't you?' Her silent assessment of him was very embarassing.

' Lofty?'

' Up in the air. Side. Hoity-toity.'

' How old are you?'

' Twenty-eight.' A note of defiance crept into his voice.

158

He was twenty-five, she thought. 'Shouldn't you be in the army?'

'Strings,' he said grinning. 'T.P.' And seeing the frown on her forehead. 'Transatlantic Press.'

'Do you like it, being a war correspondent?'

'Not bad, for a bit.'

'Then what will you do, afterwards?'

''Pends.'

'You're a scoundrel,' she said, 'aren't you?'

'I'm supposed to ask the questions,' he told her. 'What's your story?' He fumbled in his pockets for a scrap of paper and a pencil. 'Let's have it.'

'You're a funny little man,' she said.

He looked at her stonily.

'A little contemptible,' she added coolly.

His face turned red. 'You're being damned insulting,' he said at length.

'But dangerous, I should think. That makes it better, doesn't it? A contemptible little funny little dangerous little man. Especially dangerous.' She smiled at him kindly. 'Tell me, what is your work?'

'Listen, sister . . .' he lowered his head an inch or two.

'Don't pretend to be angry about the insults,' she said. 'They don't really worry you at all, do they?'

'Will you stop showing off at my expense, then?' he cried. 'Shut up, for God's sake, and let's get on with this interview.'

She laughed with her head thrown back, her arm across her eyes to shield them from the bright sun.

'Now what?'

'Come out,' she said, laughing, 'I can see you.'

'What are your war aims?' he said. 'What are you fighting for?' His hand trembled and he gripped the pencil till the muscles of his fingers ached.

'Power,' she told him, 'lots of it, unbridled, that's what

you're after, isn't it?'

' I'm just a newspaper man trying to do a job, see?'

' Sententious humbug,' she said.

' This is a madhouse I've dropped into.' He drew a deep breath. ' Now look, leave me out of it, will you? Just give me a few facts.' He bent his head over the bundle of dirty papers in his hand. ' War aims, first.'

' I'm fighting to make the world nice and safe for people like you.'

' Democracy,' he said with a faint grin, scribbling.

' Of course.'

' In this cross-section of the heart of war-torn Europe,' she began ironically, ' there is a beautiful blonde . . .'

' I give up.' He thrust the papers back into his pocket.

' Please don't.'

' I'll try again later.'

' May I see some of your despatches?'

He was surprised. ' What for?'

' Interest.'

' I don't get it.' He was suspicious.

' I might be able to help you,' she said.

He smiled. ' All right.'

' May I?'

' Yes, you can see them,' he said softly.

He nodded and left her, going away towards the bridge on his strong splay toes. She watched him. Jews, young ones, she thought, often walked like that. She wondered if there were Jewish blood in his veins and thought, yes, quite probably, a long way back. But there was something else in the young man, something other than inward uncertainty; she was interested to know what it might be and what might be done with it. Paula came to her side and stood in the doorway and touched her arm, running the tips of her fingers through the tiny golden hairs that grew there, a softening of the line of the smooth brown limb.

' Erica,' she whispered.

The woman did not speak. She watched the journalist go down the track towards the bridge, reflectively.

' Erica.'

' Ssh.'

He reminded her of somebody distantly, somebody she had known whose identity escaped her. Of two or three she had known, she thought then, not of any one of them particularly, but of all at once, having just a little of each in him, but the same quality always, and so it was familiar. For they had all been possessed by it, as even Otto was in a measure, and it was the quality in them that always attracted her anywhere, in anybody. She had a number of pieces now, a collection probably unique as such collections went, and Slater, she supposed, would make one more. But the puzzle would never be complete, would never make more than nonsense lit with flashes of vision, for she herself was incapable of understanding it. Adrian Bullivant, she remembered, had summed it up in one of those sparks of intuition that simple and clumsy men sometimes have and are hopelessly unaware of the power they wield. Not a woman, he had said, just—woman; of itself neither a particularly wise nor profound nor truly original observation —downright banal, in fact; but in its context, and for her, startling. And then the curtain dropped before the light was fairly focussed.

Unaccountably Bullivant had sensed the mystery, hinted at it and then, a little fearful of getting out of his depth, left it hastily, and because the qualities of womanhood to which he referred were in her a trifle enlarged, she understood that much better than most of her kind what he meant —and certainly better than he did; the nature of the mystery was clearer to her to the extent that she knew its bounds to be beyond the human orbit. She was a woman, an art without a medium. Only by and through men was there

161

self-expression, since her existence could not be more than complementary to theirs. That was about as far as you might go. But complementary to Slater! She looked at him, sitting on the bridge kicking his heels against the parapet, shoulders hunched up to his ears. It was so, however. She believed him to be ruthless, cruel, able, humourless, ambitious, unscrupulous . . . and these were the qualities to which she was complementary. The idea of physical contact with him brought a faint roughness to the skin of her forearms. Well, she would see. There was an order about such things; to express herself, this was first, and then the recognition of the medium and the power in him, dormant or misdirected, for which she was the life and the spur; then the doing, the achievement; contributory to all, first or last, the bed. She shifted irritably from the girl's touch.

' Erica, I'm afraid.'

' Little one,' she murmured, absently reproachful.

And what place did Paula occupy in this monstrous scheme? Sometimes she felt pity for the child, and guilt, on occasion. An animal in pain would stir the same emotion. For Paula was nothing, a plasm, and it was hard to kindle tenderness for her. She existed only as a projection of Erica.

She had found the pretty child a year ago. Her parents had vanished in the holocaust of central Europe and were in all probability dead. When Erica found her, Paula was wandering from camp to camp living on the pity she roused. It was curious that she had never been violated, a matter of luck, as like as not, combined with the simpering helplessness of her manner which was just such as might deter a certain kind of brutality. She had become a species of mascot for the group of men with whom Erica found her, each protecting her from the rest, each fascinated by his own restraint. They had been exceedingly virtuous, Erica recalled, and were deeply hurt when the child, attracted by the beautiful woman, elected to leave them and follow her. She remembered their ridiculous grief with a smile, a sudden expulsion of breath from the nostrils.

Her own feelings now towards the girl were difficult to define; boredom was probably uppermost, but she had never troubled to analyse them profoundly. She knew that the experiment had failed, certainly; Paula bored her to the point of fury at which cruelty becomes a relief and a pleasure. God knew why she had undertaken the experiment at all; she sometimes asked herself why. For it's own sake, for amusement, what other answer could there be? With a serene deliberation from which she now had at least the decency (she assured herself) to recoil with a simulation of horror, she had used the hapless child for an essay in projection that was certainly an abomination in itself and hardly less so in its effects. She had employed the willing adoring creature as a dummy wherein to recreate herself. The rapacious egoism of the artist, was what Dostoievsky called it. And she had succeeded only in stifling whatever germ of happiness there was in the girl, until there was nothing left but this frightened, bewildered parasite weeping for its nameless fears.

'Erica.' A note of panic raised the high voice to a shrill whine.

'Yes?'

'That man . . .'

She looked at the girl's face. 'Funny-face,' she said softly. She ruffled the dark hair.

'who's that woman?'

'Don't know very much about her,' Adrian Bullivant said. 'She had something to do with Toreskuj, I believe, nobody seems to know quite what.'

'Toreskuj. That's it. Provincial divorce lawyer.'

'Was.'

Slater nodded. 'Quite a story,' he said.

'That's confidential, of course.'

'Naturally.' The journalist smiled to himself. It was always an illumination of human nature that the betrayal of a confidence to the press was accompanied by the same reservation; he had never known it otherwise.

'I've just been talking to the Commander,' he said casually, hoisting himself on to the parapet and swinging his legs, 'about the reservoir.'

The officer looked at him sharply. 'Oh, yes?'

'I suppose you're all ready to go?'

'Go where?'

'Everything tied up. Just a matter of pushing the bell at the right moment.' He drummed on the wall with his heels.

'What did he say, the Commander?'

'Referred me to you, as a matter of fact. Told me you had everything pretty well laid on. As the only allied officer in the camp . . .'

'Did he say that?'

'Words to that effect. Give me the facts, will you?' He pulled the little sheaf of papers from his pocket. 'When's it to be, the day after to-morrow?'

Adrian Bullivant began, ' Look here—'

' That would just about tie up with the new offensive, wouldn't it?' He touched the tip of his tongue with the point of the pencil.

' I think I ought to make it clear right away . . .'

' What's the form?'

' Last time I saw the Commander . . .'

' The public's getting a shade restless about this front, you know. The sooner the better.'

' If you'll let me speak . . .'

' This your first job, Bullivant?'

' Yes, but that's not the point at all. The point is . . .'

' Wouldn't worry too much, if I were you. Everybody gets a touch of stage fright now and then, specially when they're pretty well alone on the stage. Just a question of getting things moving. Better if it's a success, of course, but it doesn't matter awfully if things don't go so well. Public wants action, news, that's all.'

It was dawning on Adrian Bullivant that the journalist was lying. To what extent he was lying, Adrian Bullivant did not know, nor with what object; the man's motives were oddly obscure. The trouble lay in the fact that not all the lies were complete lies; there was an element of truth in all he said. He must step carefully, he warned himself.

' I don't know what the Commander told you,' he said, ' but I do know there's a lot of opposition to the idea. I must say I see their point of view. Eleven is a bit few for a job like that. The Commander must have changed his mind since the last time I talked to him about it.'

' You can leave the Commander to me, he'll see the light. It's nothing to do with me, of course, and I don't want you to think I'm trying to chivvy you along or anything like that, but the facts, if I have to report them, and you wouldn't want me to write a string of lies, mightn't look too good in print. You never know how the public will react to a thing like that, once the story gets into the hands of the wrong people. Well, we'll see how things work out. I'd be glad of a few details this afternoon. Hope to get a couple of stories away to-night.' He slid from the wall, smiled, and nodded and went away up the track on his toes.

Adrian Bullivant watched him go, suppressing an instinct to run after him and prolong the conversation. Damn it, he had hardly had a chance to explain his own position, and the censure implicit in Slater's remarks carried a vicious sting. The fellow had no right to talk like that. His observations were simply not justified.

Slater was shaving. 'Yes?'

'Look here.'

'Cut it short.'

'This attack . . .' he paused, anticipating interruption. The silence, broken only by the whisper of the razor on Slater's chin, was disconcerting. 'This attack,' he began again, 'I've had a direct refusal from every man in the camp to have anything to do with it.'

'Got a mirror?'

He found his shaving mirror and gave it to Slater.

'Isn't that part of your job?' Slater said. 'What did you expect? That's what you were sent here for, wasn't it? to overcome opposition and stir up trouble.'

'The Intelligence people were under the impression this was a fully organised corps.'

'Organise it, then.'

'My dear man . . .'

'Why talk to me about it? Is it my job?'

'I didn't say it was, did I?'

'Sounds mighty like it, I must say. Anyway, go on.'

'Short of getting these people to help, I'll have to do it myself. And I can't possibly do it alone without armour of some sort, if only to get there in. We've got to have an armoured car. Raid it. Or buy it.'

Slater looked over the mirror at the officer. ' Buy?'

' Haven't you seen the armoury? Stiff with arms, all bought. The Boche is selling his weapons. These people buy them with the money the priest raises in Ronc.'

' You don't say? That's smart.'

' Well, we might do the same for a bit of armour. I see no other way of getting near the damned reservoir, and even that's suicide.'

' Volunteered, didn't you?'

Adrian Bullivant stopped short in the middle of the room and stared at the journalist. ' How d'you mean?'

' You didn't have to take this job. You can't complain about the chances.'

' That's a pretty lousy thing to say, isn't it?'

' It's the truth. I always tell the truth.'

' It's still a putrid remark.'

' Got a towel?'

He found a towel for the young man and gave it to him. ' Isn't it?' he insisted, feeling the slow rise of colour to his face.

' All right, all right, suppose it is.'

' Well.' He felt outraged and helpless.

' Go on about the armoured car.'

He swallowed and continued in a low voice, ' Even to raise the car is difficult.'

Slater threw the towel on to the mattress. ' I suppose I'll have to do it,' he said.

' Do what?'

' The whole bloody thing. Got a comb? Get you your armoured car, badger these old women into supporting the attack. Don't want me to fight the battle too, do you?'

Then Adrian Bullivant brought the flat of his hand across the young man's face. It was a great mistake and he regretted it at once. Slater looked up at him with a half smile of surprise on his face, his arms loosely akimbo. He appeared to be considerably amused and laughed a little, breathlessly, as the blood stained the pallid skin where Bullivant had struck.

'Well,' he murmured, 'quite a fellow, eh?'

The officer stood in front of him, arms hanging limply at his sides. Slowly the colour of his face deepened.

'I'm sorry,' he said at last. 'Bloody fool thing to do. Lost my temper. I'm sorry.' He turned away.

'That was a great mistake, Bullivant,' the journalist said pleasantly. 'I don't mean with me, personally, I mean generally, Bullivant, as a matter of tactics. You must try and conceal your hand a bit. Once you've shown your weakness you're anybody's meat, you understand. It's what the other chap does not know that he's afraid of. Matter of simple psychology. Try and keep something up your sleeve, and the less you've got the more you've got to conceal, you see? Take my own case . . .'

Adrian Bullivant turned and left the room and went out into the gay sunshine. He felt awful, wretched and humiliated as he had never been before. He wished for a moment that his father were at hand to advise him and tell him what to do. His father always knew. He was struck suddenly, as he went towards the bridge to get out of the place and walk by himself across the open country beyond, by the similarity between Slater and his own father. Precisely wherein lay the likeness he could not say, but it was there all right, fundamental and profound and evasive. And in both he detested it, conscious of its superiority over himself in any situation; he detested wherever it was, in whomever, heartily.

He walked slowly down the track, avoiding the eyes of the men and women standing in the doors of the dwellings lest they should see the pain in his own. There was plenty of time. He would go on to the plain and walk till he was tired and then find a place to sleep. Until Father Domeni-

168

cus should arrive in the camp there was nothing to be done. He crossed the bridge and left the track. The wind blew through his hair.

Father Domenicus reached the headquarters, breathless but austere, a few minutes after eleven o'clock of that night. He had no particular wish to see any member of the staff, nor had he any vital duty to fulfil; only the spur of his own unease had driven him up the mountainside this night. All appeared to be well enough in Ronc. Von Langenburg's expedition had been completed without incident except, of course, for the ugly scene in the mill of which the enemy was, and would remain, in ignorance—and the Garrison Commander was satisfied. There was nothing untoward to which the priest might point in his own mind and say, that is bad, therein lies the germ of disaster. Nevertheless the anxiety in his heart persisted. When he reached the village and was informed of the arrival of the press he knew his presentiment to have been well founded. He sought out Slater at once; indeed the journalist was waiting for him, with Adrian Bullivant and Crosby, at the bridge.

'Never mind how and when I arrived,' Slater told him curtly, 'I'm here and that's enough.'

'Your presence is a threat to the peace of the entire countryside.'

They stood together by the bridge, Slater and Adrian Bullivant and Crosby and the priest. The moon had not then risen and only such light as the stars gave shone in their eyes. The stream murmured beneath the bridge.

'These stories must leave to-morrow morning, you understand. The Anglo-American press is waiting for them. There must be people moving through the lines all the time. Don't tell me. You know all about it.'

'The allied lines are hundreds of miles away.'

'Fifty, if that.'

169

'Civilians aren't allowed on the roads.'

'You have a duty . . .'

'I have a duty to my parish.'

The journalist lit a cigarette, cupping his hands around the flame; his face shone in the light and the smoke blew into all their faces. 'To your parish. Well, that's very laudable. Don't want any fighting round here, do we?' The speed with which the fellow found the chink in every bit of armour, inserted the wedge and prised it open, was astonishing, Adrian Bullivant thought. He envied it and recoiled from it. 'Bloodless liberation and all that. Very praiseworthy, Father. But not so easy. Co-operation goes a long way.'

The priest sniffed. 'I'll see what I can do,' he said at length. 'It is just possible we shall find a messenger to take them, with God's help.' He put out his hand for the papers.

Slater did not move. 'I don't trust you,' he said. 'How do I know you'll do it?'

The priest shrugged his shoulders.

'What d'you want,' Slater said, 'money?'

'Peace,' said the priest unexpectedly, 'peace for my people.'

Slater dropped the glowing cigarette into the dust and placed his foot on it. Crosby began to whistle softly between his teeth. Adrian Bullivant suppressed an impulse to applaud.

'I'll do everything within my power to see there's no fighting in your village,' Slater said at last. 'If the enemy decides to defend it, then there's not much to be done about it.'

'And the reservoir?'

Father Domenicus was no fool, Slater thought. 'Better ask the enemy,' he said.

'What do I know of the enemy?'

'Pretty nearly everything, I should say.'

The priest was silent for a moment, watching the journalist. 'And this young man?' He indicated Adrian Bullivant. 'Has he not been sent here to destroy the dam?'

The officer answered, 'Yes,' and quickly, 'for which I'm anxious to obtain an armoured car. One of the enemy's, to buy it, short of any other way.'

'You're a fool,' Slater told him angrily.

'And if I don't supply you with the money,' the priest said, 'you launch some sort of raid in order to get what you want and thus destroy the homes and livelihood of every family in my parish.' His voice rose harshly in the soft dark air. 'And if I do extort the price from my people the attack is launched on the reservoir with precisely the same effect.' A fleck of spittle from his excited lips struck Adrian Bullivant sharply on the cheek. 'No, my sons, neither.'

'Think it over,' Slater told him.

'There is no need.' The priest turned on his heel and left them, a long black shadow against the pale surface of the street.

The journalist was the first to speak. 'That's that,' he said. 'Didn't I tell you to leave the armoured car to me?'

'I don't—'

'Doesn't matter anyway. That was all my eye. He'll be back to-morrow. You'll see.' He patted the officer's arm. ''Night.' He went away, back to the billet.

Crosby said thickly, 'Bastard!' He repeated it many times, 'bastard, bastard, bastard . . .' like little explosions on his lips, trailing into silence.

'D'you think he's right?'

''Course he's right.'

Crosby shoved his hands deep into his pockets and walked away towards the bridge, wanting to be alone with the sickness about his heart. There was no cure for it. Only when he turned it over in his mind, then and later, till the last moment, in fact, was it not wholly convincing. When

171

you have lived by an ideal all your life you are reluctant to acknowledge its flaws when they are the foundations on which the edifice is built. To prop it up is easier. You shy away from too close an examination lest the thing collapse about your ears. And the more apparent, the deeper and wider, the cracks, the heavier must be the scaffolding, till it is all poles and props and joists. It was on the mountain, for Crosby, that the rents first became visible; it was in Five Elms, long after, that he hammered home the last support.

Chubb, the policeman, understood Crosby well, but he understood him, it might be said, in his stomach. It was a phenomenon that he himself never appreciated, for it was a thing he was wholly incapable of putting into words. He knew, when Crosby was lying with a sprained, or even broken, ankle among the geraniums that grew sparsely round the old war memorial in the square waiting with the Hungarian 37 for the policeman to step into the open under the street lamp where he would be fully visible, he knew then that he had always known it would come to this. There was no escape. He understood that perfectly. Neither could escape himself. It must be decided now, finally. Chubb could blow his whistle in the quiet square and maybe summon assistance, but then Crosby would shoot— he would use the gun in any case—and there was another criminal, and innocent people whose duty was not, as Chubb's was, to administer the law would be hurt and there would be no chance for anybody. No, he must do it himself; it was his business, his private affair. And Crosby would shoot for certain, because that was the way he lived; that would be Crosby. To expect the man suddenly to behave like somebody else was absurd. In a moment now he must draw a deep breath and step into the light and go forward under the lamp.

He had not come up with Crosby again after they left the woodyard until they reached the open space behind the cinema where there was clinker on the soft earth with fragments of glass among it that glittered distantly in the starlight. Crosby was moving slowly then, evidently in great pain, supporting himself against the wall. Chubb saw him outlined for a moment against the yellow lights of the street lamp at the end of the alley. When the policeman reached the corner Crosby had vanished. He stepped into the light.

' Don't come any further, Chubby.'

He heard the voice clearly and it was not far away. The monument reared its blunt white head through the web of tramlines that hung above the square. Beyond it the windows of the shops threw back the light from the lamps that swung gently in the wind setting all the shadows on the earth moving to and fro as though to stately music. Round the monument there was a low parapet and between the parapet and the monolith the flowers grew and Crosby lay among the flowers with his head visible above the white stone, waiting for Chubb.

The policeman stepped back into the shadow.

' Don't come any further, Chubby, d'you hear?' He raised his voice sharply. ' Please.'

Chubb called to him. ' Jim, throw away that gun.'

This time Crosby did not answer. ' Jim, d'you hear me?' He cleared his throat. ' Throw it into the road.' There was a dog barking a long way away and a train drummed distantly on the rails. ' Jim.'

' Go away. Leave me alone.'

' Jim, I'm coming.'

' Don't do it, Chubby.' The voice rose on a note of alarm. ' I'm telling you.'

' I'm coming.' But he did not want to leave the wall. There was an advertisement peeling from the bricks against which he was standing of a girl nearly naked but defaced by children, having moustaches and a beard, grinning at him in the dark.

And Crosby was calling again, ' For God's sake don't do it, Chubby, get out, go home, leave me alone.'

' Give yourself up, Jim.'

The voices sped up and down the silent streets and bounced from the bald face of the cinema.

' I'm coming in, Jim. Don't shoot.' He was pleading with him now. ' Don't shoot.' He took a deep breath and stepped out of the shadows into the light, but Crosby did not fire.

' Here I am, Jim. Here I come.' He could see the head etched black against the white stone. ' Put your gun down.' He flinched against the blow of the bullet.

' Go away, go away.'

He walked across the road. He saw the bright yellow flash and stopped and crumpled slowly holding his stomach and coughing, hearing the voice crying, ' I told you, Chubby, I told you.'

He came out from the parapet on his hands and knees with a sprig of geranium clinging to the button of his dusty jacket and the gun in his hand. Then he saw where he had hit the policeman.

' Chubb,' he said, ' Chubby.'

His voice went up as though he were speaking to a man somewhat hard of hearing. ' Chubby, I didn't mean to hit you there, not in the stomach.' He sat beside the policeman in the smooth road. ' It's this damned gun, it shoots low. I'm a good shot, Chubby. Honest, Chubby. You remember how I was always a good shot. I didn't aim for the stomach, Chubby. Chubby, d'you hear? Chubby, answer me. You believe it, don't you? I didn't mean to hit you there.'

He sat beside the policeman in the road, talking.

13

FOR MANY years Adrian Bullivant remembered the conference which took place, at the journalist's behest, in the Command Post on the night following the visit of Father Domenicus to the camp. He feared its return to mind as a sensitive child dreads the recurrence of a bad dream. The intensity with which he relived from time to time those few hours in the squalid little place on the mountainside was considerably greater than that with which he lived the present. Always it was at his side, sometimes as a memory scarcely more remarkable than any other well-lived and seen and recorded, but at other times it would come stealthily and unbidden and, in the middle of a bitter quarrel with Judith or his father or of a board meeting or the most commonplace conversation, would suddenly engulf his wits so that his answers to their questions would have the irrelevance of near-idiocy or at least of a frivolity that his father found extremely vexing. It amused Adrian Bullivant at first, until it got out of all control. Then his father would speak with the voice of the journalist and instead of Henderson's saccharine baritone there would be the gentle voice of the Commander or the shrill laughter of the Breton fisherman; he listened to them closely and the walls of the great board-room would shrink, and where the vast portrait of his father hung on the wall the shadows of the candles jostled restlessly. He began to resent the intrusion of the memory and fought against it with growing panic, but it remained, impish and insidious.

He tried to explain it to Judith, anxious that she should

play the fullest possible part in his life, but she did not understand very well; she listened attentively enough, too attentively, he thought sometimes, occasionally interjecting comments of extraordinary banality or witlessness, as for example, ' Well, what happened then, dear?' It was impossible to be angry, except maybe with himself for having embarked on the story at all. She tried so desperately to associate herself with him in all things, to be at one with his thoughts and emotions; the smallest gesture of impatience hurt her. He winced inwardly and began rapidly to speak of something else, something commonplace with which they were both acquainted, overriding the bleak unhappiness in his heart, assuring himself it was only a matter of times, the awful chasm between them was the result of her illness, of the war and of the peace, of his defiance of his father's will, and that the deficiency was his as much as it was hers; more, more his than hers. But it did not always convince him. Since there was conviction in nothing he told himself, however, its very conformity to the pattern was a reassurance. It was himself who was wrong; all else was right.

The Commander, he told her, was seated at the table on which there were now three candles, the Chief of Staff having provided extra illumination for the occasion, and there was a number of glasses and mugs for the wine scattered about the map in some sort of design as though he had been running through, with the Chief of Staff or maybe Luca Pugnini, a battle and the movements of the troops involved. They were then empty. The little room was already crowded, or gave that impression. He ran over for her the names of the people present; besides the Commander, the Chief of Staff and Luca Pugnini, there was also Pierre, who seemed to have been quarrelling with the Chief of Staff, Erica, cool and remote, the journalist Slater, Crosby, Father Domenicus and somebody else, he thought, whose identity he could not recall. Ah, Otto, he remembered, Otto entered later. There was no room for them all to sit, nor indeed seats for them to sit upon; they stood, with folded arms, or leaned against the crumbling walls. He told her something of his illogical horror of the place, the residium, he supposed of his first interview with the staff shortly after his landing, an occasion he was never able to pull quite into focus. This time he was determined there should be no such naughtiness now, nor on his part, failure to keep abreast of the ebb and flow of argument.

' Had they been drinking?'

' No.' He was grateful to her for so intelligent a question. ' At least, I don't think so.' He was anxious to answer the question fully. ' There was no wine in the mugs, not at first anyway. They never seemed to drink much really. At any rate they certainly weren't drunk then.' He smiled at her, very pleased, and she returned his smile and settled her shoulders more comfortably into the couch.

He told her of the sense of oppression the place at once gave him when he entered, a little weakening of the knees, the result probably of the necessity to stoop to avoid brushing the ceiling with his head, the belief he had that everything was slightly askew as though seen in a bad mirror. The air was still and warm and heavy to breathe and the smell of mice and candlewax persisted. A great multitude of shadows thronged the yellow walls and now and then one of these would detach itself from the rest and waddle towards the candles, many-headed, vast across the ceiling. On the single dusty window a swarm of moths, drawn by the light, crawled up and down, the quivering wings abnormally pale against the night beyond.

' And the Commander?' she asked. She always liked the Commander, and liked to hear her husband speak of him with the strange puzzled affection he evidently had had for the man.

'Just the same.' He told her how the Commander sat at the table watching them all with his expressionless grey eyes, the hair a little ruffled over the temples. It was curious, he thought, looking back, how the absence of any emotion in the face gave finally an impression of all-pervading sadness. Now he had unfastened the collar of his shirt and the flesh of the heavy jowl shone in the light reflected upwards from the map pinned to the table. The Chief of Staff stood at his side, the small grey head darting from speaker to speaker with a movement that reminded one of a bird. He resented everything; he resented the conference and the participants and all that passed, deeply.

The meeting had already begun, he told Judith, when he arrived, and only Crosby came after him. As he entered one of them had said something which had drawn a volley of denial from the rest and they turned to stare indignantly at Adrian Bullivant as he let the blanket drop behind him as though the fault were his. His head struck the ceiling and the plaster fell about his ears.

'And this sanctimonious little hypocrite,' Slater said, jerking his thumb towards the officer, 'he's no help, either.'

It was not an overture calculated to set the officer immediately at his ease. He recoiled, more surprised than angry, and laughed a little. 'Oh, I say . . .'

'Why didn't you hit him?' she asked.

'My dear Judith . . .'

'No offence,' said Slater grinning, 'got to stick together, you and me.' He nodded and closed an eye and the tuft of stiff hair on the crown of his head nodded also, decorously. In a way he could not describe Adrian Bullivant was aware of the man's fears; it was obvious that he felt more at ease among enemies than among friends and so was disposed to defend himself when he was not attacked. The journalist set his arms akimbo and his legs astride and addressed the remainder of the staff. 'All right. Now listen to me. What

178

Bullivant and I want to know is this: what are your real objections to carrying out an attack on the reservoir?' He felt the woman's eyes on him and stumbled momentarily over his words. 'If you . . . the point is, those objections, if any . . .'

The moths on the window were vanishing one by one. Adrian Bullivant watched them absently, bending his knees for a few moments in order that he might straighten his back. When there was a silence he would hear a scuffle on the glass and one of the moths would disappear. He saw the bat at last, its pointed head and long narrow wings as it came swiftly to the window, hesitated, snatched at the moth and made off with it into the darkness. There were several, he saw, a whole family of bats, feeding busily at the window.

'Horrible,' she said with a shudder. 'Go on.'

He told her how accurate they were.

'Darling, do go on.'

The Commander answered the journalist. 'Mr. Slater,' he began.

'Where d'you get this mister business from? Ticks. Call me Ticks.'

'Mr. Ticks,' the Commander continued gravely, 'most of the arguments in favour of such an undertaking have already been well aired and noted by the staff. Some of them are doubtless very good ones. We have yet to hear one half as cogent, however, as the fact that none of us would survive the attack to destroy the dam, and that it would therefore fail in its real purpose.'

'That was well said, Commander,' Luca Pugnini remarked.

'Thank you, General,' murmured the Commander.

'Speak your mind,' Slater said.

The Commander raised his eyebrows. 'I do, I do.'

'What you're thinking is that I don't personally give a

damn whether you blow the reservoir or not as long as it's news. That's it, isn't it?'

'Oh, come,' Adrian Bullivant said, 'that's going a bit too far.'

'You keep out of this,' Slater told him.

'Shall we adhere to the agenda?' Luca Pugnini suggested softly. He was unusually well dressed this evening and was on the best of terms with himself and desirous that the rest should feel equally well disposed towards one another. He had recently shaved and his round blue chin was heavily powdered. 'We are dealing with principles.'

'The whole matter is in the hands of God,' Father Domenicus said testily, 'we should let well alone.' He sniffed and drew a finger surreptitiously beneath his nose. 'We must wait for the sign.'

'I'm not really trying to force the issue,' Adrian Bullivant said. He was acutely conscious of their unbelief. 'All we have to do is to discuss the thing without personal prejudice and reach whatever decision is best in the light of the facts we know.' With head bowed beneath the ceiling he looked earnestly round the room, the great blue eyes unwavering as they moved from one hostile face to another.

'God is a fact,' said Father Domenicus briefly.

'I'm staying here till I get a decision—the right one,' Slater said, 'if it takes a week.' He looked savagely at the officer. Then he looked at Erica and fell silent.

'Aesthetically,' Luca Pugnini said, 'and as a matter of fact, I for one am in favour of the attack. But, while we may attack under moral compulsion, we succeed only as a result of superiority in men and arms and, in this respect, I confess, my faith wavers. The Lord may temper the wind to the shorn lamb, but the shepherd who waits is conforming to the fact that the wind is still coolish.' He smiled. 'Shall we have a glass of wine?'

'It behoves us to remember,' Father Domenicus said,

'that more than ourselves are endangered by attacking. The effect of such a move on my parish would be incalculable.'

Slater exploded. ' Bloody nonsense!' he barked. ' If you think you can win a war without somebody getting hurt . . .'

' Keep quiet,' Erica told him.

He turned on her. ' Who asked you to shove your oar in?'

' You talk too much,' she said softly.

The Commander looked at her and then at Slater. Adrian Bullivant followed the grey eyes. He too was aware of some understanding between Erica and the journalist. A bat struck the window and a moth vanished. Pierre, swarthy in the candlelight, lugged the flagon of wine away from the wall and Luca Pugnini and Erica and Slater rearranged themselves so that he might tip the flagon and fill the mugs. He spilled a great deal of it on the floor and the smell of liquor mingled with the odour of mice and candle-grease and eau-de-Cologne and rose with the warm air to the ceiling and remained there.

' Why didn't you tell them about the armoured car?' Judith asked him.

' I was saving that. Besides, we hadn't got it then.'

' Go on, then.' She smiled. ' Then what happened?'

' Well, nothing actually happened. There was no sort of movement or anything. It's funny, that, because it always gives me the impression of having been a tremendously active night. I remember feeling frightfully tired afterwards, as though I'd done a long march or something. I can remember pretty nearly everything that was said, but not always in the order it was said. It slips out of perspective.'

She stifled a yawn. ' Yes, I expect it does.'

' Must you yawn, dear?' He looked at the pretty face. She was wearing the hair high on her head then and it gave her a peculiarly babyish air. He knew his irritation to be most unreasonable. 'It's awfully important to me.'

'But darling, it's all over now.'

'Just the same, it matters a lot.'

'Yes, all right, Adrian. It matters to me, too.' She smiled and screwed up her eyes, a habit she had acquired, he had noticed, to conceal the fact that she was not smiling. 'And then?'

'Well, Slater, I think it was, and I never can remember exactly what he was referring to, said, "Claptrap! That's all I've heard so far. That's all I've heard ever since I arrived on the mountain." He was getting really angry.'

'Horrid little man,' Judith said.

Then Erica was shaking her head and Judith said she did not like Erica either. Nor, in fact, did Adrian Bullivant. But with him it was not a matter of like or dislike. He was simply repelled by her. She was an affront to every principle of womanhood he recognised. She was not human, even. He always remembered the surprise he experienced when he first saw her eating, leaning against the wall of the kitchen in the shade, putting bread and meat into her mouth and chewing it slowly and when she had finished, feeling his eyes on her, hiding her hands in the pockets of the slacks she wore—an expression of the only understandable complex she ever exhibited. He suspected her at first, and never wholly gave up the notion, of some monstrous crime that she had thus to hide herself on a mountain where she was so startlingly out of place. Later, when he knew her a little better, she became less mysterious, but the qualities he began then to recognise in her, abnormal physical courage and pitiless cruelty and a certain wry humour, were all contradictory and only incidental. They accentuated the impression she gave that she herself was not there, was elsewhere about some other, bigger, business.

'When you're finished,' Slater continued, 'then I'll start. First I'll tell you a few home truths about yourselves and then I'll tell you about the best way to blow up the dam.'

The officer wished Slater would hold his ungainly tongue. The way he spoke to them only antagonised them, even those, if any, who were indifferent to the issue. All of those present, he believed, owed allegiance to a different concept and until they might find common ground, somewhere far back in their natures, there would be no unity of opinion. He felt embarrassed, not for the first time, that his duty in this instance went hand in hand with Slater's advantage. By instinct he would have much preferred to oppose the fellow.

'Mr. Ticks has an unfortunate manner from time to time,' the Commander said, 'but his impatience is understandable.' He raised his eyes from the map. 'We lack a judge to whom to address our arguments. We need an adjudicator.' They all listened, sipping the wine that the Breton passed among them with little whispers. '. . . somebody who, by virtue of his character and position, can sum up pros and cons and produce an acceptable decision. Blessed as we are with both the press and the Church, it might seem that one or other of their representatives would qualify for such a position. Short of Father Domenicus, then, or Mr. Ticks, neither of whom can reasonably plead impartiality in the matter, I would suggest, glad to give my reasons . . . Captain Bullivant.'

The reaction was immediate and explosive. Indeed, it seemed as though the Commander's words were a signal of some sort, a blessed release from the somewhat strained pomposity which, until then, had characterised the proceedings, an exemption from the crippling restraint of which each seemed to have been conscious in the presence of the rest. From that moment onwards, Adrian Bullivant remembered, the discussion lost all form, all relevance, all semblance of order. Every voice was raised to a shout and none cared whether another spoke or not. Sometimes the mêlée was of a general nature, at others it broke up into pairs or little groups eddying about the room among the busy shadows. And not least voluble among them was Adrian Bullivant himself who, violent in his protestations of utter unsuitability for the rôle the Commander had suggested he occupy, forced his way from one group to the other, from the Commander to Luca Pugnini, from Pierre to the Chief of Staff and back again, his head bringing down the plaster about all their dusty ears, engaging any who would listen in heated argument and few willing and none capable of hearing him. Only the Commander remained unruffled. Sometimes he spoke and by the very gentleness of his voice obtained a listener; mostly he leaned over the map on the table and drew fish and trees and little men running, and sipped his wine.

' My reasons,' the Commander continued, unmoved by the hubbub about him, ' are as follows: in the first place, Captain Bullivant is a young man of singular honour, a little confused and bewildered maybe, but in his own lights honourable, having an incorrigible sense of duty which, in a madhouse, does for escape. No matter. Now, when you ask a man of honour and partiality for a decision calling for impartiality, the bias is nearly always inverted; he at once takes the side directly opposite that which he himself favours since in his efforts to avoid leaning too far backwards he is prone to fall flat on his face if only to show just how honourable and impartial he can be . . . which illustrates well enough the mischief a man of honour can cause but which will certainly lead to postponement of the attack to everybody's satisfaction except Mr. Tick's. And the responsibility rests with Captain Bullivant. In the second place, Captain Bullivant, by the same token and for the same reasons will not lightly commit to action a party of men and women who do not willingly follow him for, while he would cheerfully undertake the operation by himself and doubtless die very bravely, he will hesitate to accept the responsibility for the deaths of so many others . . .'

White to the lips and exceedingly angry, Bullivant leaned over the table and shouted,

' I absolutely refuse to accept. D'you hear? I am not impartial. The attack must be done. It must and will be done. I've got an armoured car. You create a diversion, I'll get through somehow. I say I've got an armoured car.' He saw Crosby with his back to the blanket, standing alone, watching the journalist and pushed his way between Erica and Slater towards the soldier.

' Lend me a hand,' he said into Crosby's ear, grateful for the soldier's timely arrival. He told Crosby what had been said.

' What are you complaining about, then?' Crosby asked sourly. ' If they've left it up to you, that's what you want, isn't it? For Chris' sake.'

' They've got to agree, man. They've got to be convinced the attack should be done.'

' Do you want to do it, or don't you?'

' Of course. But they must want . . .'

'. . . the paradox is obvious, though it escapes me for the moment,' Luca Pugnini shouted close at hand. ' It's very like their foreign policy, my dear fellow, quite unhealthily typical. What's sauce for the goose is also good cooking, if you follow me. What is morally right is also in their best interests, which is very nice for them and damned annoying for everybody else.' The sally perished in the general up- roar, but he continued. ' Slater is at the back of it, of course. If the fellow had never arrived, all would now be well . . . not so much Slater himself, but the thing he represents, the voice, the dog-eared conscience of humanity, the great They, the Boyg, the rich in virtue.' Pierre's atten- tion had wandered, however, and the Divisional Com- mander, ignored but undaunted, raised his mellow voice still higher and continued, 'The press, like God—forgive me, Father—accepts all the credit and none of the blame; do not confuse my paganism with atheism, I beg. No . . .' he spluttered breathlessly in the shower of plaster that covered him as Adrian Bullivant stood suddenly upright at the touch of stiff fingers in his ribs. The officer looked round with fist clenched but saw only Crosby, watching the journalist.

'I've got an armoured car,' he said weakly.

He was convinced in his own mind that if they would but listen to him for a moment he could show them not only that it was right and necessary to carry out the attack but also that, with a good plan and a single armoured vehicle, it might well meet with success. The fact of his possession of the vehicle, he felt certain, should be sufficient to attract the attention of at least one of them, if they would only listen; thereafter the infiltration of the news throughout the entire Command Post would be a matter of a few moments only. Why wouldn't they listen? 'We now have an armoured car,' he called.

'What's that?'

At last. It was the Chief of Staff at his elbow. 'What's that, young man?' He adjusted his spectacles. 'An armoured car? Why wasn't I told? Where is it?'

'Well, we've as good as got it.' He was conscious of the awful weakness of the qualification and hastened to explain, his hand on the man's forearm, 'I've got the money, thanks to Father Domenicus, and all the necessary arrangements are made. To-morrow evening it will be here in the camp, I swear it. You have my word. That'll make a pretty big difference, won't it? You see how that changes the whole complexion of the thing.'

'It does nothing of the sort,' the Chief of Staff snapped. 'You must think we're fools here.'

Adrian Bullivant bit his lips and turned away. He thrust

186

a path through the shouting crowd in the centre of the room and leaned over the Commander's table. 'We've now got an armoured car,' he said clearly. The Commander raised his head. 'We shall have it in our possession to-morrow evening.'

'So I believe, Captain Bullivant.'

'To-morrow we shall have it.'

'Excellent.'

'It'll make a lot of difference.'

'To what?'

'I mean, it should be taken into account. It'll make the attack far simpler.'

'Then by all means take it into account,' the Commander said drily.

'Look here, sir, about your idea . . .'

'You're singeing your clothes.'

The young man withdrew a little from the candles. 'That idea of yours about leaving the decision to me . . . you weren't serious, were you?'

'It depends what decision you arrive at.'

'That's rubbish, and you know it.'

'Not at all. You'll make the best of all possible decisions.'

'Father Domenicus approves of the attack. He's found the money for the armoured car.'

'Father Domenicus is playing for time, Captain Bullivant, and has no other interest in the matter.'

'You mean he's hoping the Allied armies will arrive in time to render the attack unnecessary.'

'Precisely.'

'Yes, I know, but that's just the point, they mustn't. We have to do our part first, d'you see? Supposing we're too late and blow the thing after they've arrived?'

'I would laugh myself sick, Captain Bullivant.'

The officer turned away with a gesture of impatience and found himself face to face with the journalist, who said at once, 'What did I tell you? It's a walk-over.'

'Is it hell! These people have got to be convinced. They must appreciate that it's right and necessary. I won't push them into a job that'll be the death of every one of them unless they agree. They've got to believe in it.'

Slater's face straightened. He fingered the spot on his cheek, looking reflectively at the young officer. 'Are you trying to back out of it now, Bullivant?'

'What did you say to him?' Judith asked.

'What should I have said?'

She stared. 'Not nothing, anyway.'

'But he was right,' he said earnestly, 'I was trying to get out of it. I had been, all the time. I realised it as soon as he said so.'

'I don't understand you,' she said at last.

'Listen, Bullivant,' the journalist said narrowly, 'don't I know your father?'

His heart stood still and the shadows on the walls drew closer to listen. He felt the great weight of the ceiling on his head and the taste of the bitter air at the back of his tongue. 'I don't know,' he said lightly, 'do you know him?'

'Jonathan Bullivant, isn't it?'

'That's right.'

Slater laughed and slapped the officer on the shoulder. 'Shot in the dark's always worth while.' He laughed again. Then he tapped Adrian Bullivant on the chest and said, 'People whose fathers live in glass houses shouldn't lose their nerve,' and laughed again uproariously.

'What did he mean?' she asked at once.

'Oh, come, Judith, you know perfectly well what he meant.' She was painfully obtuse sometimes. 'He meant, to put it baldly, that he knows my father is a blackguard and if I didn't decide to do the attack he'd . . . it's really awfully obvious.'

'But Adrian . . .' she sat up on the couch.

'Let's not go on about that,' he said.

'Why didn't you hit him?'

'For God's sake, Judith, you can't run about hitting people half your own size when they tell the truth. Besides, I'd tried it once.'

'He was making beastly insinuations about your father,' she retorted.

'All of which were right and justified,' he shouted. 'You know as well as I do—'

'Your father's a famous man and a public figure, Adrian. And don't shout, I've just got rid of one headache, I can hear you quite well. If that's what you think of your father, then why are you working for him? If you think all he's done for you and me is . . . is tainted or something, then why do you accept it? Why have you accepted it all? He's training you to take his place, isn't he?'

'Yes. Yes, I know, I know all about it. You're right.' He ran a hand through his hair. 'You're always right, Judith. Don't get upset, you'll get your headache again. You're quite right.'

'I'll talk to 'em,' Slater said, 'you leave that to me. Just keep your mouth shut.'

'My mother's drinking port in her bedroom.'

Slater looked at him. 'What's that?'

'Go on,' Judith said.

Another moth vanished into the night with a little scuffle on the glass and Pierre filled his mug with wine that was like vinegar, grinning up at him mischievously. 'Bend the knees to drink,' he said. The noise whistled in his ears. He watched the window.

'Never mind about the moths, dear.'

'Judith,' he said suddenly, 'let's try and get on a bit better together.'

'But we do, Adrian.'

He said, 'Yes,' and nodded, lowering his eyes, 'Yes,

Judith,' remembering the moment, scarcely a month after his return, when he had realised that they were no longer in love and knew at the same time it was no use, it never would return. He had tried desperately hard to recover it, to track down the faults in himself and eradicate them so that they might recover the lost happiness. But they had both changed, during the years they had been separated from one another, he at war and she in a state of mental and nervous disturbance, so that when they came together again they were strangers again, having nothing in common but the memory of a few days' passion, which was insufficient; maybe they would fall in love with one another all over again, he had thought, but they did not. Wherein he himself had changed he did not know; she, on the other hand, seemed to have suffered a complete metamorphosis of nature, from the sweet enthusiasms he had loved to the balanced maturity and reason against which he now beat his head. She was his wife only in that she too agreed, formally, that the vortex between them must be bridged. So, though they quarrelled much, they made peace much, trying hopelessly to ignore or change the unchangeable things that divided them.

It was in respect of his attitude towards his father that he first realised she had changed and no longer saw eye-to-eye with him in the things that to him were most important. She recoiled, genuinely shocked, from his mention of an idea which, in the years before their marriage and just after, she had embraced with fervour. He had thought to re-arouse her enthusiasm for it, and instead she told him he was mad. They would put into practice, he told her, the plans he had pursued for years for the destruction of the great businesses his father had built and which, like most men who have founded vast fortunes on air, he was now trying to perpetuate in bricks and mortar; the Bricker's Hill Garden City, he told her, was built on a marsh, of discarded timber and porous brick, ill-drained, jerry-built, the whole wretched business a gigantic swindle to which the Bricker's Hill Urban District Council was a party, Gough, the Borough Surveyor, being completely in his father's pay and power. They were all involved; there was not an innocent man among them. And he, Adrian Bullivant, could bring the whole fantastic edifice crashing about their ears. He would buy a newspaper, he told her, and edit it himself, with Heath, he thought, to assist him. Heath would do it all right. They would publish a few truths about the Garden City, about Bullivant Enterprises, about Bullivants Refineries, and the rest. He glowed with enthusiasm. He would start a national scandal and cause a full official enquiry to be made into the state of his father's books, into the foul and cancerous affairs of the District Council. He had it planned in some detail, he said. This was no more than an outline—

'You're mad, Adrian.'

He stopped short.

'Do you really know what you're saying?'

'Love, don't you remember—'

'No, I do not. I don't know what you're talking about. You've changed, Adrian. I don't know you. You're talking like a fool, and a dangerous fool at that. You'd better not let your father hear you, after all he's done for you.'

'It's evil, Judith, the whole thing's evil, monstrous.'

'With whose money would you buy the newspaper? And what newspaper?'

'The *Gazette*. And what does it matter whose money it is?'

'But Adrian, it's your own father. And your father's money. Now don't be silly. There's nothing wrong with your father's business, Adrian, there never was. Who've you been talking to?'

And the splendid resolution faded like a carpet in the

sun. But he never forgot it. Only once, to his father, did he mention it again. That was when he told the great man to take his plans to the devil and his father only laughed. To his mother, with her loyalties divided between Jonathan and the bottle and Birmingham, he knew it was useless to talk. And Judith would hear no more of it at all. If it were to be done, or even attempted, he must first leave her; so he waited. One day, he always told himself, if only after his father's death, the opportunity would come, and then he would act. And then. And then.

'Crosby, by the way, is a murderer.'

She looked up from her nails.

'Crosby. The soldier. The escaped prisoner. It's in the papers, he's killed a policeman.'

'Is that the same man?'

'I think so.'

'Good gracious. Did he look the type?'

'Not a bit. Seemed a very decent sort of chap to me. They haven't caught him yet.'

'Let's hope they do. Why didn't you tell me before?'

'It never occurred to me, somehow. I feel in a way to blame. . . .'

'You? Why you?' She stared at him.

'Oh, I don't know. I knew the fellow.'

'Rubbish.'

Then the Commander was speaking softly in the uproar. It was curious that the gentle voice was audible.

'. . . so I think it is fair that he is given a hearing at least. What he may have to say is certainly relevant and may be of interest to Captain Bullivant.' He looked up over the candles. 'Mr. Slater?'

The journalist grinned. 'Yes, I've a few things to say. Plenty. Not for Captain Bullivant's benefit, either.' He set his arms akimbo and stared round the room, drawing in his lips. 'Lots of people just now are worrying about a state of affairs known by and large as democracy. Nothing very positive about it, we don't pretend there is. You simply get a lot of things that way you don't get any other way. I won't fool you about it. There's a lot of folk who think it's just a racket. So it is. Far as I'm concerned all political faiths are rackets, fine sentiments and dirty play, but that's human nature and you can belly-ache about that till the cows come home, it won't make a ha'porth of difference. It's just that we think our racket's a better one than any-body else's, d'you see? So it is. Plenty of scope, not so many damn policeman about, plenty of pretty music. What d'you think we're fighting so damn hard for? Not for what it is, but for the way it is. It's all right. You outsmart the other fellow, he outsmarts you, that's all right, you started level, didn' you? Well, it's on its way, we're bringing it to you fast, and if you don't like it you can lump it, because that's the way it's going to be, at any rate to begin with. Little me, I represent it. I have to tell people what the form is, what you're doing about it. And the answer right now is nothing, damn all, talk. And when they know that, the way I tell them, they're liable to get up on their high horses. They store it up against you. You don't want to find yourself on the wrong side of the fence one day, do you? I'd have thought you'd had just about enough of that. Which brings me to blowing up the reservoir. You do your stuff now so that you get a look-in afterwards, d'you see? From your own point of view it doesn't matter a tinker's curse whether you blow up the dam or not, just so long as you try. You got to show willing, see? From my point of view, as a newspaper man trying to do a job of work, I don't care either. Success is a better story, but failure's not bad, not bad at all. You know what Bulli-vant wants. So there you are. Take your choice, there's only one.'

The Commander drew a little man on the map. 'That

was very interesting, Mr. Ticks,' he said. ' Thank you.'

And they began again to shout at one another. Pierre moved among them replenishing their glasses and laughing in a high treble and Luca Pugnini's clear tenor was heard above the clamour : ' How can it matter, my dear fellow, what political creed you die for . . ?' his voice was drowned in the Chief of Staff's unintelligible rasp. The moths were nearly all gone now, Adrian Bullivant noticed. His head was swimming in the noisome air beneath the ceiling and the back of his neck ached. On the table the candle-grease ran across the map and dripped to the floor till there was a small stiff stalactite of white wax beneath the edge. Several people seemed to be addressing him at once but he took no heed of their remarks.

' I can't hear what you're saying,' he said.

Then the Commander was speaking again. ' Mr. Ticks has more or less unhindered access to the columns of some eight or nine hundred newspapers, perhaps more, and may therefore number his readers in terms of hundreds of millions . . .' the voice waxed and waned in the din . . . ' a power for evil, it might be for good, at which the ordinary mind baulks . . . the truth but not the whole truth, the terrible weapon of omission . . . whose qualifications for the position from which he may sway the opinions and destinies of nations are limited to the fact that he happened to be first on the scene of a notorious murder.' He went on a long time, his voice rising and falling tonelessly. '. . . without honour, scruple or integrity, to whom the measure of truth is speed and for whom the incalculable responsibility of his position is of interest only as it relates to a spectacular career.' There were now only four moths left on the window. '. . . wearing the shabby cloak of freedom which, in his world, is not freedom, but only licence . . . should dare to utter a protest then the drums roll and the trumpets sound and the tattered banner is unfurled under which they may hide and the rest must cower. And those in high places are afraid and those in low places have no voice. . . .' Adrian Bullivant watched the lips and saw them moving but he could not hear.

' Be quiet !' he shouted.

' What Captain Bullivant must decide, therefore, is, are we to conform to the news, or shall the news conform to us? For Mr. Ticks has two despatches in his pocket, one for victory and one for defeat. Which must it be? Mr. Ticks' career stands or falls to some extent by Captain Bullivant's decision.'

' I absolutely refuse . . .' he could no longer hear his own voice.

'. . . and I am attuned to genius,' he heard Erica say.

' Stand or fall.'

' *Aut Cæsar, aut nullus,*' said Father Domenicus sonorously.

' More than a grain, my dear fellow.'

'. . . being perpetually bossed about.'

' All beautiful women are fascist. It's not a political opinion, it's an instinct.'

Pierre was laughing crazily and Adrian Bullivant heard himself shouting again. ' I refuse, I refuse.'

The blanket over the door was whipped aside and Otto stood in the doorway. For a second he recoiled from the turmoil of men and shadows and the dirty yellow haze, narrowing his eyes and coughing. The red hair stood on end and the skirt of the smock he wore and his hands and his face were all smeared with gay vermilion, and in the red beard drops of spray glittered prettily in the candlelight. Only the officer noticed him, and fell silent, waiting, feeling that maybe this was the climax of something. But it was not.

' Erica,' the artist shouted.

She ignored him.

He pushed his way to her side. ' Erica.'

Then Adrian Bullivant saw that others were watching, the Commander was watching her, and Pierre and Slater.

' It's nearly light. Come.'

Then he was pleading with her and she was shaking her head many times, always slowly.

' Erica. Little one.'

She shook her head. In a little while he left her and stumbled from the room. The Commander bent his head over the map and drew a horse, grazing, carefully.

Adrian Bullivant did not remember leaving the place. When he awoke he was lying fully dressed on the mattress in his billet with his eyes open. He could not have been there long, he thought, for the day was barely broken. In the window above his head a plump diamond bristled in the green sky, green as sea on a sandbank. A pillar of grey light spun slowly in the middle of the room and the shadows trembled in the corners and among the litter on the floor. He shivered, for it was chilly. There was something on the floor . . . legs, Slater's legs, in the stiff abandon of exhaustion, grey in the dim light. He listened to the man's breathing. He sat up presently and ran a hand through his hair and groped for his glasses, finding them where he normally left them, on the floor at the bedside. He put them on and got up and went quietly out into the street. The stream sang softly beneath the bridge and the air shook in the distant thunder of the cataract and the sighing of the trees on the edge of the forest. A little spiral of dust rose on the wind and ran a few feet, caught a scrap of paper and carried it to the wall, and subsided. To his left, above the village, the peak thrust upwards to the sky. The summit was not visible. Below him, towards Ronc or maybe even beyond, a cock crowed and a dog began to bark.

The Commander was asleep. He sat at the table in the Command Post with his head on his arms. The three candles on the map had burnt themselves out and the wicks lay deep in the rigid wax. There were four mugs on the table, one of which was nearly full of wine.

Adrian Bullivant leaned over him.

' It's me,' he would say, ' Bullivant. I'm very sorry to wake you up.' He put out his hand to touch the heavy shoulder, and then withdrew it.

' The decision,' he would say.

' What?'

' The decision about the attack.'

' I was asleep,' the Commander would say irritably.

' It's about the attack. You remember.'

' What is it?'

' We'll have to do it. I'm frightfully sorry, but we'll have to do it.' That, or : ' My decision is that we attack.'

And the Commander would say, ' Of course, Bullivant. I knew all the time.' Maybe he would smile.

He laid his hand on the bulk of the Commander's back and he stirred.

14

'WITH THE UTMOST severity,' the man said. Crosby listened, turning his glass round and round in the little pool of spilled beer on the table. The man spoke with the overwhelming unction of one whose opinion is morally unexceptionable, addressing only his neighbour but aloud, loud and firm, so that all those in the bar might hear. Soon they fell silent and his remarks were punctuated only by the occasional chirrup of the till.

'Twenty years minimum, I say, if not a hanging.' He caught sight of himself in the painted mirror behind the counter and raised his chin. 'The fellow ought to be made an example of, as a warning to the rest of them. They've got to be taught the war's over now and they're back home and we don't settle things that way in this country or anywhere else for that matter. They are all the same, you can see it in their faces, in their attitude. Think they're going to run the country their own way. Nobody's denying what they went through, nobody, least of all me. I know what it's like, mud up to your bloody armpits, I had some in the last one. Were we allowed to take the law into our own hands when we got back?' 'Pity we didn't,' somebody murmured, but the speaker ignored the comment. 'And why should they, that's what I want to know?' A man in a soiled felt hat ordered another pint of bitter and the woman in the shiny black dress behind the bar stared at him resentfully and lugged at the tall black tap and thrust back her hair. 'They've got to be taught a lesson, that's all there is to it. If they can't come to their senses by themselves then they've got to be shown and the sooner the better. Seem to expect some sort of special treatment. We had bombing, didn't we? Years of it, bombing and rockets and one thing or another, and look at Dover. Shelling. These fellows seem to forget the people who stuck to their jobs weren't exactly having a holiday. Coming home riding roughshod over law and order like this.' The till chirruped briskly and the woman slammed the drawer. 'Who's to say how many thousands of guns have been brought into the country? Souvenirs. Souvenirs my aunt Fanny. Gangsterism, that's all it is. Chicago, that's all the place is becoming. If steps aren't taken soon there'll be a public outcry. Shooting down unarmed policemen in the execution of their duty . . . their own chums, that's what gets me, their own buddies. Decent people are getting so they dare not go out now after dark. Dollis as never hurt a fly beaten up in front of his own house. Crosby ought to hang for that alone. As an example. They're all the same. Mischief-makers. Worse than fascism, that's what it is. Nihilism, the *Observer* called it, and that's about right: nihilism.'

They did not recognise him. He listened for a little while and presently got up and went out quietly. He stood in the doorway and felt the gentle evening breeze, redolent of fruit and vegetables and the interior of trams, running through his hair. There were still a few people about, mostly women with shopping baskets. It was growing dark and the shops were closing one by one and the cars passing in the road below him eyed him brightly as they rounded the bend. His eye travelled down the hill to the junction. He knew the place quite well, it was not far from Five Elms. Where the old showroom had been there was nothing now, an open space. A direct hit, he supposed. With a deep nostalgia he thought about the direct hit and the way a big building would melt if it got it in the right place and of the curious deep satisfaction it gave you like the feeling you had when you hit the man at whom you had aimed because the tremor, the something you could never hope to explain, came back up the barrel to your shoulder. He shook the thought out of his head and moistened his lips. He could see the new slates on the roofs everywhere scarlet against the brown old ones. The flat brow of the library towered above the junction and he could see the stains the oil bomb had flung aslant the white stone when it had dropped there in the road. Iris had written to him about it; they dropped an oil bomb yesterday, she said, in Norfolk Common, to-day I made some jam and aunt Flo is going to have another my God that makes seven. He grinned to himself and went down the steps into the road. His ankle was still swollen, he could not walk easily even yet. Now where would he go? There were many things he might do. He could go to the cinema again, for example, but he had seen the film twice already, once this week and once in Italy or Austria or somewhere. He could walk, yes, he ought to keep moving in any case, though God knew why, the instinct of self-preservation, he supposed. He could go and see Mrs. Chubb, he had been meaning to go and see her for a long time; but then they would be after him at once; she would tell them; he would go and see her when he knew they were catching up with him and seeing her would make no difference. He might go and see Captain Bullivant. No, it was too far, too far, and would be frightfully embarrassing for Bullivant. But there were really many things he could do. When you have very little time left, there must surely be many things you want to do. And damn it all, he had been wanting to have the time like this for years. It was really wonderful. He went along the street slowly.

He was surprised they had not caught him yet, for he was making no particular effort to evade capture. Certainly he was not giving himself up, let them search, but neither was he running away. He moved about in broad daylight in public places, used trams and buses, ate food and drank beer and slept in the parks or the doss-houses if it was raining. Maybe they did not expect to find him so near home, a five-minute tram ride from Five Elms. A description must surely have been circulated, even if they had not found a photograph. There was the wedding group on the mantelpiece at home. Maybe he would go and see Iris, too, but there again they would be waiting and watching. He wondered if there was anything he could do for her, for Iris or Mrs. Chubb, or even both, something splendid, something truly magnificent. Even the fools and the fat men sometimes died doing something big, he had seen them. Take the Divisional Commander, for instance, Luca Pugnini, who went down, they said, with six holes in him and a wounded man on his back. The man must have known what was coming to him, they must all have known. He remembered well the way nobody on the mountain was surprised or indignant about Adrian Bullivant's decision.

' We shall attack the reservoir on the evening of the day after to-morrow,' the Chief of Staff told them.

' To-morrow,' Slater corrected him irritably, ' to-morrow evening.'

The Chief of Staff glanced at his notes. ' Of course, I meant to-morrow evening,' he said.

Then they started to talk, as though they must get it all said. Nobody objected. Nobody protested against the crazy order, no dissident voice mourned the passing of sanity and reason. The decision was accepted as if there had been no other thought in their minds, as if indeed it were an occasion to which they had been looking forward with more than casual interest. Nobody mentioned the matter to the officer, for which he was deeply grateful, and their attitude towards him changed only in that it became if anything even more friendly and accommodating. It was incomprehensible to Adrian Bullivant and the soldier. At first they had thought the cheerfulness with which the camp was suddenly infected was a veneer, a pose, but it was not so at all. They were genuinely excited. Adrian Bullivant found it uncomfortably moving. Even the irascible Chief of Staff had difficulty in concealing his good temper. Adrian Bullivant had seen similar phenomena before, among hardened troops. It was a good sign.

They went over the attack in great detail. It was a pity, Luca Pugnini said, that they could not use the plan laid down by the staff, for it was a good plan. And yet in another way he was not displeased; it might always have succeeded. 'An unsigned canvas may always be a Giotto,' he said.

The plan upon which they finally decided was as follows: to begin with, all would carry automatic weapons so that the enemy would receive a first impression of greater strength than the staff in fact amounted to in numbers of men. There would be three distinct phases, for which the headquarters would be split into three groups. The first group, to consist of Luca Pugnini, Pierre, Otto and Maria, would attack from the slopes due east of the reservoir. The second, to consist of the Chief of Staff, Roberto, Slobadov and Hans, would reinforce the first party after an interval of ten minutes, but attacking somewhat from the south-eastern side so that the enemy, holding his reserves for the real attack, might think this was it and throw in his main strength. The feint or diversion was to be confirmed, as it were, by the arrival of the third group, comprising the Commander, Erica and little Josef, the latter to act as runner, a capacity wherein his tendency to follow movement would be most useful, which would add its fire to that of the first two. Thereafter all three would advance as best and as far as they might, and indeed there was no saying how far they might not go, occupying the enemy's attention while the last phase of the operation was put into effect. Adrian Bullivant, in the armoured car, would enter the village of Ronc from the eastern side and, with turret closed, run through the village as if hastening to the assistance of the defenders of the reservoir. There was a ramp, steep and narrow, running from the Ronc road to the top of the wall. Once they had gained the summit they would make immediately for the gates and the control-house; these they would open from the control tower or by blowing; Crosby would have to deal with any sentries not called to repel the attack on the eastern wall. Charges would have to be prepared. The officer had arrived on the mountain armed with detonators and small charges; these would have to be reinforced by the stripping and emptying of grenades and mines such as the armoury possessed an abundance of; he showed Roberto how to do it. Once the gates had been blown, of course, it would be a matter of every man for himself. A rendezvous was arranged among the rocks of the Old Town beneath the edge of the forest. The attack would naturally be launched at dusk so that the occupants of the armoured car might be less conspicuous and the weakness of the diversion less apparent to the enemy.

'And Father Domenicus must be told nothing,' Luca Pugnini added.

'Why not?' Adrian Bullivant was puzzled. 'He might be very useful.'

'He would at once inform the enemy.'

'Good Lord, would he? Is the man an enemy agent?'

'Ours and the enemy's.'

'Well, I'm damned.' He began to understand the activities of the priest. 'Does the enemy know that, too?'

'Naturally. Everybody knows except Father Domenicus.'

'You mean he doesn't know that everybody else knows. . . .'

' Just so.'

There was one item of equipment, however, not yet in their possession and without which nothing could be done. The necessary preliminaries for the acquisition of the armoured car had been put in hand by Luca Pugnini during the conference. He had arranged with the priest that a message would reach the most slovenly and bibulous of the crews of the armoured car platoon of the garrison suggesting a parley that evening at the point where the minefield ran closest to the Ronc road; it would be made known to the crew that in the event of a sale the priest would assist the two men to desert should they feel it advisable or convenient to do so. It remained only to negotiate the exchange. The Divisional Commander was confident enough of success, but Adrian Bullivant felt he should be at least in the vicinity, well-armed and supported by Crosby, lest the enemy took fright and attempted to withdraw. The issue must be forced, by persuasion, threat or in an extremity, action.

They would leave the camp at six.

It was shortly after the Chief of Staff's address to the headquarters on the subject of the attack and the parts each would play in it that certain conversations took place between members of the staff such as often precede action after a long period of idleness. The premonition of death led them into attempts to elucidate their misunderstandings to wind up, as it were, their affairs. One of these was between Erica and the artist Otto. He had been somewhat restive all the afternoon. Slater watched him. The lids over the yellow eyes hung as heavily as ever; there was no outward sign of inward turmoil. Yet the man gave an impression of profound anxiety.

' Yes, what is it?' she asked when he came to the door of her billet and called her name. She went towards him.

He said, ' The attack to-morrow . . .' and stopped. The voice was deep and husky.

' Well?' She stood in the sun in the doorway.

' My work,' he said.

' Yes?'

' I cannot finish.'

' I suppose not.' She raised her shoulders. ' It can't be helped, can it?'

' You must see it.'

' No, Otto.'

' It's you . . .' he stopped again. He dropped his eyes and swallowed. ' Please.'

' There's no time.'

' I want you to come and see it.'

She shook her head.

' Erica,' he whispered.

She turned and went into the dark room and the Slav lumbered away up the track.

Then the Commander sent for her, asking that she come to the Command Post. He was waiting for her.

' You want to see me?' she said.

' Yes.'

It was a long time since he had faced her alone. In the past there had always been others present and neither had sought the opportunity of private conversation. He had watched her and she had been aware of it and made no effort to disguise her life. Of all the men in the camp only in the Commander's eyes had she never seen open desire, or indeed anything but a gentle mockery. If only for this reason, though irritated sometimes by his manner, she had once or twice thought him worth her attention. But he was already mature and the vitality that was necessary was already gone in the erosion of the years. She preferred rawer material and was interested in him only in that he had the self-respect to conceal his lust. Now she looked at him. He was getting heavier, she thought. When the chin was down the flesh beneath lost all its shape; only when he raised it and the folds of flesh sank into the neck was there a line to the chin.

' Paula shouldn't be taken on this attack,' he said.

' No.' She waited.

' What d'you propose to do about her?'

' Leave her behind.'

He nodded. ' Walk with me, Erica.'

They left the gloomy place and went out into the sun. She walked slowly at his side, suiting her pace to his heavy limp. They passed through the village among the curious eyes and over the bridge. There on the bank of the stream Luca Pugnini was explaining to the staff the movements of the piston of the light machine-gun while Roberto, occasionally adjusting the brim of his trilby, stood at a little distance ready to drop on his face behind the gun and demonstrate. They went on beyond the bridge. A wisp of cloud passed across the face of the sun and its shadow sped over the plain in front of them.

' Your leg pains you? she enquired.

' Yes, a little.'

They leaned against the broken fence that ran from the bridge a little way into the open country and there petered out in a few rotting stumps. She waited for him to begin.

' You ought to get married, Erica' he said at last.

She looked at him in surprise, having defined his thoughts but not the manner of approach. This was somewhat crude, she thought. ' D'you think so?'

' I've thought so a long time.'

' Really? To whom? To you, you mean?'

He stared at the distant forest. ' I wasn't thinking so much of myself . . .' he looked at her.

' Liar,' she said.

He smiled. ' Yes.'

' Yes, of course. Why not say so?'

' Because I'm a silly old fool.'

' You are.'

' I only wanted to hear you say it. You understand?'

' Perfectly.'

' And so . . .' he raised himself from the bar of the fence.

' Please don't go,' she said. And when he sank back on to the fence and looked at her she could not think why she had wanted him to stay.

' Try persuading me,' she said, smiling.

' I love you,' he said drily.

' Is that all?'

' I can't think of anything else to say.'

' Well, enlarge on that.'

' You're as big a fool as I am, Erica.'

She threw back her head and laughed immensely. They left the fence and walked back towards the bridge.

' Satisfied?' she asked him presently.

' Oh, yes, quite satisfied.'

They were silent then until they reached the door of her billet. She turned to him there and touched his arm. ' And thank you,' she said. She went into the cottage.

Slater watched them. And Paula watched them. Otto followed them with heavy eyes and Luca Pugnini smiled to himself. ' The surplus gases are then discharged,' he said, ' through the . . .' he stifled a yawn.

In the early evening they set off, Luca Pugnini and Roberto briskly and with purpose, Adrian Bullivant and Crosby, each carrying a machine pistol, furtively, several hundred yards in the rear. The officer was determined that this time there would be no bungling and he did not altogether trust the Divisional Commander, who to his mind took the matter much too lightly. ' My dear fellow,' the general had said, flourishing the bag of money, ' we could buy the entire garrison for this.' Crosby plodded through the grass at his side down the long green slopes towards the spur of land beyond which lay the reservoir. On the Commander's map the Ronc road and the minefield converged at a point roughly corresponding to the end towards the spur of land beyond which lay the reservoir. Thereafter the minefield swung sharply to the east, ran along the crest of the spur a little way, and then dropped to the flat country beyond. From there it ran roughly parallel with the edge of the lake. At the angle, however, close to the road, there was a knife-rest in the wire, a movable section of timber and dannert. It was for this point that the party made. None knew for certain whether there were mines on the other, the enemy, side of the knife-rest or not; it was thought not, since the enemy patrols had been seen moving about quite freely in this vicinity. They would see very soon. Luca Pugnini and his assistant made for the knife-rest while Adrian Bullivant and Crosby climbed the spur and moved through the scrub that covered the lower slopes to a point from which they might overlook the site.

' There it is,' the officer whispered, ' keep down.'

The little armoured vehicle was drawn up at the side of the road below them. Two German soldiers leaned against it smoking, the one tall and having a pronounced stoop, the other inclined to stoutness. They were wearing forage caps and carried no arms.

' Keep them covered,' Adrian Bullivant said. ' You take the tall one. If they make as though to get in and drive away, now or any other time, let fly.'

They settled down in the scrub. In a very short time they saw Luca Pugnini and Roberto approach the knife-rest and call the two soldiers. Then they were through the wire and in the road. ' No mines,' Crosby muttered. The general began a short tour of inspection of the car, bending to look at the tyres, examining the interior. He was gesticulating to the crew. Evidently his intention was to drive a hard bargain. There was a great deal of shouting among them. Adrian Bullivant's anxiety increased; there should not be all this delay? What had gone amiss? Were they asking too high a price? Was the general quibbling over trifles? He lifted the gun and set his elbows firmly on his knees. He glanced along the sights: it would be very easy indeed to pick off the crew.

' What's going on?'

The officer turned and found Slater's face at his shoulder. The journalist was breathing hard with the exercise of climbing the hill but he was grinning cheerfully and the point of the tongue flickered between his lips.

Crosby said, ' For Chris' sake . . .'

' What's happening?'

Adrian Bullivant said angrily, ' How the hell did you find your way here?'

Slater tapped his nose. ' The Slater nose,' he whispered. He peered over the officer's shoulder. ' What's going on down there?'

' They're arguing about the price,' he told Slater bitterly. ' Pugnini is, anyway.'

' That so?'

' Sit down and keep quiet.'

' I'd like to be in on that,' Slater said softly, ' very much indeed.'

' You stay where you are.'

The journalist stared at the little group about the armoured car below as though hypnotised. Then he stood up in the scrub and Adrian Bullivant reached out to pull him down. But Slater was already walking away down the hill towards the wire, the frond of hair rising and falling like a wing on the crown of his head, and Adrian Bullivant was cursing and calling to him to get down, did he want to wreck the whole affair? But the young man ignored the hoarse abuse and went on down the hill towards the group about the vehicle.

'That's about mucked it,' Crosby said.

'Must have gone off his head,' Adrian Bullivant said. He was very near to panic. 'The man's a maniac.'

Crosby looked along the sights of his gun. 'I could just fix him up nicely,' he said.

'Don't shoot. Keep them covered.'

He watched the little scene on the blade of the foresight of his gun, the sweat moist on his forehead and cool in the evening breeze that came across the slopes from the great lake. He wondered whether he should not get up himself and go down the hill covered by Crosby and take command of the situation; it was obviously getting out of hand. The soldiers would have to be killed in that event, in cold blood; he wanted no prisoners; but he knew he could not bring himself to shoot down two men like that. He wished they would make as if to get into the vehicle and drive away so that he could shoot with a clear conscience. Now he saw the journalist offering them cigarettes and Luca Pugnini kicking the tyres and Roberto examining the tool kit. Then they were on the other side of the vehicle and he could distinguish only their heads above it. The dusk stole across the plain.

'Listen,' Crosby said.

The low voices were audible.

'What are your war aims?' he heard the journalist asking in clumsy German.

And then Luca Pugnini, to the tall soldier who stooped, his voice melodious on the scented air: 'There is a law of moderation, my dear corporal . . . this is inflation . . .'

They went on until the twilight had deepened into night and the two men waiting on the spur could no longer distinguish one from the other of the five men below. Adrian Bullivant stood up stiffly when he heard the engine of the vehicle break into life and the car swung through the gap in the wire towards him. He went down the hill and Crosby followed him.

'Hallo, there,' cried Luca Pugnini, 'we'd forgotten about you two. Come along.'

'You've been hours.'

General Pugnini raised the bag of money and the officer saw that it was nearly half full. The general smiled.

'The tyres are very poor,' he said.

Roberto drove and Luca Pugnini took the gunner's seat. Crosby and Slater and Adrian Bullivant clung to the pitching turret. The wind blew in their faces and sang shrilly in their ears. It was exhilarating. The stars glittered excitedly above the lonely peak.

15

ADRIAN BULLIVANT awoke very early on the following morning. The day had not broken and there was no light in the sky other than that of the stars. He lay still with his eyes on the window, conscious of his own unease, and wondered what it was had disturbed his sleep. Many miles away thunder muttered sulkily; a storm somewhere, he supposed. Soon it would begin to rain and the heavy drops of water, each at first alone and slow, then faster and heavier till it was all one breathless roar; but not yet, it was still far away. He closed his eyes. Something had disturbed him. The journalist snored lightly where he lay against the wall and a rat scuffled somewhere in the roof; nothing untoward there. Maybe Slater had cried out in his sleep. He drew up his legs and dozed and rejoined the people waiting patiently in his mind, Judith and his father smiling and Liza Bullivant singing tipsily. Then he sat up on the mattress with his heart beating violently in his throat, knowing at last what it was. He felt for the glasses at his bedside and pulled on his boots and jacket and went outside into the open air.

The clouds had come to rest on the foothills of the mountain scarcely fifty yards below the edge of the plateau. They stretched for miles white and cold and serene as new snow, so impenetrable that he might go down the mountain a little way and step up on to them and walk away from the dawn whose breath had already misted the glassy sky in the east and lit the slender arteries of ice on the flanks of the towering peak. For he did not want this day, nor any moment of it. He hated it, dreaded it. To suspend this moment, to prolong it into an infinity of time, to embrace the stillness and turn his back upon the inevitable movement towards himself, that was the thing to do. Now that would be something, he told himself in the empty generalities of spoken speech in which he felt more at home. Take the mountain, stuck there above everything like a finger, the finger of God raised in warning or admonishment. Yes, the mountain. Well now. There was something mystical in the attitude of the mountain towards him. It would seem to carry some special significance for him. A lot of nonsense, of course, but an interesting hypothesis. He remembered then that he would never now walk up through the forest, it was too late, of course, it was too late. It was almost a relief. Some other time, he told himself, he would return here and then he would see. The leather of the inside of his boots was cold and harsh to his bare feet. In the south he saw the gunflashes; they flickered like summer lightning through the floor of cloud and the earth trembled imperceptibly.

But the camp was astir early and when Adrian Bullivant and the journalist went out to the stream to wash and bathe Roberto was already running a nicely-oiled armoured car up and down the track with little Josef following at a purposeful canter. There was other activity. Slobadov and Hans were grooming the Commander's mare and General Pugnini, having already completed his task of laying out a number of guns and belts of ammunition on the dusty earth outside the mill, was watching the progress of the vehicle with a pride that he made no attempt to conceal. The Chief of Staff, important and humourless, went from one to the other of the billets and finally to the kitchen, where Maria Pugnini and Paula were preparing a number of sandwiches for distribution. Adrian Bullivant's heart sank when he saw that the clouds had not shifted. They lay motionless against the mountain, a floor beneath God

213

alone knew what was toward, and he would gladly have forfeited such minor advantages as they offered for a glimpse of the valley. The barrage had dropped to an intermittent rumble. He imagined it to be a little nearer than it had been when it first disturbed him. They would be moving up and soon it would swell to a steady thunder as troop and battery and regiment swung into position. He began to long for the oblivion of battle.

They washed in the stream, the officer in silence, Slater shouting with laughter and splashing about like a gipsy. The man's ebullience was infuriating at this juncture and he seemed to know it and delight in its effect. He had a nerve indeed, Adrian Bullivant thought. That was, primarily, the trouble. You could hardly take exception to the man's light-hearted derision when you knew quite well that when the attack would come he would be there in the van taking as many or more risks than the best of them. That was the mystery of courage, the way it would lodge in the most unlikely people, wholly irrespective of other, baser, qualities, however paltry and ignoble, and there defy every law of reason and average. Not that he thought the journalist capable of the impersonal bravery that has sometimes the beauty of the divine, not at all; Slater's courage would be nicely calculated. He would go where he could best fulfil his duty to himself. It made no difference that his despatches were already written; his strange code demanded that he should also go and see.

Slater himself was well satisfied with the course of events. The affair was developing excellently well and he saw no reason why it should not reach an end entirely satisfactory to himself. His fears of competition and the loss of exclusiveness which was the story's only real merit had diminished with the final settlement of the time and the manner of the attack to a point at which he was able to ignore them; they were a small dark cloud, no more, and it was moving away from him with every moment. After a sandwich in the kitchen and a mug of bitter coffee he settled down with his back to the mill to write the story of the arrival of the allied spearhead in Ronc and of the affecting welcome the troops received there.

He heard the throb of the engine at the beginning of the third line of the second take. It was then five minutes after eleven o'clock, somewhat less than an hour after he had settled down with the typewriter upon its lid between his knees. He looked up into the sky, shading his eyes against the glare, and saw the little biplane circling the plateau. The blood ran out of his lips.

The aircraft dropped steeply, the engine chirruping nervously as it levelled and dipped, wavered, dipped again and lightly touched the resilient turf. It hopped from hummock to hummock for a distance of maybe fifty yards and then the tail went down and the aircraft lurched to a standstill on the flat ground above the mill. The journalist did not move, though he heard the excited clamour in the village. He saw two men climb stiffly from the cockpit, the one appearing on account of his uniform and careless bearing to be the pilot, the other unidentifiable except that he was carrying, with a blanket roll and a raincoat, a small black box. The two men lit cigarettes and then walked down the slope towards the mill chatting pleasantly. When they were close enough Slater saw that the box the second man was carrying was a portable typewriter. He recognised him as Bernard Hendrick.

' Just fancy,' Bernard Hendrick said gravely to Slater. His sound blue eye—the other was glass—travelled from Slater's white face to the typewriter between his knees. ' Ticks Slater, of all people.'

' Who'd you get it from?' Slater said huskily.

' Oh, fie, fie . . .'

He walked on with the pilot towards the silent gather-

215

ing at the foot of the slope. Slater ran a trembling hand across his eyes.

The second aircraft landed approximately twenty minutes after the first. He watched it taxi over the plain and come to a standstill alongside its companion. George Dilling climbed laboriously from the cockpit and gathered his paraphernalia into a heap. As he passed Slater on his way to the village, he nodded and said with scarcely a trace of derision,

'Been here long?'

Slater did not speak.

The pilot of the first plane passed him returning to his aircraft and the journalist watched him absently as he started up the engine and taxied across the level ground and took off. Then there was a third circling the landing strip, coming in skilfully along the tracks of its predecessors. Mary Willis eased her long body from the cockpit and, instructing the pilot to follow with her suitcase, strode down the slope to the mill. She nodded and smiled sourly.

'Writing your memoirs, sonny?'

Slater did not answer. He lit a cigarette and watched the second plane taxi into the wind and take off.

It became something of a procession, with plane and pilot and passenger and pilot returning to plane and the air busy with the hum of engines. He knew them all, there were none missing.

'Too bad, Ticks,' Woronski murmured as he passed the younger man and went on down the slope to join the others.

''S a small world,' Percy Demetz said heartily.

'Didn't think you'd get away with this, did you?' Dicky Willis asked him bitterly. He did not wait for a reply, ambling down the slope to the village where he began a noisy quarrel with his wife.

'Send my love to T.P., won't you?'

'Feeling bad, little one?'

' Getting your name in the papers?'

Mowbray and Brenda Phillips did not speak to him at all.

He sat still for a long time, watching the planes land and take off. And presently he got up and threw away the cigarette and went down the slope into the village. He ignored the throng outside the Command Post and went across the track to the woman's billet. He knocked on the door and when she came, he said briefly,

' My despatches.'

' Your . . . ?'

' Despatches. Stories I gave you last night.'

' Oh yes, I haven't read them all yet. I want to talk to you about them some time.'

' Quickly. I can get them back in one of these planes. I'll beat 'em to it yet. Talk later.'

' They're not good enough,' she said. She leaned against the door and looked at him smiling, shaking her head. ' Not those you showed me.'

' We'll argue about that later maybe. Give me them.'

' I destroyed them,' she said.

' Listen.' The faint colour rose to his face. ' I'm in a hurry. I want my stories, see?'

' But I destroyed them,' she said, ' really. Perhaps Paula used some for hair-curlers . . .' she turned into the darkness of the cottage. ' Paula, those bits of paper I gave you last night.' She spoke again to the journalist. ' We're very short of paper,' she said.

He moistened his lips. ' You destroyed them?' he whispered.

' I think so, most of them.'

' You wouldn't be fooling?'

' Fooling? No, why should I?'

' You destroyed them . . . just like that?'

217

' Of course. You don't do yourself justice with stuff like that, you know.'

He listened to the blood singing tenuously in his ears. ' So you just . . .'

' Tore them up. Not completely. Into strips. For hair-curlers. Paula,' she turned her head into the room again, the white throat dazzling against the ancient timber of the door.

He heard the girl's voice in the darkness, petulantly, ' But you said I could use them, Erica.'

She turned to him. ' This afternoon I'll tell you what to write,' she said smiling.

He turned away.

The aircraft came and went all the morning and during the early part of the afternoon. Though there were seldom more than two on the ground at the same time the still air was filled with the yarr and burr of the excitable little engines and the village with the voices of the correspondents raised high in protest at all they found and saw and learned there. They were very numerous indeed. When they had all arrived they numbered nineteen and the track between the frightened dwellings was strewn with their equipment, type-writers, recording machines, cameras, paper and blanket rolls. Only the conducting officer had failed to arrive. Maybe his plane had crashed, Mrs. Willis suggested, hitch-ing her corsets a little lower.

' For God's sake leave your corsets alone, woman,' her husband said. His bald pate glistened in the sun.

The staff of the headquarters had been greatly excited by the arrival of the first of the flush, partly because his presence lent their enterprise a solemnity and a consequence that Slater, too deeply immersed in their affairs himself, had quite failed to do, and partly because Slater's dis-comfiture afforded them considerable pleasure; he had not endeared himself to them. The arrival of the second aircraft after an interval of some twenty minutes served as confirmation, unnecessary but acceptable, of the first. The third, they thought, was neither here nor there, while the fourth and fifth bordered on the redundant. Thenceforward, as the total soared steadily to that of the strength of the headquarters, passed it with hardly a backward glance and rose to a figure approaching double that of the entire staff, the emotions of the little gathering at the foot of the slope veered from amazement to anger, from anger to laughter, to boredom, and finally baulked altogether.

' I am numb, dumb and aghast,' Luca Pugnini said.

' You should be happy, general,' the Chief of Staff said viciously. ' This is what you wanted, isn't it? Some friends for Mr. Slater?'

Nobody else spoke.

16

THE PACK roamed the village. The leaders, who were somewhat older and therefore more astute than the rest, at once
sought places in which they might, then or later, curl up
and sleep. The rest entered the kitchen. They snuffled the
floor and uttered little yelps of joy when they came upon
scraps of offal in the corners; when the floor was clean they
followed Maria Pugnini about with piteous eyes and drew
blood from her frightened fingers when she, to humour the
ravenous beasts, offered them morsels of bread and meat. But
it could not continue indefinitely and at last, deeply anxious
lest they might take it into their heads to seize what they
wanted, she left the kitchen and sought the Chief of Staff
with her tale. Feed it to them slowly, he advised her, keep
them satisfied. When she returned to the kitchen all the food
was gone, they had devoured everything, all the sandwiches
she had prepared for the staff, the last loaves of bread. She
burst into tears. For a little while they watched her, tongues
drooping from red mouths and white teeth; when they
were bored with the tears they left her.

The more cautious in the larger body of the pack were
later greatly alarmed when the Chief of Staff told them,
with a certain bitter relish, that they were trapped. There
was a move to quit the place at once, but as they were at
pains to point out to one another, you never knew what
those remaining might run to earth; if one stayed all must
perforce stay. And so they stayed. The quiet hamlet
resounded to their lusty voices. Mrs. Willis bickered wearily
with her mate outside the Command Post, Brenda Phillips,

of whom it was said that she invariably seduced her prey before devouring it, trotted in melancholy fashion from man to man among the staff, and Percy Demetz, Bernard Hendrick and two others, who had settled down in the shade of the mill to a quiet game of bridge, bid sonorously above the aimless clamour of those who sought only casual distraction. Ezzy Allison moved stealthily from door to door and from man to man taking photographs and clicking his tongue appreciatively after every careful shot. Somewhat removed from the crowd the radio correspondent chatted confidentially into a microphone; his measured tones were recorded on a spool of wire, part of the unwieldy paraphernalia he carried with him.

The staff, frightened, outraged by the rude invasion and profoundly aware of its own numerical inferiority, kept out of sight. Only Adrian Bullivant and Crosby were so indiscreet as to show themselves and they were at once encircled by a dozen or more correspondents who made so much noise scrambling over one another's backs to get to the front, trampling their weaker neighbours underfoot and whipping round to snap at any who complained, that the officer and the soldier were unable to make themselves heard at all; presently they were able to sneak away unobserved.

The pack found Otto. The artist was sitting alone on the dusty earth among his pots of bright paint. He flinched a little as they came up to him in a rush. He lowered his arm and looked round the circle of faces timidly. But he understood nothing.

' You just don't like newspapers, that it?'

He shook his tousled head.

' Well, what the hell is it, then?'

He opened his lips to speak, but no sound issued from them.

'Listen, coppernob, you've been waiting for a chance like this for years, haven't you? Come on, then.'

'Air your views, Ginger.'

'So you're a painter?'

'What d'you paint, Rembrandt?'

'Shut your trap, you.'

These two fell out and scuffled a little while in the dust. They seldom hit one another very hard, however.

Then they left Otto and scuttered across the track to the door of the Command Post, where the Chief of Staff had just appeared.

'When's it happening, general?'

'Do we get a press conference?'

'What's a matter wit' de chief's so cagey?'

'What's he like?' Brenda Phillips asked at once.

'Oh, for Chris' sake . . .'

'Cut it out, Brenda.'

'I dissociate myself from that question.'

'Absolutely.'

Ezzy Allison knelt dramatically and took a photograph of the Chief of Staff of the Twenty-third Corps being interviewed by representatives of the Anglo-American Press at his Headquarters in the Mountains, and clicked his tongue with infinite appreciation.

The Chief of Staff cleared his throat. 'You are making the place into a madhouse,' he said.

They fell silent, surprised and offended.

'A madhouse,' the Chief of Staff said, 'a zoo, a jungle.'

'Nasty, eh?'

'Captain Bullivant will tell you all you want to know.'

'You ought to be more polite, mister.'

'Later the Commander will speak to you himself.'

'Just a minute—'

But the Chief of Staff had turned and stepped back into the Command Post without another word.

' Ill-mannered bastard,' Ezzy Allison remarked.

Adrian Bullivant faced them nervously, wishing for a little of his father's inscrutable suavity. Jonathan Bullivant would make short work of them . . . a little flattery, a betrayal or two of other people's secrets, a bland riposte at the expense of one for the amusement of many. But the son's confusion was only increased by the apparent fatuity of their questions, a simplicity that verged on the inane. Indeed, if he had not not known that the pack was directly responsible for the informing of the vast majority of at least the English-speaking peoples of the world he might well have thought them congenital idiots. Their exterior ignorance, in these circumstances, could only conceal some profound inner wisdom, and this was most alarming. He grappled feebly with their questions. They seemed satisfied with answers which seemed to him quite puerile.

Later he attended the press conference.

They sat or lay or squatted on their haunches on the banks of the stream and some dabbled their feet in the water while they waited. They talked among themselves and Mrs. Willis bickered with her husband. All the staff was present, with the exception of Erica, and all the pack, with the exception of Slater. The air was unnaturally still then and the stream sang quietly. The sea of cloud about the mountain shut them from all but the vast unhurried sky and the peak sailing serenely through the wisps of cumulus that seemed to have escaped the mass beneath to straggle northwards with the wind.

The Commander came at last, limping slowly along the track with the Chief of Staff at his side. The pack scrutinised him and Ezzy Allison took a photograph and clicked his tongue. The Commander stood with his back to the stream and addressed them where they sat, the hair above his temples standing on end and his eyes narrowed against the sun.

'I must apologise first,' he began, 'for the poorness of our hospitality—'

'Can't hear,' cried Dicky Willis, greatly irritated by the confidence in the Commander's voice.

'Shut up,' said Mrs. Willis.

'But I can't hear,' her husband retorted. 'I have a right not to hear, haven't I?'

'I don't give a damn whether you can hear or not. A lot of good it would do you anyway. You're only trying to draw attention to yourself,' she told him. 'And if I can hear, you can.'

'If I don't want to hear, I don't have to.'

'For pity's sake,' said another.

In the succeeding clamour Mr. and Mrs. Willis dropped their stridulous voices to a whisper, and continued the argument throughout the conference.

As the hideous din died away the Commander raised his head again. 'We have no food, no communications, and very few men. Doubtless you have already been informed of these matters. I can only offer my apologies. It must be very trying for you to come so far for so little. I think perhaps the office responsible for your movements was misinformed. This evening, however, we shall endeavour to blow up the reservoir in conformity with the Allied plan to trap and destroy the German armies in the valley. So perhaps your time will not have been altogether wasted. If the attack should fail, the Allied armies should be here in a day or two, and you should be able to manage till then. If it succeeds it may be that we shall all be able to escape in the confusion. It is likely that in any case there will be some sort of punitive expedition by way of reprisal, except in the unlikely event of the enemy withdrawing completely.' He hesitated and his eyes ran over the circle of hungry faces. 'When Captain Bullivant has explained his plan of attack . . .' the officer started and flushed . . . 'I will try and answer any questions you may have.'

Brenda Phillips rose to her knees in the grass. ' Commander,' she said, ' would you mind telling us where you got that so attractive limp? Our women readers . . .'

Her clear tones were drowned in a bedlam of voices.

' For Chris' sake.'

' Dry up, Brenda.'

' Give it a rest.'

' Why doesn't somebody strangle that little bitch?'

' I dissociate myself from that question.'

' Absolutely.'

' Change the record.'

She appealed to the Commander. ' I'm just a newspaper woman trying to do a job . . . If these people . . .'

She was not permitted to continue. A young man gave her a sharp nip in the small of the back and she uttered a cry of protest and turned on him.

' Quiet.'

' Will you shut up?'

' I thought we agreed . . .'

The Commander said at length, ' Now, will you be so good as to explain the plan, Captain Bullivant?'

He rose uneasily to his feet and faced them. They scribbled and licked their pencils and flicked the flies from their twitching ears and Mrs. Willis bickered hoarsely with her husband. He began to tell them, sensing the hostility they radiated, about the attack, about how it was broken into phases and how they would try to get on to the wall of the reservoir and one thing and another.

And he was saying to his father:

' But why don't you throw me out? You know perfectly well I hate the whole vile business, that I'm opposed to every move you make. I simply don't understand what you keep me for, I'm not even decorative.'

225

P

'Adrian, I've always had a very considerable respect for the inevitable. I recommend it to you.'

He was sitting upright at the great mahogany desk and spoke quietly with the fixed formal smile he used for recalcitrant employees without families: if they had families they were seldom difficult; he always filled positions of responsibility with men with wives and many children. It was odd, when you came to think of it, that so little remained in the face of the filthy yard in which the man had been born. You would have thought that at least something of its angular vulgarity would have clung to the lines of the mouth. But its origins were unidentifiable. You must learn to recognise the inevitable, he would tell his son, so that you may turn it to account.

'I've practically begged you to throw me out.'

'I am not unaware of your attitude, Adrian. It's very provocative at times.'

'D'you think I shall change my ideas or something?'

He blew a fleck of ash from his sleeve. 'Everything changes, Adrian, if it's human. Your tummy gets empty every so often.' He smiled. 'That's about all that doesn't change, you know.'

'My opinions won't change.'

'It doesn't matter much whether they do or don't, laddie. The extent to which you allow your opinions to affect your advantage . . . that's the important . . .'

'I hate it, dad, I hate every minute of it. I don't fit in and I never will.'

'I'm not stopping you from going, if you want to.' The velvet voice rose a little at the end of each sentence, as it had always done. He smiled slightly.

'I'm not your son, I'm just an investment.'

'I won't argue with you, Adrian, on that or any other score. You'll grow out of it. Be patient with yourself.'

'I'm not a child.'

226

· Then you really should stop talking like one,' his father said gently. ' You'll have a heavy responsibility later on and the sooner you begin adapting yourself to it, the sooner you'll enjoy it. I'd start, in your shoes, by getting a few facts arranged. That politics, for instance, are expressions of opinion and not of law.'

' Who said anything about politics? I didn't.'

' Very well, I did. If you want to have a revolution or something of the kind, and I gather from Judith that you do, go ahead and fix it up. But remember that when it's all over and done with and you've destroyed everything you can lay your hands on, the fellows who'll come out on top will be the fellows like me. Same chaps, another name. They can't follow, they can only lead. You can't destroy me, Adrian lad. People have been trying for hundreds of years. If your society is a sack of potatoes I'd still be the biggest potato in the sack.' He grinned suddenly, mischieviously. ' Eh? That's one of the inevitables.'

And the young man, aware of the supreme truth of his father's words, knowing only that the point at issue was not a matter of politics or social orders or potatoes but a thread in the warp and the weft of the human destiny that he himself could not recognise and certainly could not explain, found nothing to say. It was not really his father from whom he sought escape, but from himself, and there was none. He had to be a fanatic to do what he asked of himself, he had to be able to turn a blind eye to the distant truth and acknowledge only its more immediate illusion and if he could not do this, and he knew he could not, then the necessary fanaticism was not in his nature. He must accept the inevitable, the good and the evil.

' Evil, Adrian? Evil? What evil?'

' The concentration of so much power in the hands of one man, whether benevolent or not.'

' Oh come, you and I are not street-corner agitators—'

'Your road is paved with little envelopes.'

'Bribes, you mean?'

'Presents, little presents.'

'Who is the more to blame, the giver or the recipient?'

'Both equally.'

'That's too easy.'

'Then you don't defend it?'

'Neither defend, nor attack. Accept.'

'Well, I don't. I don't and can't.'

'Then you must follow your conviction, Adrian. Only make sure that you haven't made a mistake.'

And face to face with the mistakes he had made and the disasters in which he had already been involved, his omissions, his errors of judgment in pursuit of his convictions, he wavered. He thought of his wife and their unhappiness for which he was responsible, of the attack into which he had forced a handful of otherwise harmless people and of its terrible consequences, and uneasily he thought of his father's mute distress that his son should scorn as evil and worthless the labour of a long hard life. He did not want to destroy his father, only the thing his father had built. And his father was defending it, as he must. Good or bad there was art in such a labour and the artist grasps at perpetuity, as Jonathan Bullivant looked to his son to catch and hold the flame he had lit. It must be dreadfully galling, Adrian Bullivant had realised, that a man so rich and powerful should have nobody at whose feet he might throw the prizes and know they would be appreciated and loved. Liza wanted nothing. Birmingham. Poor mother, he thought, with her bottles of port in her wardrobe and her fear of the servants and her dream of her husband's ruin—and Birmingham. And it was curious, too, that Jonathan had never taken to himself a mistress, a woman on whom he could rain the diamonds he earned, the fruits of his great endeavour. He remained, so far as Adrian knew, loyal to her as if he were punishing himself for his error, his hastiness in marrying that grotesque girl at all, finding relief in the weight of the burden he forced himself to endure. And then, as though knowing precisely the thoughts that were passing through his son's head at that moment, asking,

'To what, then, if it isn't to me or to your wife or even to yourself, to what in heaven's name do you owe allegiance?'

The young man answered desperately, 'To a dream. Something you don't know anything about, an earnest little dream of the worthwhileness of some sort of honour and dignity and integrity . . .'

'Grow up, boy, grow up.'

'It's indestructible—'

'It's not even relevant.'

'It's always relevant.'

He slams the heavy door as he leaves the study.

And then, on the banks of the stream on the mountainside, the questions beginning:

'When's the war going to be over?'

'That's a fool question if ever I heard one,' her mate remarks.

'Who asked your opinion?' She turns on him.

'I'm telling you.'

'Why don't the partisans stop squabbling among themselves, they might get something done then, mightn't they?'

The Commander continues to shake his head, smiling.

'Is it true that no personal relations are permitted among members of partisan bands?'

'She means sexual, she's shy.'

'Our women readers . . .'

'Got any new war aims, general?'

Till finally: 'Could it be arranged, please, for the attack to take place at dawn instead of at dusk? I represent a morning paper and I haven't had a decent break this war.

The afternoon papers always get the best stories . . .' the man continues to expound his plaintive theory but his voice is no longer audible as the pack gives tongue. The Commander waits patiently, immovably, but the clamour continues without abatement. Indeed, it seems there will never be an end to it, and presently he steals away.

17

IT WAS SHORTLY after the Commander's unobserved withdrawal that Slater came down the bank of the stream with his hands in his pockets and a cigarette dancing between his lips. He joined the fringe of the crowd, drawn by the clamour, and listened. Almost at once he heard a remark that piqued him and he opened his mouth to make a sharp rejoinder. But then he thought better of the intention and said nothing. Several times during the twenty minutes he listened he was tempted to throw his weight with one side or the other, but each time he checked himself and held his peace. It was certainly entertaining, if it did not concern you. Perhaps there was something in the woman's suggestion after all; maybe she was right. But whether it was for him or not, that was another matter. It needed thinking about, weighing, considering. It would be a dangerous step; there would be no going back, once he had begun; the boats would be burned. In a little while he left them and went back to the billet.

He sat on the edge of Adrian Bullivant's mattress and set up the typewriter on its lid. He ran a sheet of paper into it. He always thought better and more clearly with the machine open and ready. He scratched his chin and fingered the bright new pimple that was forming on his cheek beneath the scar of the old one and stared at the clean paper in the machine.

She was no fool. He would never forgive her for her unwarrantable destruction of his despatches; but she was no fool, not by any means. He tried to recall what she had said, in her own words—

'You will have to carry corruption to the point at which

it becomes the absolute of moral rectitude,' she had said. A woman after his own heart. ' And the first essential is complete detachment. You must be, in that respect, in-human.' Well, that was easier said than done. She went on, ' Begin by recognising your own attitude to your work. No false virtue about it, you're interested in your own career and nothing else.' He had interrupted there and she waved aside his interjection. ' All right, international newspapers, then, but always owned and controlled by Mister Slater. So. Now you say to your hundred million readers, Come with me. Come with me, I'm a cheap little rogue like many another, with a vast ambition. Confess it, tell it openly, frankly, flatly; you'll have a public practically at once. Then you begin.' There was no nonsense about her, cer-tainly, none whatever. ' Then you start to write about—yourself and your work and about the people who think and live as you do : but these only indirectly, you under-stand : you mustn't be caught out in libel or calumny. Simply confess yourself as typical of your kind and then by achieving your own betrayal you achieve also theirs.' And the Lord only knew how the city editor would react; with a laconic cable of dismissal, as like as not. No right-minded agency would so foul its nest as to offer its own clients material lampooning—by inference, condemning—them-selves and their service. And then what? after dismissal. ' Then,' she told him, ' then you offer your notorious services to a privately-owned newspaper.' There were such, a few, such as would print what he had to write, lonely pirates in the ocean of complacency who would be attracted by the piquancy, if not by the loftiness of motive, of his despatches. ' Walk down the hill now,' she said, ' and listen to your-self. They're having a conference. Go and listen to it. Join them as you normally would, only keep your mouth shut. And listen. Watch yourself when we attack the reservoir this evening. There's the true and significant story of the attack . . . you. Not the futile death of a handful of paranoics, but the antics of yourself and your colleagues in relation to it.' He began then to understand what she meant. ' Use this evening as a preliminary canter. By all means describe the attack, if you must, but put it in its context by describing also yourself and what you have to do and say and what your colleagues do and say. You're writing about Mister Slater, before, during and after. Your readers must see the attack through Mister Slater's eyes, all of it.' He was very doubtful.

' Suppose it fails and I've made myself look a fool and a scoundrel for nothing?'

' Then,' she said, ' you will have at least the satisfaction of martyrdom.'

He shook his head. ' Crusading isn't my particular cup of tea.'

' The kind of power you're after,' she said, ' is never the result purely of hard work. It's a gamble. You must remember always that you are a scoundrel and that you'll look a scoundrel—for a time. Later they'll understand that what you're really doing is conducting a private and most heroic war against a dragon whose nature they never suspected. And then great virtue will accrue.' He would wear the shining armour of the crusader, she said. He would probably become something of a messiah for a lot of people, with a column in every paper in the world; and how far was it from there to ownership? There was no saying how far he might not go. ' Perhaps to heaven.'

He grinned. ' What you're really suggesting is that I clean up the press a bit, that's it, isn't it?'

' It's a contingency that shouldn't be lost sight of,' she admitted.

' Well,' he said at last, ' I never thought there was any future in virtue before.'

She answered, ' It has several possibilities.'

18

ERICA DIED in childbirth in May of the year following the attack. There were seven bullet-holes in her body, including the severe graze on the left side of her head which had been caused most probably by a ricochet, when she was carried into the hospital by the allied stretcher-bearers that night. The right femur was broken high up and the left knee quite shattered; she had sustained also a bullet through the hand and one through each shoulder and the chest in a kind of triangle. One might have thought she had been propped up in some way and subjected to a burst of machine-gun fire at fairly close range.

The surgeons who interested themselves in her case did not understand why she was still alive and even less why she continued to live. The wounds were of course re-dressed and further plasma units administered and she was heavily injected with morphine so that her last hours, if she recovered consciousness, and she seemed all the time to hover between life and death, might be less painful to her. She did not die, however, and remaining unconscious herself, was unable to throw any light on the phenomenon.

The question of identity became troublesome. None came to claim her, there were no callers of any kind. Her clothes bore no mark. In the course of time the nurses came to call her among themselves, somewhat irreverently, Olga, and the name took the general fancy to such an extent that within a few days she was not known by any other. The fact that they dropped upon a name having a certain Russian flavour was attributable mainly to the detection by

Dr. Kuhlaj, the old Czech surgeon, whose patient she finally became, of a distinctly Mongolian cast to the bones of the shrunken face; perhaps Italo-Byzantine, he admitted later, but then it was much too late and she was irrevocably Olga.

The weeks lengthened into months and the broken body clung to life with extraordinary persistence. Though with the passing of the delirium and the slow healing of the lesser wounds the body came to bear functionally some semblence to life, in every other respect she appeared to be dead. The house physician stuck to his theory of sleeping-sickness, but it had no other adherents. She never spoke, nor moved, nor opened her eyes. There was a good deal of speculation among the surgeons as to the exact nature and extent of the wound on the side of her head : chronic con-cussion, total paralysis of the nervous system; only Kuhlaj abstained from conjecture. He would stand at the bedside for hours, watching her, watching the dead face. Sometimes the thin blue lips wore a faint smile, a smile of such genuine amusement that the old man found himself sometimes smiling with her as though they had a little joke in common.

It occurred to him before long that she wanted to die, was indeed trying to die, and only the body refused. He studied her with this theory in mind and grew more certain of its truth as the time passed and the likelihood of signs and symptoms to support the notion diminished. And for some reason she was amused. He was conscious of the struggle within her as he stood at the bedside and looked down on the inscrutable face and the torrent of pale dull hair that streamed down the pillow from beneath the ban-dage with which the head was still swathed, a struggle that was little and mute and yet titanic, like that of the trapped scorpion which stings itself to death. But she could not.

It was not until the end of the fifth month that the

nurses, busy about their routine jobs of washing those patients unable to wash themselves, noticed the shape of the belly. They exchanged startled glances across the bed and sent at once for Dr. Kuhlaj. The old man did not take long over his examination. He reprimanded the nurses for not having noticed it long before, ordered a slight change of diet, and left her. He was very thoughtful for the rest of the morning. In the common room shortly before lunch, however, he announced at random that he had discovered why Olga was still alive.

The hum of conversation petered out and they turned to look at the old man by the fire. He waited patiently for the question they must ask and without which he would not continue.

'She won't die just yet, either,' he added.

And when the necessary question was asked, he said:

'She's going to have a child.'

They smiled incredulously.

'Well?' he demanded.

They were more or less accustomed to the old man's idiosyncracies and held their tongues.

'You skitter of godless louts . . . explain that one away.' He got to his feet and went into the dining room smiling to himself, very well pleased.

Thereafter he was rarely far from her bedside watching the slow intake and exhalation of breath . . . 'renewing my faith in God,' he told the house physician. She would not die, he said, before the child was born. It would have to be a Cæsarian, he thought, almost certainly, there was no power left in the muscles. He looked down at the still face and wondered what she would think if she knew.

The snow fell silently in the yard and there was the bitter rasp of shovels all day on the ashphalt beneath and then more snow and more till there was nothing outside but silence and then the shovels again and the slow erosion of the dirty grey heaps in the rain. The crocuses blossomed timidly in the window boxes and cast slender shadows across the beds when the sun shone and then over the polished floor. The whole ward would be filled with the pleasant stink of warm wax when they opened the doors in the afternoon to let in the sunlight and wheel the beds out on to the bald terrace where the sparrows waited. Later there were swallows in the evening.

He often asked himself what was the nature of the life she was living in her mind, for that she was doing so he had no doubt whatever; there was a coherence about her, a simplicity he felt in her company he was aware of and able to accept without analysis; sometimes he would tell himself it was so much nonsense, this blessed tranquillity he felt at her bedside, and that it was only what he wished to feel and not at all what she offered him; he was thinking himself into it. But he was an old man and very sage and soon gave up the effort to trace its origin : it was there and it mattered little how or why it came. It sufficed that he was glad to be near her. She never moved. She smiled sometimes, but no more. Only once he thought her conscious, or even near to consciousness, but for so short a moment that the illusion was gone before he could overcome the start of surprise, almost of red-handed guilt, he gave when the lids of the eyes lifted suddenly and there was a gleam of light in the misty pools beneath. The nurses had been polishing the floor again—he wished sometimes they would devote as much attention to the patients as they did to that damned parquet —and the slender arrow of sunlight which had pierced the shadows above her bed was dense with the dust that glittered in it and every tiny hair of the soft green blanket where the sunlight lay shone separately like blades of grass on a green hillside. And the eyes watched it as though puzzled and the misshapen hand moved across the blanket towards it. But the light left the eyes almost at once and the lids drooped and she returned to the life in her mind without acknowledgment of any other. After a few days the body began to move a little as the child within her stirred.

Her preparations on the afternoon of the attack had been as slight as those of the remainder of the staff were elaborate—and punctuated from time to time by a certain self-conscious levity, an almost hysterical lightheartedness such as often marks the preparations of children for a long journey. Certainly they would carry a blanket each, as laid down by the Chief of Staff, but there were other belongings of greater importance whose stowage was more troublesome; trinkets and mementoes and oddly-shaped pebbles and all the little items of personal fancy they had collected during the long months and stored away and forgotten; now they came to light again and the owners could not bring themselves quite ruthlessly to discard them and so, magnanimously, gave them away with much running to and fro, and accepted others, so that in the end the sum of their litter remained the same. The village rang with their voices and with the chatter of typewriters as the pack settled down as best it might to compose the preliminary despatches. The four who had been playing bridge in the shade of the mill took up their cards again and continued and Mary and Dicky Willis argued bitterly as they wrote. The staff, busy about its own affairs, did not disturb them. And in the mill there took place another of the many conversations designed by one or other of the parties concerned to ease a strained relationship, to settle an ancient feud. Pierre, tight-lipped and determined, sought out the Divisional Commander.

General Pugnini was in the mill, surveying somewhat wistfully the remnants of his collection.

' Look here, Luca,' the fisherman began defiantly.

Luca Pugnini recoiled, ' My dear fellow . . .'

Pierre, also startled by the harshness of his own voice, cleared his throat and moderated his tone. ' Well, there's something I've got to tell you,' he said doggedly.

' There can be no necessity to shout, surely?' He leaned back against the millstones and, folding his arms, composed himself to listen with an encouraging smile. ' Now then.'

' It's been worrying me a long time,' Pierre said.

' If there's something you wish to tell me, old man, and there is anything I can do, rest assured it shall be done. As for my discretion, shall I say it has been described as proverbial?'

' Thanks very much . . .' he hesitated.

' Well?'

' It's Maria,' Pierre blurted.

The Divisional Commander froze. Horror and embarassment and chagrin fled across his mercurial features and a faint moisture became visible on his shining head. He was very angry. He might have known, he told himself, he ought to have realised what was coming; great heavens, it could scarcely have been plainer. He cursed himself for having blundered so innocently into so guilty a trap and felt a swift eruption of resentment against the Breton who stood before him now with head slightly bowed and the twist of black hair tumbling guilelessly over his eyes. Ingrate! So heedlessly to inflict pain, so clumsily to cause such vexation of spirit was alien to the general and in any case a shabby return, he thought, for the restraint he had shown during the last few months; and once or twice the vulgar affair had been almost too flagrant to ignore. Now to drag it into broad daylight like this where it might no longer be decently overlooked showed an impoverishment of taste from which the general shrank appalled. If your soul is paltry, he held, you should abstain from laying it bare, since the greater your enjoyment the deeper the suffering you may cause your confessor. A man owes himself a secret.

' Maria and me . . .'

' You need say no more,' he told the Breton coldly.

Pierre raised his head. ' I must.'

' I beg you, not another word.'

' I must and will, Luca.'

' Then I fear I cannot listen.' He made a move towards the door but Pierre gripped his arm and swung him back to the stone.

' You shall listen, it's my right.'

The general went pale. ' I am fully aware of the liaison between yourself and my wife,' he hissed.

' No.'

' Yes.'

' I'm her lover,' Pierre said, ' you can't ignore it any longer, d'you hear?'

' Insensitive clod,' Luca Pugnini said dully. There was no escape. Now they must pick over the stinking carcass. ' I'll never forgive you for this,' he muttered, ' never.'

' We love one another,' Pierre said simply.

The Divisional Commander raised a haggard face. ' How can you do this to me?'

' We couldn't help ourselves, Luca.' He was deeply moved.

There was a long silence in the mill. Outside they heard the hum of the engine of the armoured car and the garrulous prattle of the typewriters and the song of the stream in the great blades of the millwheel beneath. The fisherman waited patiently. The Divisional Commander stared fixedly at the floor. And presently his face wore a slight smile. He looked up.

' You love one another?'

The fisherman nodded dumbly.

' Then it can't be wrong if you love one another, can it?'

240

His voice rose. 'Can it?'

The fisherman frowned.

'Can it?' Luca Pugnini insisted.

'I suppose not.'

'Of course not. My dear fellow, why in heaven's name did you not mention that before? Don't you understand? If you love one another, who am I to come between you?' He flung back his head and laughed triumphantly showing the shining gold teeth. He threw wide his arms. 'Who am I?'

But the Breton, puzzled and wary, was reluctant to be comforted.

'Come, Pierre, cheer up, cheer up, my dear chap.' He put his arm about the fisherman's shoulder and led him to the door. 'God hasn't given you a love like yours to make you unhappy.'

'I've betrayed your friendship,' Pierre said sulkily, 'and you tell me—'

'Betrayed nothing. Never heard such nonsense. Go to her, go to her and tell her all is well. Tell her what I've told you. She will understand, she is a woman. A trifle simple perhaps, a shade elemental, but a woman.'

And Pierre, dissatisfied, uncomprehending and unhappy, knowing only that he had been swindled in a manner wholly beyond his understanding, left the mill with the sting of the general's slap across his burly shoulder and went slowly down the track towards the kitchen.

The air was still and scented. The deepest inhalation did not satisfy, as though the air had already been used, breathed in by the earth, the grass and the forest. Outside the village there was an immense silence, the frightened unhappy immobility that precedes a violent storm. The clamour among the old dwellings was small and lost in the spaces of the sky. It would rain, the Chief of Staff predicted, it would certainly rain. Upwards from the clouds below them in the valley, or out of a clear sky? He ignored the question: it would rain, that was all. He looked at the big silver watch he lugged from his pocket; it was ten minutes past five. At seven o'clock the first party would move out of the village towards the reservoir.

At twenty minutes to six Erica left her billet followed by Paula who was carrying a bundle of clothing in a blanket. She turned quickly away from the street and led the girl down the steep incline between the cottages so that she might not be seen and followed by the pack. Until then she had not been noticed but she was well aware that as soon as she showed herself she would be harried and pestered until she had told them a string of lies about herself, an excruciation for which she had neither the time nor the stomach. She took the girl by the hand and finally the bundle from her slight shoulders so that they might move faster. Paula, frightened, ignorant of the purpose of the journey, wept pettishly. They stumbled down the mountainside towards the clouds in which the minefield lay.

The fringe of the mist clung raggedly to the earth; wisps of grey cumulus drifted along the edge, for the air was stirring. But inside, in the mist, there was no movement. Where it was shallow the light was pale and golden; as they went on slowly down the slopes it turned grey and dark and the heavy moisture clung to their clothes. Erica was grateful for its density; the girl held fast to her hand.

She was confident of finding the gap in the minefield. If Father Domenicus had used it so long and apparently with ease it must surely be marked, at least by the passage of his feet; the grass would be a little threadbare, the wire would bear traces of movement or interference of some kind. When the tangle of dannert came up out of the mist she turned to the left and led the girl along the wire slowly.

'Where are we going?' Paula whispered.

'Ssh.'

Below the fence there was another entanglement, running parallel. She supposed the mines lay between them, buried not far beneath the turf. They walked along the wire, their feet whispering in the sodden grass. Nothing changed; the black wire trailed across the slopes without a break. They walked for nearly twenty minutes and at the end of that time Erica knew they were lost. Certainly she knew the way back to the village—straight back up the mountainside; and to Ronc—straight down; but where the gap might lie she could not tell. When they had reached the wire Erica had turned to the left, but only instinctively; she might equally well have gone to the right. They turned and walked back the way they had come.

' Where are we?'

Erica did not reply. The white walls receded shyly, keeping their distance. There was nothing else to see, only the wire and the grass. She began to watch the earth between the belts of wire. Almost at once she found what she wanted, a place where the earth had been disturbed. She stopped and narrowed her eyes; quite distinctly there were circular patches of turf slightly yellow in colour, discoloured by the mines beneath. She memorised the pattern and withdrew up the slope a little way, and then back to the wire, the girl watching her and following her to and fro. When they were close to the wire nothing was visible and the grass was a uniform green; a few yards away the difference in colour was quite clear. She committed the design to memory, closing her eyes to try it in her mind, and opening them, looked again. She thought she knew it then.

' Listen, Paula.'

Paula knew what was in the woman's mind. ' No, Erica . . .' her voice rose to a wail.

' Be quiet and listen to me carefully.'

' Erica, I'm afraid.'

She told the girl to climb on to her shoulders and bent forward a little so that the girl might clamber on to her back. 'All right, now get down.' Paula slid from her back and stood trembling at her side.

'Get a blanket out.' Together they knelt over the bundle and pulled out a blanket. 'And another.' She folded the blankets together.

'Stop shaking,' she told the girl.

'I'm cold,' Paula said. Her face was very white but the sounds in her throat had ceased and the tears had dried in her eyes. Erica glanced at her. 'That's a good girl.' She went down the slope to the place where the mines were visible and threw the blankets across the wire. They settled uneasily there.

'Now give me the bundle.'

She swung the bundle and pivoted on her toes and flung it. It fell heavily in the lower fence, on the other side of the minefield.

'Now listen. I am going to lie on the wire. You will walk over me as far as you can and then stand perfectly still. You understand? Then I shall take you on my back and carry you to the other side.'

Paula looked at her wide-eyed.

'You understand?'

'Why are you doing this?'

'Never mind about that. When we get to the other side, you'll go straight down the hill till you come to Ronc. Go to the priest and wait there. I will come later.'

'Erica . . .'

She threw off the girl's hands and went back a little way, narrowing her eyes again so that she might not forget the pattern. Then she ran towards the wire and Paula screamed and clapped her hands over her open mouth. Erica threw herself on to the blankets and the wire sagged under her weight; she seemed to bounce once or twice and

244

then lie still with her head buried between her arms and the long shining hair spread across her shoulders. Paula heard her calling.

'Walk over me now.'

'I can't.'

'Do as you're told.'

'Erica, I'll hurt you.'

'Walk over me.'

The girl stumbled over the prostrate body and stood in the wire beyond the woman's head while she got to her feet with blood on her face and arms and the wire rising about her. She picked herself free of the barbs that clung to her clothes through the blankets and stepped clear of the wire. 'Get on to my shoulders.'

Paula began again to weep and her teeth chattered loudly. She climbed on to the bent back and wound her arms about the woman's neck. She closed her eyes. Erica carried her across the little space between the fences and set her down in the wire on the other side. Then she turned and looked at her footprints in the wet grass. Paula retched mournfully and shuddered from head to foot.

'Now. You needn't think I'm going to lie down again, my girl, because I'm not. Step on the wire after me. Come along, hold my hand. There.'

The wire sprang up about them and the barbs struck their arms and legs viciously and once Paula's face, leaving a red weal across her chin. It took a long time to get through the fence. Then the girl retrieved the bundle of clothing from the wire and waited for Erica to step out of the entanglement and join her.

'Come here to me,' Erica said.

Paula went to her.

'I'm not coming any further, Paula, not now.' The voice was strangely lifeless in the mist.

'Erica.' The panic rose swiftly to her eyes.

' You're free now, d'you understand?'

The girl shook her head dumbly, looking up into the cold dark eyes. ' No . . .' she whispered.

' Go straight down the hill and ask for the priest.'

' No !' She uttered a scream. The mist sparkled in the fluffy hair like rain on a spider's web. She reached out to grasp the hand Erica held to her, but the wire sprang up across her breasts and she fell back.

' You're free.'

And then the woman turned and began to force her way back through the wire towards the minefield, grasping the malevolent stuff with her big hands, treading on it, tearing herself free of the barbs. The girl screamed behind her. This time in the field she made no attempt to remember the pattern of the mines but followed simply her own footsteps in the wet grass, crouching from time to time the better to see the contrast between that which had been disturbed and that on which the moisture still lay thickly. The screams were already muffled a little in the fog.

' Erica, don't leave me . . .'

She went on slowly through the second fence. This time she fell twice and when she reached the other side her hands and arms and legs were covered in blood and the left leg of her slacks hung by a thread from the thigh. She pulled the upper blanket from the wire and threw it on to the ground and sank on it. She lay still for a long time listening to the beating of her heart and the girl's unintelligible cries.

When she came out of the mist, walking slowly back up the mountainside, the sun was still shining. She felt its warmth on her face and neck.

Her absence from the camp had not been noticed. She slipped into her billet and changed her clothes and bathed the cuts in her hands and arms and legs. The shouting had ceased and there was only the tapping of a typewriter a

246

long way away. The sun was low and turning red and the paper she had glued over the glassless window thrummed in the gently rising wind. She went across the track quickly and into the Command Post.

' I've got rid of Paula,' she said.

The Commander looked up. ' How?'

He looked at her steadily. ' I found a way through the minefield,' she said.

' Won't she find the same way back?'

' No.'

His eyes dropped to the bandages she had tied about her hands. They were working loose and already the blood was showing pink through the flimsy material. ' Shall I tie those bandages?' he asked gently.

' That would be kind,' she said.

He bent over the hands and retied the bandages carefully. She stooped suddenly and kissed his head.

' And that is unkind,' he said.

' Forgive me.'

He released the hands and leaned back. ' There, that should be all right.' He raised his eyes to hers. ' You're quite sure?' he said quietly.

She nodded. ' Quite sure.'

' You're not making a mistake?'

' No.'

' Is it for my sake?'

She raised her shoulders beneath the blouse. ' Both.' She smiled faintly. ' Yours and mine.'

' I would gladly—'

' We shall be moving off in a few minutes,' she said.

' Yes.' He drew a deep breath. ' It's going to rain.'

' The wind's rising.'

The Chief of Staff entered. He stopped short when he saw the woman. ' Pardon.'

' What is it?'

'General Pugnini is ready.'

'Tell him I'm just coming.'

She followed him out into the street.

Already the sky was dense and the sun a great red ball above the floor of cloud in the west. The smoothness of the floor was already broken and wisps of red cloud trailed aimlessly through the restless air. Below the mill the first party was assembled, the three men and the woman, with the pack about them like boys at a bicycle race. Luca Pugnini was laughing immoderately, fumbling for wit and finding only banality; he was as bulky now, with the rolled blanket strapped across his shoulders, as he was tall. Maria, festooned with belts of ammunition, looked frightenedly at the correspondents and simpered when they spoke to her, while Pierre on her left, leaning on the gun, stared darkly at the Divisional Commander. Otto, head and shoulders above the throng, seemed remote and detached from all that passed.

A little way away from the rest Adrian Bullivant and Crosby leaned against the armoured car and watched Luca Pugnini shepherding his party into single file.

'Christ, I don't know . . .' Crosby muttered.

They bristled with weapons and ammunition and blankets and bundles of clothing. Small parcels swung from their belts when they moved.

'A bloody tragedy, that's what this is,' he said.

The officer did not speak.

Luca Pugnini raised his eyebrows to the Chief of Staff and the Chief of Staff turned to the Commander. The Commander nodded. Then there was a lot of shouting and waving and the photographer took some photographs lying on his belly looking up and little Josef had to be held back by force as the party moved away and over the hump of the bridge towards the open country beyond. The three men and the woman bent to their clumsy burdens and

248

shuffled through the dust on the bridge and turned to wave. Then they were small against the great spaces waving and calling.

'Makes you sick,' Crosby said.

Bullivant wished only that it was time to get into the armoured car and drop the turret over his head and drive at a perilous speed down the mountainside into the merciful sea of mist where it would be too dark to see anything and too late to stop it. Slater came towards him with a grin whose quality the officer understood only later to be lascivious; and later he did not believe it had been so.

'Now we're off,' the journalist said.

'I wish you as much joy of it as I wish myself,' Adrian Bullivant said briefly.

Crosby said, 'I'm just in the mood for you. If I were you I'd get the hell out of here.'

The journalist's face straightened. 'Getting a bit above yourself, aren't you?'

'Am I?'

'Better watch your step.'

'Oh? Why?'

'Save it till later,' Adrian Bullivant told them.

'Because,' said Slater smiling, 'just because.'

Crosby pushed himself away from the vehicle. 'I didn't ought to do this,' he said, jabbing his fist into the journalist's face, 'but now I've done it.' He leaned back against the vehicle.

Slater turned pale and a trickle of blood ran from the corner of his mouth.

Adrian Bullivant spoke sharply to Crosby, 'What the devil d'you think you're doing, man?'

'I socked the bastard, sir,' Crosby said.

'That's the second time,' Slater said. 'One each, eh?'

'Get into the car,' the officer told Crosby.

Crosby turned and climbed into the vehicle and Adrian

Bullivant said to Slater: ' I'm very sorry that happened.'

' I imagine.'

' The man will be punished.'

' You can leave that to me.' He wiped the blood from his chin, smiling.

' He'll be dealt with in the proper way.'

Slater looked at him. ' You bloody sanctimonious little upstart,' he said softly. He went away on his toes towards the crowd at the bridge where the second party was preparing to move. The officer swung round to the car; Crosby was leaning out of the turret smoking.

' That was a bloody fool thing to do, wasn't it?'

' I hardly touched him.'

' You ought to be horse-whipped.'

' Do him good. Did me good, I know that.'

' Crosby, for heaven's sake when will you realise you can't put things right just by socking chaps in the mouth?'

' Tell me another way.'

' Showing off to yourself, that's all it is.'

They said a great deal more, but it was this last remark that came back to Crosby's mind, a long time afterwards, when Mrs. Chubb used the identical words, and then he was puzzled to know where he had heard it before. The first time it had slipped from his consciousness with no more of a stir than any other casual observation might make in an argument; the second time, he began to wonder if that was really how it must seem to other people. It worried him, it was so palpably wrong. Such a motive for his behaviour had never occurred to him. Good Lord, was that what it looked like? Showing off to himself? After all this and Chubb and the rope that was waiting for him now? Showing off? He was suddenly desperately anxious to convince the unhappy woman that it was not like that at all, she was wrong, terribly wrong. For her own sake and for his, Crosby's, sake. It was of tremendous importance suddenly, sitting with her in the neat rectangular room with the bit of Delft on the mantelpiece, that whatever he had done to her she must understand he had not done it for that. She must believe him, else the whole ghastly business were without a single coherent feature. Chubb had died for nothing if that was what she thought, and Crosby would hang not for his convictions but for his petty vanity. He felt sick at the thought and, now for the first time, frightened of death. The light-heartedness he had been feeling during these last few days, the sense of freedom, of release from the burden of a lifetime, gave way to horror. He must make her understand, so that his faith in himself was not swept away. The desire to convince her became a yearning that emptied his stomach and sent its emptiness rocketing to his head while he groped and fumbled for the word that would silence the lethal tongue she wielded. Maybe she understood something of his despair and the reason for it; if she did she gave him no comfort. She telephoned for the police.

Only Iris did not care. Iris would not even listen. It made him very angry and impatient that she would not listen to what he was saying and give a reasonable reply, express a considered opinion. He had only a few minutes with her, for they were close on his heels, and all she said time after time till it drove him crazy and he began to shout, was:

' It's all my fault, Jim. My fault, Jim. It would never have happened if it hadn't been for me,' with the tears streaming down her face. He might not have been there at all. Both the words and the voice had the quality of a prayer too often used, of a chant that has lost its significance. He felt himself outside her, already dead and she was mourning his death. ' It's all my fault, my fault, my fault . . .'

He took her by the shoulders and shook her and shouted.

'For pity's sake, listen,' he cried, 'I'm asking you a question. Why did I do it? Why?' He dropped his voice to a whisper, hoping to penetrate the veil of tears with the urgency of sibilation, 'Why did I kill old Chubby, eh?'

'You didn't do it, Jim. I did it.'

'Was it because I was showing off to myself?'

'I went and saw Mrs. Chubb and told her, told her it was me.'

'Answer me, Iris.'

'I did it.'

'Iris, for Chris' sake,' he cried.

'The kettle's boiling,' she said, 'your tea's nearly ready.'

'Tell me just this, just this one thing . . . did I do it to show off to myself?'

'Your tea's been ready every afternoon, Jim. Ever since.'

'God damn the tea. Listen, for the last time. Listen to me.' He gripped her by the shoulders again. 'Look at me. Look straight at me. There. Now.' The swollen eyes lit unsteadily on his face. 'I've got to know why,' he said slowly, 'I've absolutely got to know why you think I did it.'

She shook her head. 'It's not you, Jim. It's me. It's all my fault.'

He dropped his face into his hands and rocked himself to and fro while she ran her fingers over his hair. Then he heard the car draw up outside in the street and he was gone, out through the kitchen into the yard and over the walls one by one behind the houses all the way down to the railway.

The second party had left, shuffling over the bridge to the wide green land in the tracks of the first which had already vanished beyond the shoulder of land that linked the great spur with the mountain, the Chief of Staff and Slobadov and Hans and Roberto one behind the other. Now only the third remained. The pack encircled them, seeing Erica now for the first time. She shook her head

252

sadly and told them in excellent English that she did not understand English and they were deeply hurt. The Commander watched the second party. And when he saw the Chief of Staff approaching the copse that lay at the foot of the shoulder of land between the spur and the mountain he said to Erica that they might start now and hoisted the machine-gun to his shoulder. She took the machine pistol and the ammunition and the Commander took little Josef's hand and they went towards the bridge. The pack gave tongue and the photographer took many photographs lying on his belly. The man and the woman and the child went over the bridge and out on to the flat land. The wind stirred the dust on the track and the cloud which had hung heavily about the towering wall of the peak all the afternoon now shifted a little and clung streaming to the summit.

The correspondents gathered together their property and shouldered it; since the majority had elected to carry their baggage with them, all were forced to do likewise. They followed one another over the bridge, shouting and crying to one another to wait, wait for me, and jockeying for position. Soon they had all gone and were far out on the plain, the Chief of Staff and his party very small in the distance, then the Commander and the child and Erica, and finally, strung out and lumbering beneath their clumsy burdens, the pack.

It was quiet in the empty hamlet then. The Commander's mare cropped the turf behind the kitchen. A wisp of blue smoke spun about the chimney on the wind. And as Bullivant and Crosby threw away their cigarettes and climbed into the armoured car, the storm broke across the mountainside and the sun was obscured.

19

THE RAIN did not fall till later, when the wind had subsided somewhat. First came the wind and then the lightning and then the scudding purple clouds and the rain. For a few minutes the wind was very strong and fell upon the mountainside with a wail of fury and the force of an avalanche. The forest staggered under the blow and the great trees cracked and strained and some fell, bringing down their neighbours with a rending of outflung arms. The grass lay flat and the spume of the cataract fled across the plain before the whip. In the village slates clattered from the broken roofs among the rubble and a wall collapsed without a sound and the mane of the Commander's mare, silver in the murky light, tossed wildly about the eyes of the lonely animal as it plunged against the tether; the dust hissed on the trembling flanks and rolled on across the open spaces. In the kitchen the embers of the dying fire spun with the débris on the floor and some escaped to join the frightened litter that scurried along the street towards the bridge, Otto's bright scarf and a cap and the empty tins and the torn shirt that had belonged to Erica and a football. And at last the sea of white cloud broke, recoiled from the mountainside and the wind, catching it, flung the mists upwards and away to the empty sky jostling and bumbling through the dingy spaces. For a little while the mountain was enveloped. Then it was gone and the vapour trailed from the roofs for a minute or two.

It was about that time, when the lightning began to play about the peak and the thunder rumbled sonorously above the forest, that the first party came within sight of the wall of the reservoir. Vapour still clung to the lee side of the spur and visibility was variable; but they could see the tiny figures on the wall quite well. They were extraordinarily active.

It would do no harm, the Divisional Commander thought, to attract some attention; his party was still a thousand yards from the wall, and so neither side was exposing itself to great danger by firing, always provided that they were gentlemen enough to confine their defence to small arms. Then, later on, they could perhaps advance a little way. The ground over which they must move was ideally suited for movement—roughish, pitted, with rocks and tufts of marsh grass waist high and hollows here and there.

He held up his hand. ' I think we shall stop here and fire a few token rounds,' he said.

They gathered about him, Pierre and Otto and Maria. The Breton observed sulkily that they would never hit anything from where they stood now.

' Just to attract attention,' Luca Pugnini said.

It was a waste of ammunition, the Breton said.

' Just to draw attention to ourselves,' Luca Pugnini explained. It was no use their being here unless the enemy was aware of their arrival.

' I don't like it,' Pierre said.

Nor, in fact, did the Divisional Commander. When it came to the point he found that the idea of inflicting mortal wounds was repugnant to him—on friend or enemy equally. He was no soldier. ' Nevertheless, that is what we must do.'

So they mounted the guns in a row and got down behind them. The wind, less weighty but still brisk enough here below the spur, tugged at their legs. Maria Pugnini sat in the grass behind them and drew the skirts about her bare brown shins and watched. She watched them pull the butts

255

of the guns into their shoulders. Then she put her fingers in her ears.

Pierre shouted suddenly, ' Listen !'

The Divisional Commander lowered the butt of his gun and turned towards the fisherman. ' What is it?'

' The bells.'

The general put his hand to his ear but he could hear nothing but the sighing of the wind in the tall grass and the beating of his own heart. ' I can't hear them.'

' Listen.'

The thunder mumbled among the rifts and crevices of the peak. There was no other sound.

' Imagination,' Luca Pugnini said.

Pierre shook his head. ' I thought I heard the bells,' he said. He raised the butt of the gun to his shoulder. On his left Otto stared across the dusky land and made no move at all.

In the belfry of the church Father Domenicus began the long climb to the tower and the battlements. The splinters in the ancient ladder caught at the skin of the palms of his hands which were already raw and blistered with the bell-ropes and he looked upwards to the square of light as he climbed. He was breathing sterterously and his vest was already moist with sweat and adhered to the small of his back. Even yet the fusty air vibrated with the clangour of the bells and the walls tossed the low sweet music to and fro across the tower. The cassock wound itself about his long legs and he closed his eyes and prayed aloud that he might be given strength to climb faster; he stumbled and flung his arms about the ladder and the drop fell from his nose down through the trembling air to burst on the flag-stones far beneath him.

When he reached the belfry he leaned against the wall above the trap and passed a shaking hand over his face. The bells hummed and the cold air entering through the open arches carried the reverberation hither and thither and out into the waiting wind. In a moment he started for the spiral stair that went up to the battlements, ducking beneath the bells across the rotting lime-splashed beams that groaned under his weight. The pigeons returned to the arches when he had gone.

The weeping girl had found him only a few minutes before the first of the armoured units entered Ronc. He was alone in the dark church, on his knees before the altar where the candles leaned this way and then that in the ebb and flow of the draughts and lit the edges of the great brass crucifix and the tinsel with which the saintly dolls were draped and cast the shadow of the priest far down the aisle to the girl's feet where she stood waiting for the mournful ululation to finish so that she might approach him and tell her story. He had been aware of the muffled sobbing for some time before he turned and got stiffly to his feet.

She told him whence she came and why. He questioned her and she misunderstood the rising tide of alarm in his voice, taking it for anger with her, and wept the more. At last he left her and she heard the footsteps going away from her and then a great door slammed and soon the peal of bells above her head. She sat on the bench that ran beneath the windows. Presently she fell asleep on the bundle of clothes.

The tanks were entering the square at that time so that it was fitting that the bells should toll. The people stood quietly under the trees and watched. The wind played excitedly with the joyous clamour of the bells as the low ceiling of cloud broke and streamed towards the north across the evening sky, and the people stared at the rusty pageantry about the fountains in the square where the armour slithered to a standstill and the oil on the grinning faces that rose from the turrets shone gallantly in the few moments of yellow sunlight that burst through the wild confusion of the sky.

It was with a glad triumphant heart that Father Domenicus stood at the roadside and clapped his blistered hands as the tanks rumbled past him on the road; he moved among his people and encouraged them to applaud also but they were not a demonstrative race and were a trifle ashamed of their priest and slipped away from him. And after the tanks the infantry trudged along the roadside in the dust with their eyes on the ground as though embittered by defeat when it was in fact by victory; they seemed to resent the priest's applause and stared at him expressionlessly. He went with them towards the square, overriding the unease in his mind. No, they must have heard them, must have heard the bells, must have understood their message. In the square he saw the little car return from the road to the reservoir and pull up with a squeal of brakes among the tanks resting there; the driver spoke to the officer and in a minute the turrets went down and the monstrous creatures moved off one after the other along the road to the reservoir. In a few moments the square was empty. It was very surprising, he told himself. He stopped a man running past him and the man said the enemy had launched a counterattack on the reservoir.

He began to run towards the church unwieldily, with the cassock bellying between his legs. As he approached the gate the second column of infantry wound slowly into the village street and he spoke to the young man who seemed to be in command. It was the partisans, he said, who were attacking the reservoir, not the enemy; it was all a ridiculous mistake; they did not know the allies had arrived; they must be stopped.

20

THE OFFICER raised his eyes to the face. Yes, he answered, they must be stopped. His eyes fell again to the gutter and he went on down the road with his men.

Now, on top of the tower, Father Domenicus leaned against the battlement to regain his breath and still the violent beating of his heart. The wind pulled and shoved at him as he looked about for something with which he might attract the attention of the little figures far away on the plain. There was nothing. The old lamp he had once used to signal to the village on the mountain lay useless and rusting in the corner beyond the trap-door. He looked over the edge of the battlements. Beyond the ordered symmetry of the graveyard the infantry shuffled along the road. Now they had stopped and were waiting, leaning on their rifles or sprawling in the gutter. Then there was the row of cottages and the wood and the lower slopes of the mountain where the goats grazed sometimes in the good weather. And on the plain, on the spur itself, he thought, the machine-guns were chattering question and answer one to the other across the level land. Father Domenicus waved. He prayed that they might see his signal and waved his long arms to and fro over his head. He climbed on to the wall itself so that they might perhaps see him against the sky, holding on to the slender flagpole there and waving and shouting hysterically. He pulled the black sash from his waist and waved it back and forth, aware of the futility of it and yet wholly unable to dismiss the possibility that somebody might see and understand.

One soldier saw the figure on the tower. The soldier was lying on the lower slopes of the mountain at the edge of the wood. He watched the priest for a moment and then called to his companion.

'Look at that.'

'Looks like a signal,' the second soldier said presently. He raised his rifle tentatively.

But the first soldier was less hasty. 'Hold on a minute,' he said, 'who's he signalling to?'

'The bastards up there,' said the second. He raised his gun to his shoulder.

'Better make sure.'

'Oh, what the hell.'

'Bet you don't, anyway,' the first soldier said.

'Get him? What d'you bet? Give me that automatic.'

'Too far.'

'What's the betting?'

'Packet of cigarettes you don't.'

'Right.' He pulled the machine-gun into his shoulder and drew a deep breath and held it. The gun leaped as though startled by its own voice. The soldier opened his eyes and peered through the trail of pale blue smoke that drifted from the lock.

'No,' he said. He saw the grey dust start from the battlements at the feet of the man signalling.

'Yes,' said the first soldier.

They saw the waving cease, hesitantly as though he had been reluctant to stop. The black cloth dropped from his hand and fluttered down the wall a little way till the wind caught it fully and carried it away twisting furiously into the trees in the graveyard. The man leaned forward and back and forward again too far and fell, turning over two or three times in the air with the cassock billowing about him, a straight swift drop to earth. There was no sound. The pigeons began to return to the belfry.

' Golly,' said the first soldier.

Old Gregory, summoned from the inn by the bells when they had tolled nearly half an hour before, seduced from his purpose by the tanks and the guns and the marching men, forgetting and remembering, straying but always returning, stupidly drunk, reached the great door of the church a few seconds later. He was very surprised. It was a grievous business. He sat on the cold stones beside the shapeless bundle and wiped his nose on the sleeve of his jacket and shed potulous tears. It was a terrible thing and he did not understand it, but he knew it was grievous, and he wept.

When Adrian Bullivant and Crosby came within sight of the wood there they were fired upon, the little missiles rebounding with a melancholy wail of frustration from the armour of the car. Adrian Bullivant looked at the soldier, his ears singing with the din inside the cabin, but Crosby kept his eyes on the ground ahead. The car pitched wildly over the rocks as they went down through the rough country. They had found the gap in the minefield without great difficulty; the clouds had gone when they reached the wire and the track was easily found; it was wide and the ruts in the wet earth were quite fresh; probably the enemy had used the gap returning from the sweep across the mountainside.

When the second swarm of bullets struck the steep flanks of the vehicle Crosby said:

' Wouldn't be our people, would it?'

Adrian Bullivant said no, not possibly, they were miles away. He wondered idly what he would do now, now that the Allied armies had arrived in Ronc and the attack could not be stopped. He hoisted his handkerchief on the crank handle he found on the floor of the vehicle, a white handkerchief, through the turret, thinking presumably he would go back and try and stop the thing.

The firing had ceased. There were little groups of soldiers standing under the trees on the edge of the wood smoking, looking curiously at the passing car. He would run back up the mountainside to the village, if there was enough petrol in the tank, and then across the plateau to tell them what had happened. They would be very surprised, and amused, he supposed, by the absurdity of it. But of course it was too late already. The horror of being too late welled up inside him and his thoughts shied away but there was only his father and mother and Judith. My mother said that I never should, play with the gypsies in the wood. He sang softly and Crosby turned to look at him strangely in the dusk. For if I did then she would say, oh, you naughty little girl for to disobey. They went down through the wood to Ronc.

The brigadier was non-commital. Yes, he could lend the officer a tracked vehicle of some sort or other, and would see about informing the fellows on the reservoir. Difficult job to stop a battle. He thought it was too late. It was just one of those things. They would do their best, but what could they do? A small flight of aircraft flew low over the village going towards the reservoir and the brigadier's voice was drowned in the noise they made.

The soldier leaning against the fountains in the square —Bullivant had not thought it necessary that Crosby return with him—lit a cigarette and supposed soon he would have to go and find himself a bite to eat and somewhere to sleep. To-morrow he would have to start the long search for his unit. He wondered where they were now and what they were doing, Nicholls and Chubb and Hazeltyne and the rest; sweating it out somewhere, he supposed. He detested the idea of return, detested it, though he supposed it wouldn't be so bad once he was there, things never were. A nameless irrelevent grief clung to all his thoughts. He ran over in his mind all the things he could think of, and places and people, and the grief was on all of them. It never really left him indeed, from that moment on the fountains in the square, onwards, not until he entered the tunnel after he had left Iris and gone down to the railway with the police on his heels. There was no point in flight, there never had been, and from time to time he had promised himself that next time he would stand fast and let them come and take him, but he never did, he always ran. It was only when the ankle he had sprained in the woodyard had gone again and they picked him up off his hands and knees where he had fallen across the greasy sleepers that he understood at last that he was not running away from anything at all, he never had been, never all his life, but towards something.

He had recognised the tunnel as soon as he had entered it. He had been there many times, maybe always, at night, driving himself along it towards the pinpoint of light at the far end in the simple effort to sleep. He recognised the acrid smell of soot, the murmurous silence, the faint glimmer of light along the rails, though he supposed all tunnels to be very much alike in these particulars. It was chiefly the light he recognised; as big as the head of a pin, but white, dazzling. He went towards it again, as he had done before, had always been doing, he thought, and broke into a run and when he slipped on the oil and fell and knew the ankle had gone again, he began to crawl on his hands and knees hearing the voices behind him and the patter of running feet and trying to go faster, not away from them, but so as to reach the end before they might reach him. Already he could feel the wind on his face, clear and strong and cold. His wrist gave way when he put his hand on a blot of oil on the wood and he went flat on his face. He got up again and crawled towards the light. Now it was a full half-circle, blinding his eyes. Already he could see the great trees and the snowdrifts across the track and the shadow of the great escarpment.

'Come along, Crosby.' The voice was very kindly. They lifted him to his feet.

'Yes, this way,' he told them excitedly. He could see their eyes oddly glassy in the darkness. 'Yes.' He turned to go and fell sprawling across the rails and they hoisted him gently to his feet.

'No, sonnie, this way now. Come along.'

His voice rose. 'No, it's this way,' he insisted, 'this way.' He pulled them towards the light at the end of the tunnel.

'Come along, laddibuck.'

'No . . .'

'This way.'

'No.'

They took him back along the sleepers in the dark, their arms about him so that he would not fall again.

21

BUT THE OFFICER went back up the mountainside through the wood in the vehicle the brigade commander had lent him. It was all but dark then and there was light only on the western wall of the peak. It had begun to rain, a thin fine downpour that seemed less to fall that to have been there a long time and only now became visible. He stood up in the vehicle to direct the driver and the rain ran down his glasses and his face into the neck; soon he was wet to the skin. The vehicle pitched sickeningly and skidded on the wet turf from side to side. They went up to the empty hamlet and stopped there in the street and Bullivant told the driver to switch off the engine for a moment, but there was no sound. The wind played among the deserted dwellings and the mare tethered beyond the kitchen whinnied softly. They went on again, over the bridge and out on to the level land where they could move a little faster. Bullivant sank into the seat to warm himself at the fumes rising from the hot engine, bracing his feet against the bucketing over the hummocks, now barely visible in the dusk. He felt quite sleepy in the warmth.

At the foot of the spur he left the driver, telling the man to wait for him, and went through the scrub to the crest on foot. There on the summit and down the slopes to the marsh above the reservoir there were dead trees and the boles of trees squatting among the brambles; scraps of paper littered the ground among them. The pack, he supposed, had used the crest of the spur as a grandstand from which they might observe the course of the battle, sitting on the boles and the tree trunks with their typewriters on their knees. And among the cries and the shouting and the stammer of the guns and the whispering bullets there would be the prattle of the machines and the querrulous tintinabulation of the little bells.

The first he found was Maria. She appeared to be sleeping, but he saw when he bent over her that she had been hit over the heart; she lay on her back in the long marsh grass below the more solid ground where Luca Pugnini and Pierre had first opened fire; there were two small piles of empty cartridge cases on the turf and the marks of their bodies in the grass where they had lain. He wondered whether Luca Pugnini had noticed the loss of Maria when he led his party forward again. Then there was nothing for a long way, no empty cartridge cases, no tracks; then there were a couple of small shell-holes close together. And then the Divisional Commander and Pierre.

The fisherman was alive and muttered in his own language when Adrian Bullivant touched him. Luca Pugnini was beneath and dead. Bullivant wondered how far he had carried the wounded man before he had been hit himself, and why he had carried the fisherman forward, towards the wall of the reservoir, instead of to the rear. He pulled the Breton off. He was more shocked he remembered afterwards, by the way the Divisional Commander looked than by the fact that he was dead: a middle-aged gentleman with dishevelled hair and mud on his face lying in the rain in the dusk.

The officer shouted to the party of men he could see below him with the stretcher, their flashlamps twinkling in the rain, and they came towards him slowly. They bent over the fisherman and Bullivant left them and went on down the incline to his left, where he supposed the others would be. He found the Chief of Staff, the small grey eyes oddly indecent without the pince-nez, and then Hans; Slobadov was not hurt, nor was Roberto; there was a hole in his trilby but it sat firmly and jauntily on his head. Afterwards the doctor thanked him cordially for his services, he was a very able fellow, the doctor said, and Roberto was extremely pleased. Little Josef followed the doctor.

Further still to his left Bullivant saw the little lights swinging over the earth; and then they steadied and he knew it was towards this group he must go. Certainly he might turn now and go back to the vehicle he had left in the scrub on the southern side of the spur and none would question his movements but himself; there was no valid reason why he should drag his feet down the slope towards the circle of light the flash-lamps made, no reason in the world except that it would be easy and a great relief to him and therefore in some obscure way morally indefensible. When an action of that nature was distasteful, then it became a duty, and your duty you fulfilled so that you might afterwards look yourself in the face, for this over-rode all other considerations. He went down towards the lights slowly.

No, they said, glancing up at the tall figure, they had found nobody yet who answered to that description, only this woman who was dead, or dying. The relief he experienced then was blessed, but he knew he must search the plain himself, there was no way out. He wandered across the dark country seeking the body for quite a long time, but he found no sign of it. Later he would have to organise a search party and comb that quarter of the battlefield, he told himself. He went back to where they were and stood over the motionless woman while they administered the plasma units and dressed the wounds by the light of the flash-lamps they focussed on her. She moved once and sighed. The falling rain glittered in the yellow light and the faces of the men shone eagerly against the darkness behind them.

It was there on the plain, Kuhlaj said, that the child was born. The processes of nature dictated a certain lapse of time for gestation and delivery, but as far as Olga was concerned the commonplace notions of time and space were not operative and they could take it or leave it, he added belligerently. The staff listened to him with the amused tolerance they normally allowed the old man. It irritated him. If they require proof, he told them, they had but to harken to that delirium : she died on the plain beneath the mountain. Certainly, from the few audible and intelligible words that bubbled now from her lips—the first sounds she had uttered since her admittance to the hospital—you might have thought she was still lying on her back in the wet grass with the blood flowing out of her as fast as it flowed in from the bottles. She was crying out at the pain of wounds long healed and calling urgently to somebody she called Commander and then to somebody to hold the gun she was firing and then to her mother and a person who must have been a dancing master of some kind.

' Come and listen to Olga,' Kuhlaj told the house physician. He was tremendously excited. ' Quickly, quickly.'

They listened.

' There you are, you see. What did I tell you? She's still on that damned battlefield, she's never left it. She's in the moment of death, dying of multiple wounds. Should have died months ago really. She is dead, now, to all intents and purposes. It's suspension of time.'

When she was wheeled out of the ward with the rubber tyres of the table whimpering on the polished floor and all the other patients staring from their beds, Dr. Kuhlaj walked at her side down the long white corridor towards the lift with his hand resting on the edge of the table she lay on and a foolish complacent smile on his lips. He nodded happily to the nurses.

But the muscles were weak and bed-ridden and alone they were insufficient. Without her conscious help they could not accomplish a natural delivery and it became necessary to use the knife. Under the knife the broken body yielded the child, since it must, but then there was no life remaining in it.

The Commander had thought her dead and when he saw the stretcher-bearers working over the field and knew they must find her soon he left her and went back through the long marsh grass towards the scrub and the spur. His leg ached mercilessly and he moved only with considerable effort, bracing his hand against the muscles of the thigh to still their fluttering. The rain streamed down the broad face and dripped from the jowl to the sodden shirt. In a little while he was counting the strides he took and swearing to himself he would not rest except at every hundred. There was no need for haste, there was plenty of time, but it occupied his mind and kept him moving. He would go as far as the ruined shepherd's hut on the brow of the spur and there rest for a bit, he promised; he could see it already, a shapeless irregularity against the skyline; he had ridden past it many a time; once he had heard the sharp shrill whoop of a marmot from there, somewhere down among the rocks.

Then he was climbing. He beat time to the slow rhythm of his gait, blowing out his cheeks like a trumpeter. It was a long way, a long climb, and the scrub was littered with bramble and tree-stumps and rotten branches pallid as ancient bones against the black earth. He raised his head when he heard the sound and saw the light in the door of the cabin.

The journalist half rose and the machine slipped from the lid between his knees and the candle lurched and he put out a hand to catch it. He sank back, grinning.

'Gave me a start,' he said.

He replaced the candle on the framework of the type-writer and settled it firmly on the lid. Then he looked up at the man in the doorway. 'Wet?' he said. He touched the spot on his cheek and said, 'You look wet.'

The Commander leaned against the door, the rain shining on his face and in the hair, and looked down at the young man.

'Didn't go too well, did it?' Slater said.

He settled again to the machine and lit a cigarette at the candle. He inhaled deeply. 'No good looking at me like that,' he said at length, 'wasn't my fault, was it?'

The Commander's hand moved to the broad black belt about his middle and the thumb was hooked in it so that the fingers fell limply across the belly. He looked at the journalist with expressionless eyes.

Slater frowned. 'Well?'

The Commander did not speak.

Slater said angrily, 'What the hell's up with you? Either come in or go away, for God's sake.'

The Commander did not move. He might have been alone, thinking.

Slater grinned and moistened his lips. 'War of nerves, that it?' He shook his head. 'Wasting your time.'

He waited, leaning back against the beams of the wall watching the Commander reflectively.

'Cigarette?'

The Commander looked at him without expression.

'Cigarette?' He extended the carton.

He stuffed the carton back into his pocket. 'Don't, then.'

Then he cried, 'I didn't make the bloody decision, did I?' violently. 'Did I?'

The Commander did not reply. Slater shrugged his shoulders and read through what he had written and in a moment began to type again. The Commander turned from the door and went out. The journalist paused to look at the square of darkness where the man had been; the raindrops shone as they fell across it.

When the Commander reached the village on the edge of the plateau he was very tired indeed. The crickets were trilling sweetly in the kitchen where the fire had been. Beyond the wall the mare whinnied and stamped. He went out to her after a time and let her nuzzle his chest, feeling the warm wet lips in the palm of his hand. It was only when he led the animal into the street where the ground was level that he remembered he could not mount without assistance. It was a great nuisance. Now he had to leave the mare and go into the Command Post and grope in the utter darkness for the box he used as a chair and, having found it, carry it out into the street and set it down beside the restive animal and climb on to the creaking timber. The mare shifted and shied away as he took hold of the mane to pull himself on to her back. He cursed and jerked savagely at the bridle. But it was no use, the mare would not permit him to mount until he had shoved her by force against the wall of the Command Post, set the box down at her side, and held her there with his weight while he clambered on to her back. Then it was all right. He felt the warmth of the wet flesh against his legs and pulled the head round and kicked at the ribs. He rode out of the village and up on to the plateau, kicking all the time at the trembling flanks of the mare. The wind drove the rain across his face.

Where the ground was excessively rough he allowed the animal to move at its own speed and with head low. Where it seemed smooth he kept the head up and kicked continuously. He took the track that skirted the southern side of the chasm; it was shorter and the wind would be carrying the mist towards the north. The roar swelled dully. When he reached the crane the artist had made he drew in the reins and looked down at the platform. He looked at it a long time till it was as fully in focus as the night allowed and then he saw that the cradle was not there. The rope went down without interruption. So the artist must be there, he thought. Otto must be working. It was very pleasing.

He shook the bridle and touched the ribs and drove the mare up toward the mountain. The wind boomed in the forest.

THE END